Laura Marshall grew up in Wiltshire and studied English at the University of Sussex.

After almost twenty years working in conference production, in 2015 Laura decided it was time to fulfil a lifetime's ambition to write a book, and enrolled on the Curtis Brown Creative three-month novel writing course. Laura's debut novel, *Friend Request*, was a *Sunday Times* bestseller and an ebook number one bestseller and was shortlisted for both the Bath Novel Award and the Lucy Cavendish Fiction Prize 2016. *Three Little Lies* is Laura's second novel.

Laura lives in Kent with her husband and two children.

Also by Laura Marshall

Friend Request

Three Little Lies

LAURA
MARSHALL

sphere

SPHERE

First published in Great Britain in 2018 by Sphere

1 3 5 7 9 10 8 6 4 2

A CIP catalogue record for this book
is available from the British Library.

Hardback ISBN 978-0-7515-7305-3
Trade Paperback ISBN 978-0-7515-6836-3

Typeset in Caslon by M Rules
Printed and bound in Great Britain by
Clays Ltd, St Ives plc

Papers used by Sphere are from well-managed forests
and other responsible sources.

MIX
Paper from
responsible sources
FSC® C104740

Sphere
An imprint of
Little, Brown Book Group
Carmelite House
50 Victoria Embankment
London EC4Y 0DZ

An Hachette UK Company
www.hachette.co.uk

www.littlebrown.co.uk

For Michael

Olivia

July 2007

My little boy. He looks so alone up there. It's the first time he's worn a suit since he left school, which God knows feels like five minutes ago, although it's over two years. It seems only yesterday that I was sending him off to school for the very first time, his hands lost in the sleeves of a jumper I'd bought with growing room. I can see that boy in his face, which is the same to me as it's always been. Yes, of course he's changed, but the new faces have just been layered on top of his original face, the one that only I can see now – smooth-skinned and perfect, a sprinkling of freckles across his nose, his expression completely open.

It's closed now, seemingly emotionless, although I'm not fooled. I'm the only one that can feel the tremors running through him, because they run through me too. Flesh of my flesh. Until a baby is around six or seven months old, it has no idea that it's a separate person to its mother. Up until then, it thinks they are one person, which is why separation anxiety kicks in around this time. Eventually, the baby gets it, but for the mother it never goes away. You and your child are, always and forever, one. You feel every cut, every mean remark, every heartbreak.

'Court rise.'

There's a bang on the door signalling the judge's imminent arrival, startling Daniel, who looks instinctively up at me for guidance. I try to smile but my lips won't press themselves into the right shape. His eyes sweep the public gallery hopefully, even though he knows Tony won't be here; can't face it. I can't face it either, but I'm here. It's merely the latest in a lifetime of things I couldn't face but did anyway – getting up five times a night to feed him or soothe his crying, spending endless Sunday mornings watching him playing rugby in the freezing rain, driving him all over the country to play piano concerts, sitting beside him all night the first time he got drunk, too petrified to sleep in case he choked on his own vomit. Everything I've done has been to protect him, to make things better. This is what we do, we mothers. I need to keep reminding myself of that, whatever happens, whatever I've done. It was never about me. It was for Daniel.

The judge sweeps in, a caricature in a frayed wig with florid cheeks, the jury watching him expectantly. They are nervous, overawed; it's probably the first time most of them have been in a courtroom, let alone been a crucial part of the process. Some of them let their eyes flicker to Daniel, but they don't linger on him long. What is it that makes them look away? Disgust? Fear? How much do they already know about him, about what he is accused of?

I lean forward, resting my arms on the rail. I will be here every day until this is over. I can only let myself see a positive outcome, where he is exonerated – the witnesses discredited, the ... *victim* admitting she lied. We will take a taxi home and I will put him to bed and he will sleep, and his body and mind can begin to restore themselves.

I can't countenance the alternative. I shudder at the idea. For me, as for most people, prison has always been an abstract concept; at most, I have driven past them, imagined the prisoners inside, but as a race apart: criminals, not ordinary people. Completely alien to me and my way of life, something I will never come across or have to think about. Well, not any more. When you have other mothers as friends, the conversations move on over the years. First it was all sleepless nights and nappies, first words and potty training; then schools, friendship dramas, puberty. Most recently, it was drugs, sex and alcohol. I thought they would be the last problems we would have to deal with before I forged a new relationship with my sons, an adult one. I imagined them taking me out for lunch, consulting me for advice on home improvements, hugging me again, like they did when they were little, but this time it would be them making me feel safe instead of the other way around. I never in a million years imagined I would be here, in this unknown landscape where none of my friends can, or would want to, follow me. I would swap places with any of them in a heartbeat.

The judge sits down, and so does everybody else apart from the prosecution barrister, who turns to the jury to make his opening statement. And so it begins: my little boy's rape trial.

Ellen

September 2017

Sasha's not in when I get home from the studio, so I put on a CD of Olivia's recording of 'Dido's Lament' by Purcell, full blast. Of course I've got everything she's ever recorded downloaded, but this is my absolute favourite, softer and more intimate than some of the showier arias. It was the first thing I ever heard her sing live, and there's something about slotting the CD into my old hi-fi that feels right. I played it on the show today, shoving down any misgivings I had about whether Sasha might be listening. She was at work; there's no chance they were playing Simply Classical in her office. I don't suppose any of her colleagues have even heard of such a tiny digital radio station unless she's mentioned it, which I doubt. She hardly even talks to me about it – a silent signal that she disapproves of my choice of work, redolent of the Monktons as it is. Classical music was their world and she rejected it utterly, as she has done everything connected with them since the day she moved out.

It was different for me, though. I loved it as she never did. My parents weren't ones for listening to music. My mum listened to Radio 2 in the kitchen sometimes, and they had a few CDs in a dusty stand in the front room, one of which might be put on if they had friends round, but they didn't care about it. It didn't stir any emotion in them. I went through the motions of fandom when it came to the bands other girls liked, blu-tacking posters to my wall and even going to a couple of gigs with Karina, but my heart was never in it. It wasn't until that first concert where I sat in the darkness next to Daniel, heart pounding, tears in my eyes, Olivia's voice pouring over me, into me, like warm water, that I understood what music could be.

I lie down on the sofa, wanting to relax into the music but keeping one hand on the remote control, alert for Sasha's key in the door. I hadn't been expecting her last Friday – I thought she was going out straight after work – but she'd come home around 7 p.m. in a foul mood and found me listening to Olivia. She hadn't said anything about the music, but I could feel her displeasure, radiating out like soundwaves, invisible but powerful. I'd switched it off and tried to talk to her, but she'd stomped off to her room, saying she was tired. There was definitely something up with her but I never got to the bottom of it. This Friday it's not Sasha's key but the door buzzer that interrupts me, jerking me upright like a marionette. I hastily turn off the music and take the few steps into the hall.

'It's Jackson,' says a terse voice on the intercom. No hello, how are you. Not for Jackson the fripperies of the normal greetings that oil the social wheels. I sigh and buzz him up, waiting until I hear his footsteps in the hallway before I open the door.

'Is she here?' he demands, sweeping past me into the front room.

'No, she's not back from work yet. Was she expecting you?' I am chilly, matching his brusqueness note for note.

'Clearly not,' he says, flinging himself down on the sofa, legs apart. 'I went to meet her from work ... as a surprise.' He has the grace to look shamefaced about this last bit. We both know he was checking up on her. 'She hadn't been there all afternoon. The receptionist told me she left at lunchtime, and her phone's going straight to voicemail. If she's not here, where is she?'

'How the hell should I know? I'm not her keeper.' I try to maintain a cold note of indignation, but a thread of worry tugs at a far corner of my brain. Where is she?

'You're not far off,' he says. 'Best friends, aren't you? So close? Tells you everything?'

A small voice in my head wonders if this is true, but I want it to be, so I agree.

'Yes, she does, and whatever you're thinking, it's not true. She's not seeing someone else, Jackson. She's really not. She loves you.' This last part sounds weak even to me. I'm not sure she does. The rest of it doesn't ring entirely true either. Twelve years of friendship should give you a certain understanding, a shorthand. We shouldn't

7

have to tell each other what's going on, how we're feeling. We should just know. Usually I do, but in the last week or so, since she came home in such a strange mood, Sasha's been distant, evasive, brushing off any attempt on my part to get her to open up. Jackson deflates a little with the realisation that I genuinely don't know where she is, and I lower myself on to the edge of the armchair.

'What's going on with her, Ellen?' His bluster has evaporated, and with a jolt of surprise, I realise how much he likes her. 'I mean, she's always blown hot and cold, but this is something else. It's not the first time I've caught her out in a lie recently.'

'What do you mean?' I say, torn between my discomfort at discussing her like this and my need to know. What has she been lying to him about?

'Oh, I don't know ... Not being where she said she was going to be, or being ... evasive. Cagey.'

'She's always been a bit like that, though.' This is true. She liked to retain an air of mystery, even when we were teenagers and had little to be mysterious about. 'That's just how she is. It doesn't mean—'

'That she's shagging someone else? Oh, grow up, Ellen. She's not this perfect superhuman being, you know. She's as flawed as the rest of us. If not more so.'

'I know,' I say, stung. 'I never said she was.'

'No, you never said it,' he says scathingly. 'But we can all see it, what you think of her, how much you love her.'

'She's my best friend!' My cheeks are hot. 'And what do you mean, "we can all see it"? Who's "we"?'

'Forget it.' Jackson picks moodily at a loose thread on his jeans.

'Look, she's not here, and I have no idea when she's going to be back,' I say as firmly as I can, standing up and moving towards the door. I don't want him here, cluttering up our flat with his accusations and insinuations. 'When she gets back, I'll tell her to call you, OK?'

'I think I'll wait,' he says, taking out a pack of cigarettes and a lighter. 'She'll have to come back sooner or later.'

My instinct is to acquiesce, but I force myself to speak. 'I'd really rather you didn't. And you can't smoke in here.'

He sighs theatrically and puts the cigarettes back in his pocket. 'Fine, I'll go. But make sure she rings me as soon as she gets back.'

'I'll tell her you were here, Jackson. It's up to her if she wants to ring you or not.'

After he's gone, I go into the kitchen, where my phone is charging, and call Sasha. Her voicemail clicks in straight away. I listen to her message as if there's going to be some clue contained in it. 'Hi, this is Sasha's phone. I'm not available right now so please leave a message.' She's smiling as she speaks, you can hear it.

'Hey, it's me. Jackson's been here kicking off about you not being at work. Where are you? Call me when you get this.'

I replace the phone on the side and lean back against the worktop, staring out of the window. There's not much to see from this side of the flat. The next block of flats is about five metres from ours, a strip of potholed concrete in between. A couple of old-style punks with Mohicans live in the flat opposite. Sometimes they smile and wave when they're in their kitchen cooking, but there's no sign of them today. You can just see a section of pavement on the route that leads to and from the station, and there's a steady stream of commuters making their way home from work. None of them is Sasha. That thread tugs at me again; memories push against the door I closed on them years ago.

I sit down at the tiny kitchen table by the window, taking a biro that has found its way into the fruit bowl and twiddling it round and round, ink staining my fingers where it's leaking. She would normally be back from work by now, entertaining me with tales of her day, pouring us both a large glass of wine, rooting around in the fridge for something to cook. It's one of my favourite times of day when I'm in, although I'm not a traditional nine-to-fiver, what with irregular shifts at the station and other freelance work.

I'm hungry, but there doesn't seem much point cooking just for me. I toast a slice of bread and eat it without a plate, gazing out into the evening. As the sky darkens, the frequency of the passers-by decreases, but there's no sign of Sasha. I call her again, but it's still going straight to voicemail. The nagging voice in my head that I've been trying so hard to ignore is louder now. I put Olivia's CD back on to try to drown it out, but it's a mistake because it brings those days back, and what had started

10

as a whisper – a question, a suggestion – becomes a voice that I cannot quiet.

What if he's back? it says. *What if he's had enough of his new life in Scotland? What if he's been waiting, biding his time, lulling us into a false sense of security? Waiting for one of us to let our guard down, to slip up? What if he was waiting for her outside work? What if he followed her down the street, cornered her in a dark alley, bundled her into a car?*

No. She's gone out somewhere, her phone's out of battery, that's all. She'll be back soon, smelling of wine and cigarettes; she'll take me in her arms, hug me, affectionate and silly, slurring her words, full of gossip, indiscreet as ever. We'll sit and talk late into the night as we often do; in the morning I'll take her in a cup of tea and we'll half-watch *Saturday Kitchen* on the telly in her room while we look at clothes online, planning an afternoon shopping trip.

It's almost completely dark now, but still I sit here. I haven't turned the kitchen light on, so I am able to see outside rather than staring at my own reflection. The pavement is more or less empty, just the occasional late-comer from work, head down, speeding along, or groups of friends on their way to the pub, chatting and laughing. Meanwhile I sit here, watching, waiting; trying to stop the voice that forces its way into my brain, seeping around the walls and locks I have constructed to keep it out, reverberating through me. The voice that reminds me that ten years ago, Daniel Monkton was sentenced to ten years, five of which he spent in prison, and five on probation, his every move scrutinised. The voice that tells me Daniel Monkton is free to go where he pleases now, and contact who he likes. The voice that says Daniel Monkton is back, and he wants to make us pay for what we did.

Ellen

July 2005

The day the new family moved in to the house on the corner, Karina and I sat pretend-casually on the front garden wall of Karina's house opposite. Karina was painting her nails a vivid shade of electric blue, the bottle balanced precariously on the uneven brickwork, as I leafed through a copy of one of her mum's magazines.

The summer holidays had only begun that week, and already they promised to be the most boring since records began. Yet again we weren't going anywhere on holiday. Lilly Spencer's mum and dad were taking her to Dubai, and she hadn't stopped going on about it for weeks. We weren't even going to Bournemouth.

The corner house had been empty for years. I'd heard my dad saying they wanted too much for it, it was too big for the street and no one who had the money they were asking for it would want to live round here. I didn't really understand what he meant, but the house was certainly bigger than any of the two- and three-bed terraces and semis that lined the rest of the street, and its corner plot meant the garden was huge compared to mine and those of my friends. It even had a garage, unlike any of our houses. Karina and I had got into the garden one day a few years ago, through a gap in the fence. The grass was up to our knees and it soaked the bottom of our jeans until they clung wetly to our legs. We'd peered in through the windows at the empty rooms with their high ceilings and bare wooden floorboards. One of the windows was loose and Karina had wanted us to pull it open and go inside but I wouldn't. Instead we had explored the garden, our early-teen self-consciousness preventing us from playing the game of hide and seek it really demanded. In the end we had climbed the mulberry tree right at the bottom of the garden, and imagined lives for the people on the top deck of passing buses.

The removal van arrived first. The new family must have given them the key because they started unloading straight away. It wasn't normal stuff, though. The first thing I saw come out of the van was an ornate birdcage, the kind of thing you'd see in an old film on the telly. No bird. Then box after box, marked in big, bold letters: BOOKS. So many books.

'Do you have a lot of books in your house?' I asked Karina. I mean, I'd been there obviously, and hadn't seen any, but I didn't know where people who had a lot of books kept them. Maybe they were in her mum's room. We weren't allowed to go in there.

'No,' said Karina. 'Do you?'

'No, hardly any. My mum's got these old cookery books with pictures of weird stuff that no one would want to eat. She never cooks out of them, though. And we've got the Bible, I think.'

'Do you think they've read them all?' she said. The removal men scurried back and forth, getting redder and sweatier each time.

'Dunno. Maybe they're teachers?'

She sniffed. Neither of us thought much of teachers.

A second van drew up, smaller than the first. Specialist Removals, it said on the side. Two men got out, one old and bald, the other younger with curly hair and glasses.

'What's this?' said Karina, settling herself more comfortably on the wall and screwing the top back on the nail varnish, her fingers splayed out like claws.

The two men went into the house and we could hear them talking to the normal removal men, although we couldn't make out what they were saying.

'We'll have to go round the back, through the French windows,' the curly-haired one said as they came back out of the front door and started opening the van. Karina and I waited, holding our breath, to see what was going to come out.

'Oh,' said Karina, as the younger man backed slowly out of the van, down a ramp, wheeling something on a trolley. It was huge and wrapped in a blue blanket. The older man gripped the other end as though his life depended upon it. 'What is it?'

As they manoeuvred it carefully up the kerb and

through the garden gate, there was a faint plinking noise.

'It's a piano,' I said, in wonder. 'One of those big ones. They must have taken the legs off. I wonder when the family will get here.' I was impatient to see the exotic creatures who owned all this stuff.

'It might not be a family,' said Karina. 'I think it's a weird, old professor who lives alone.'

'Maybe,' I said, trying not to stare too obviously at what might come out of the truck next. Whatever it was, we never saw it because our attention was drawn to a rusty old car that had pulled up behind the removal van. I clutched Karina's arm and hissed, 'They're here.'

The first one we saw was the dad. He unfolded himself from the driver's seat and stood by the car, yawning and stretching. He was tall and broad-chested, with wavy dark hair swept back from his face. He was wearing a navy jumper with a paisley scarf knotted artistically around his neck. I tried to imagine my dad wearing a scarf like that, but I simply couldn't do it; I kept getting a picture of him with the grey, woolly one my mum had bought him for Christmas last year. I didn't think he'd even worn that.

'Ooh, Ellen, he's good-looking,' said Karina.

'Good-looking?' I whispered. 'He's about forty-five!'

'So what?'

I struggled with these conversations with Karina about boys, and whether they were good-looking or not. We were late starters, both of us having had our first kiss in the summer term, at Tamara Gregg's party. Since then,

Karina was forever demanding whether I would get off with such-and-such a boy, and debating the merits of all the boys in our class. Part of me longed to reply that I'd rather die than get off with any of those smelly idiots, but I didn't. Even though I had turned sixteen just before her, Karina had a way of making me feel young and stupid when it came to stuff like this, so I joined in, usually agreeing with her assessments. I'd only kissed that boy at Tamara's party so people at school didn't think I was a total freak for never having got off with anyone. Karina always ended up concluding that the one she most wanted to go out with was Leo Smith. Leo had hair the colour of golden syrup and dark brown eyes. He wasn't the coolest, best-looking boy in our year, or the star of the school football team, but there was something about him. He was clever, but it didn't seem dorky on him like it did on some of the others, the nerdy ones who spent all their spare time in the computer room. I didn't fancy him, exactly, not like Karina did, but sometimes I imagined having meaningful conversations with him, in which he truly understood me like no one else ever had.

Next out of the car were two boys, dark-haired like the dad. One looked about our age, the other a bit older, maybe eighteen. They were both wearing Converse trainers with jeans. The younger one had a grey T-shirt with a long-sleeved white top underneath, and the older one was wearing a shirt with a skinny tie. They lounged out of the car, heads down, muttering to each other, toes poking at tufts of grass sticking up between the cracks in the pavement. I felt the heat from Karina as she pressed her leg into mine; I could almost hear her brain computing their suitability as potential boyfriends. In complete contrast to their languor, the mum came bursting out of her side of the car, a whirl of embroidered purple material, jangling silver bracelets and flowing, dark hair. She rhapsodised over everything: the house, the sunshine, the size of the garden.

The four of them started up the garden path. Karina drew breath, and I readied myself for an exhaustive dissection of the two boys, but then the car door opened again at the back, and a head appeared. The first thing we noticed was her hair, a shining sheet of bright gold all down her back that made me think of the shiny paper around chocolate coins. Then it swung round like a cloak and we saw her face, heart-shaped and perfect apart from a thin, red scar on her right cheek. I heard Karina gasp and I knew I'd done the same.

As if she'd heard us, the girl swung her head around and gave us a scornful, challenging glare. I dropped my eyes guiltily and Karina became absorbed in her fingernails, blowing them dry as if her life depended on it. The girl let us wither for a moment more, before flicking her hair around again and sauntering into the house without speaking a word to the mum, who was standing just inside the front door, wittering on about the size of the bedrooms and the views across the London skyline. As the front door shut behind them, the mum's voice was abruptly cut off, leaving Karina and I staring at each other in the sunshine.

'Did you see . . . ?' Karina whispered.

'Her face. Yeah.'

'What do you think happened to her?'

'Dunno.'

Karina shuddered theatrically. 'God, Ellen, imagine having that on your face. I wonder if it's permanent. She's really pretty, too.'

'I know.'

The removal men continued their work, swarming back and forth like worker ants, but we had lost interest in the family's possessions, our imaginations caught by this beautiful, disfigured stranger, peculiarly romantic, like a character in a fairy tale.

As we went back into Karina's, I turned for one last look at the big house, my gaze drawn skywards to the bedrooms. There was no one at the bay window on the right, but at a smaller window on the left I saw the blonde girl. She wasn't looking at me; she was resting her forehead against the glass and staring out across the rooftops. Somehow, though, I didn't think she was admiring the view.

Ellen

September 2017

I wake early, still in my clothes from yesterday, sticky-eyed and thick-headed. I spent a fitful night where every cell of my body was alert for the click of her key in the door, the creak of the loose board in the hallway, the peculiar groan of the kitchen tap. I go straight to her room, even though I know I would have heard if she'd come in during the night.

As always, it's a mess. I'm reminded of her usual joke – that if the police came to our flat for any reason, they would assume her room had been broken in to. Fear rises in me at the thought, and I give a little half-sob. There are clothes all over the floor and spilling out of drawers. The wardrobe is half-open, bursting at the seams as ever. She has a mirror propped on the chest of drawers behind a mishmash of make-up, tangled necklaces, half-drunk glasses of stale water. There's a magazine open at a page detailing how to achieve perfect contouring, smudges from her fingers evident on the shiny paper. She was

20

here yesterday morning. Her perfume lingers in the air, infused into her clothes, her unmade bed.

The leaden feeling in my stomach deepens, and the panic I've been trying to suppress begins to swirl through me. Something is wrong. I know it. She would have called me if she was going to be out all night. We always let each other know where we are. It's one of our things, always has been. When we first lived together after university and she was forever rolling home with some man or other, she never forgot to text me. *Still alive!* Her message would often say, or *Not dead in a ditch!* Only then could I go to sleep, safe in the knowledge that she was OK. I joked once that I was like her mum, but her face darkened and I quickly changed the subject. There are a few topics that, despite our years of closeness, she won't ever discuss, and her mother is top of the list, closely followed, of course, by the Monktons.

We've never discussed the trial, not properly, not even at the time. Not even when the letters came. We were together the day we got the first one, written and posted the morning he was due to be sentenced. Sasha was living with us by then. I'm sure Mum had been secretly counting down the days until she went to university in the October – Mum's heart had never been in it, although even she could see that Sasha couldn't have continued to live with the Monktons, not with Daniel out on bail and living there. I'd padded down in the morning to make Sasha a cup of tea, leaving her asleep on her back on the fold-out bed in my room, arms neatly by her sides, a

21

marble statue. Unreachable. I almost ignored the post on the mat, but Mum had been on at me to do more around the house, to take notice of the little things that needed doing every day, so I picked it up. The top letter was handwritten, which was unusual enough to make me take a second look. It was addressed to me and Sasha. I chucked the rest of the post down on the mat and scurried back upstairs, all thoughts of tea banished from my mind. She was awake, and I laid the letter carefully on the bed in front of her.

'That's Daniel's writing,' she said. We both stared at it, as if it might grow teeth and bite us. There was a full-length mirror on the wall and I glanced into it at the same time as she did, our scared faces reflected in the silence that lay between us.

'Shall I ...?' I reached out a tentative hand. Sasha nodded. I slid my thumb under the thick, creamy paper of the envelope and tore it open, pulling out a sheet of Olivia's monogrammed notepaper. I was probably imagining it, but I thought I could smell her distinctive musky perfume. There were a few lines scrawled on it, and I read them aloud to Sasha, my throat constricted by fear.

To Ellen and Sasha
    Today I will find out if I will spend the next few years of my life in prison, or whether I am free, found innocent, as I should be. If I go to prison, it's not only that liar Karina that won't be able to sleep easy.

You both lied in Court. You chose to do this to me, and I will never let you forget that. You will pay for this one day.
  Daniel

I think about that letter now, every word of it burned into my brain. Sasha kept it, as she did the others that came later, after he was released from prison. We had five years of blissful silence, of knowing exactly where he was. Either he didn't write during those five years or his letters were confiscated by the prison before being posted, considered too threatening. Then five years ago, when he was released on licence, it began again. Where are those letters now? I leaf through her bedside drawers, subduing the guilty, snooping feeling by telling myself she wouldn't mind, not under the circumstances, although I'm not sure this is true. I sift through old birthday cards, out-of-date medications, dried-up nail varnishes and broken jewellery. I find her passport, but there is no sign of the letters. I take everything out from under her bed and go through every file, every box, but I do not find them. I look in every battered shoebox in her wardrobe, each old bag hanging on the back of her door; I take her clothes out of the drawers, even pulling each drawer out to look on the back, as if she might have taped them there in the manner of a bad TV movie, but there's nothing. She has kept all her old school essays and notes, appointment diaries going back to her university days and earlier, clothes and shoes I haven't seen her

23

wear for years, and yet she doesn't appear to have kept these letters. It's not so much that I want to read them – I can remember every accusatory word, every expression of hatred, every threat – I just need to see them, to satisfy myself that they are here. In the end, I admit defeat, slumping on her bed and looking around me. If anything, the room looks tidier now I've methodically searched every inch of it, replacing things as I went. My phone trills from the bedside table and I snatch it up. It's Jackson, and as I answer, I pray she has turned up at his flat, contrite and armed with a reasonable explanation.

'Have you heard from her?' he says without preamble.

My heart sinks. 'No. So you haven't either?'

'Shit. Where is she?' He sounds more worried than angry, and my stomach turns over with a painful flop. It's not only me that's scared now. 'Do you think we ought to call the police?'

'Oh God, I don't know, Jackson. She hasn't even been gone twenty-four hours. They won't do anything, will they?'

'I don't know. I suppose we should call around first, see if anyone's heard from her? And maybe call the hospitals?'

'Yes, of course.' I've been so preoccupied with my private fears I haven't thought of these simple things. 'Will you do the hospitals, and I'll try her friends?'

'OK. Call me if you hear anything, won't you?'

'Of course. You too.'

It strikes me when I cut off the call that I don't know

Jackson as well as you might expect someone to know their best friend's boyfriend. They've been together a year, it's not as though he's some fling. I'm not sure if it's because I haven't made the effort, or he hasn't, or whether Sasha has kept him at arm's length for some reason.

I decide to start with Rachel, Sasha's friend from university, who I've got to know in the years Sasha and I have lived together in London. We form an uneasy threesome, spending evenings hanging out in the Forresters, our local pub, and Saturday afternoons going up to Oxford Street or Covent Garden clothes shopping. They often try and persuade me to buy things I've tried on for fun but can't afford. Neither of them have much understanding of the tight budget I'm living on. Rachel has a well-paid job as a management consultant, and as well as her job in marketing, Sasha owns this flat outright, paid for by her mum. She only charges me a peppercorn rent – I couldn't move out even if I wanted to.

The three of us went on holiday together once. They wanted to go to Thailand but there was no way I could afford it, so we settled for a week in Malaga, Rachel and I taking it in turns to be the spare wheel.

I have a sneaking feeling Rachel wishes she had the friendship with Sasha that I have. What she doesn't understand is that it's borne out of years of shared experience, and no amount of drunken nights out, girly days shopping or getting her nails done with Sasha can ever replace it, or even come close. We've been through things together, Sasha and I. Things we can't even begin to explain to Rachel, or to any of our other friends. Rachel will relish being the first to be called. She's always going on about how Sasha is her '3 a.m. friend', the one she can call on in an emergency, any time, no matter what. She's not Sasha's, though, I am, and she is mine. Every heartbreak, every drama, I've been the one she calls on, on the other end of the phone when we were at separate universities, and in person ever since we've been living together. Whether I like it or not.

I suppose Karina was that type of friend too once, years ago. But I always knew I wouldn't be able to stay friends with her, not after everything that happened. We both needed to move apart, to move on. To try and find a way of living with what had happened, to knit our ripped-up lives back together.

Rachel picks up on the first ring.

'Hello!' she says, sounding surprised, and I realise how rarely I call her. 'Is everything OK?'

I briefly wonder why she thinks it might not be, but don't have time to give it more than a second's thought. 'I don't know,' I say. 'Have you seen Sasha? I mean yesterday, or today.'

'No, I was at work yesterday, then I came straight home,' she says, as if providing an alibi. 'I haven't been out yet today. Why?'

'Jackson came over here last night looking for her. He'd been to meet her from work.'

Rachel snorts. She has no time for Jackson's jealousy and paranoia.

'Anyway, apparently she hadn't been at work all afternoon, and she didn't come home at all last night.'

'Have you tried phoning her?'

'Of course I have,' I snap. 'I'm not completely stupid.' I suspect Rachel thinks I'm a flake, not having what she sees as a proper job. She's always flying off to Paris or New York in a fancy suit at a moment's notice. If I presented on Classic FM or Radio 3 she'd probably be impressed, but she sees Simply Classical as lame – an indulgence, barely more than a hobby – and has probably never even read any of the articles I've had published in the classical music press.

'Yes, I know, sorry,' she says soothingly. 'Maybe she . . . I don't know, bumped into someone, and they ended up going out, and she stayed over at theirs?'

'Who, though? Anyway, she would have phoned or texted. She always does.'

'Perhaps she forgot this time.' She struggles to keep out a note of triumph at the idea that Sasha and I are not, as she suspects, as close as I think we are. 'Or she's out of battery.'

This is the only explanation that doesn't scare me, and I've been clinging to it like a limpet to a rock. 'Will you do me a favour, Rachel? Call around anyone you can think of and see if they're with her, or if they've heard from her.'

'No problem,' she says, instantly efficient. We divide up all the friends we have phone numbers for and agree to call each other the minute we have any news of her.

*

Ten minutes later I've worked my way through my list with no joy, and five minutes after that I get a text from Rachel: No one has seen her. Police???

Do you think? Or wait a bit? I text back.

There's a hiatus, during which Rachel evidently decides she doesn't want the responsibility of making this decision, because she replies: Up to you. x

I curl my feet under me on Sasha's bed, trying to stop myself picking at the raw skin around my fingernails. I don't want to make the decision either. I'm aware of my tendency to catastrophise, and it makes it hard for me to know how realistic my fears are. Will the police laugh at me if I call now? She's a grown woman, after all; she doesn't have to tell anyone where she is. Or if I leave it, am I placing her in more danger? Will the police be angry if I don't tell them straight away? But she might be back later, or at least have let me know she's OK. I don't want to waste their time. A text from Jackson to say he's called all the London hospitals and none of them has any record of Sasha confuses me further. In the end, I pick up my phone and do what I always do when I have a decision to make.

'Hello, sweetheart,' she says. Straight away I feel calmer. Mum and I grew apart during what I think of as the Monkton years, but ever since the aftermath of New Year's Eve 2006, it's been her I turn to for comfort. 'How are you?'

'Not great, actually.' My voice wobbles. 'It's Sasha. She's ... gone.'

'What do you mean, gone?' Along with thankfulness that I haven't been in an accident, or diagnosed with some terrible disease, there's a tiny hint of irritation. Although she had been pleased at first that I'd found a new friend, it hadn't lasted long. As I had begun to spend more and more time at the Monktons' house, Mum had sensed she was losing me. She couldn't even encourage me to hang out with Karina more, because she was round there every chance she got too, both of us seduced by a life so different from the one we knew in our own homes. My hackles rise as they always do when I sense criticism of Sasha by people who don't know her as I do.

'She's disappeared,' I say bluntly. 'No one's seen her since yesterday lunchtime.'

'Oh!' She wasn't expecting that, and I experience an uncomfortable throb of self-satisfaction that reminds me of our former prickly relationship. 'Maybe she's met someone, or ... I don't know, taken herself off some-where. It wouldn't be the first time, would it?'

I know what she's referring to. Summer 2006. Sasha disappeared without warning, causing no end of worry for twenty-four hours, until she called Olivia to say she'd bumped into some old friends and taken off to France with them on the spur of the moment. I was devastated. We'd planned to go on holiday together, but I was left to endure deathly dull days working in the Body Shop and evenings cloistered in my bedroom in the stifling heat, listening to Olivia singing on my hi-fi and wondering what Sasha was doing.

'She would have told me, Mum, honestly. She's different now.' Or at least I have to believe that she is.

'I'm sure she is. I haven't seen her for … goodness knows how many years. She certainly never visits the Monktons.'

'Of course she doesn't, she hasn't seen them since … Hang on, how would you know, anyway?'

'I can see their house from our front window, can't I? Not that I'm looking, particularly.'

'No, of course not,' I say, smiling. Not for nothing do her friends call her a one-woman neighbourhood watch.

'Nicholas, now, he does visit. I suppose he's the only one they've got left, poor things.' She can afford to be magnanimous now that Olivia and Tony's lives have played out so badly. 'Although …' She trails off, as if she's thought better of whatever she was going to say.

'What?' I pounce, knowing it's something I would want to know, but that she thinks it would be better if I didn't.

'It's probably nothing, don't worry about it.'

'Oh, for God's sake, just tell me, Mum.'

'Well … the other day, I happened to be looking out of the window and I thought … I thought I might have seen Daniel.'

The room blurs before my eyes and I swallow hard, concentrating so fiercely on staying calm that I can't speak.

'Ellen?' Mum says cautiously.

'When?' I manage.

'Last weekend, I think it was,' she says vaguely.

'And when you say you *thought* you saw him . . . '

'It was getting dark, and he came from the other direction, rather than past our house, so I didn't get a really good look at him. It could have been Nicholas, I suppose; they were very alike, weren't they? I don't think so, though – it was something about him, the way he was walking, maybe.'

My heart is thumping and I try to breathe deeply, the phone burning hot against my ear. If Daniel really is back, then I have no choice but to call the police. *You will pay for this one day.* I pretend there's someone at the door and say a quick goodbye to Mum.

Alone, I lie down on Sasha's bed, burying my face in her pillow, wrapping her duvet around me, trying to bring her back to me. It doesn't warm me, though. Nothing can, because lying here surrounded by her things, breathing in the scent of her, all I can think about, ice creeping through me, is Daniel Monkton.

Ellen

September 2005

Karina wasn't in school. It was the third day back after the summer holidays, our first term as sixth-formers, and she'd been off sick for all three of them, making me realise how much I relied on her. We were the only two girls who had gone on from our primary school to this school, and having her there had made me lazy about making other friends. I got on OK with everyone, it's not that I was bullied, or even unpopular, but I wasn't part of any of the little groups that had formed over the five years we'd been at secondary school. And usually that was OK, because me and Karina were our own gang. She lived down the street from me, and we'd been in and out of each other's houses for as long as I could remember. It wasn't so much that we had chosen each other – in fact, sometimes it felt more as if we were stuck with each other – but it seemed too late, somehow, to change things. Karina and I weren't studious, A-grade students, we weren't sporty, and we certainly weren't part of the cool group who went out drinking at the weekends and hung out with the good-looking boys. There was nothing about either of us that would encourage new friendships, so we tried to feel grateful that we had each other, at least.

By the Wednesday, I was running short on people to hang out with, so after gulping down my lunch alone in the cafeteria, I headed to the library where, although I would still be alone, at least no one would see me except those who had their own problems to worry about. I was passing one of the maths classrooms, near the library, when Leo Smith barrelled out, bumping into me as he did so.

'Oh God, sorry,' he said, putting his hands on my shoulders. 'Are you OK?' His palms were warm, his eyes dark chocolate pools. A hint of a thrillingly masculine fragrance lingered around him.

'I'm fine,' I said. 'No problemo.' *No problemo?* I groaned inwardly.

'Great,' he said and sped off down the corridor.

I tried not to stare after him and was about to walk on, when I saw the girl from the corner house standing by the open window of the classroom, her golden hair lifting in the breeze. She held her hand to her face, the tip of her finger stroking the place where I knew the angry red scar was, although it was either fading or she was so skilful at hiding it with make-up that it was barely visible. I hesitated at the door, torn between my natural shyness and the curiosity that had been growing inside me since the day Karina and I had watched her family moving in.

We had come to an unspoken agreement over the summer that meant we had spent much of our time sitting together on the seat in the bay window in her front bedroom, pretending to read or play board games, our heads whipping round at any sign of movement opposite. With the windows open, we could hear the faint strain of music floating through the still, summer air; sometimes the piano, sometimes what must have been the mum singing opera, sometimes a musical instrument we couldn't identify. We watched the boys loafing off in the direction of the station, and the mum and dad coming and going, sometimes separately and sometimes together, at all sorts of different hours, and in a variety of outlandish outfits. The dad was often holding a black case that we could only suppose contained the instrument. We were fascinated by them. My dad left and returned at exactly the same time every day, wearing the same cheap suit and carrying a bag with his sandwiches in, as had Karina's before he died a couple of years ago. Our mums worked part-time, a remnant from the days when we needed to be collected from school every day. They rarely went out in the evenings.

Of the girl we had seen very little. She didn't often leave the house, and when she did, she walked swiftly down the street, sunglasses on, head down, as if she was in disguise, or trying to escape something. The boys had friends over, arriving in jostling groups holding carrier bags clinking with beer cans; the scent of barbecuing meat would float across to us, mixed with cigarette smoke and sometimes the sweet tang of marijuana. On those days I could feel the longing to be in that garden oozing out of Karina like blood from an open wound. I was happy to be observing from our vantage point in her bedroom, heat rising to my face at the mere thought of having to make conversation with all those strangers. We couldn't see the main part of the garden at the back, but the boys and their friends would sometimes spill into the scrubby patch of grass at the side of the house by the garage, where we would get tantalising glimpses of them, and catch scraps of snatched conversations. More than once we heard the boys refer to their sister as 'Lady Sasha', and you could tell from the way the conversation often turned to her, and from their clumsy jokes, that their friends were taking more than a passing interest in her. She never joined them, though, as far as we could tell. Once or twice on the days when the garden was crammed with people, the parents moving easily among the teenagers in a way I could never imagine my parents doing, we saw her face at the window where we had seen her that first day, staring blankly out across the London skyline.

Today in the classroom she was also staring out of the window, her lips pressed together as if she was trying not to cry. I turned to go, but the movement must have caught her eye and she looked round at me, her face hard.

'Sorry, can I help you?' She was well-spoken with a back note of Estuary English.

35

'No, I ... I was just passing and ...' I twisted my hands together, the rough skin on my palms crackling like paper. 'Are you OK?'

There was a silence, and all the possible answers to that question hung in the air between us.

'I'm fine,' she said, wiping a finger under each eye where her mascara had smudged; because what else could she say to someone she'd just met?

I nearly walked away then. I was desperately intrigued, but I could tell already that there was an edge to her; in fact, she was all edges. I was used to the comfortable familiarity of my friendship with Karina, where neither of us had to try too hard. But the pull of that house – the books, the music, the exotic parents, those dark-haired boys – I couldn't resist.

'You live in the big house on the corner of Stirling Road, don't you?'

'Yeah,' she said, frowning. 'How do you know?'

'I live down the road from you. I saw you moving in.' I tried to sound casual. I didn't want her to know that Karina and I had maintained a surveillance operation worthy of the Metropolitan Police on her and her family all summer. 'My friend lives opposite.'

'Not that girl who's always staring over at us?' Ah. She had noticed, although thankfully she didn't seem to recognise me. Karina must have been putting in extra hours when I was at home. 'Daniel and Nicholas think it's hilarious.'

'Daniel and Nicholas?' I said, trying to hide any trace

36

of excitement, while storing away their names to tell Karina on the phone later. 'Are they your brothers?'

'God, no.'

I waited for her to elaborate but it soon became clear she had no intention of doing so.

'So, have you moved from far?'

'Not really,' she said, looking out of the window again.

'Oh, right. Well . . . ' I sensed I was fighting a losing battle here, and was about to leave when she spoke again, and this time she sounded warmer.

'What a creep.'

'Who?' I said, confused.

'That boy who was in here, before you came in.'

'Leo Smith?' He'd never struck me that way. There were boys in our year you knew to avoid, boys with wandering hands and worse, but he wasn't one of them. Sarah Penfold had got completely pissed at a party and woken naked in a strange bed to find David Weekes with his hands all over her. She'd managed to push him off and get out, but who knew if the next girl would be so lucky.

'If that's his name,' the girl said, shrugging.

'Why, what did he do?'

'Oh, nothing,' she said, closing herself back up. 'Are you doing anything?'

'What, now?' I was struggling to keep up with the constant changes of pace.

'Yes, of course now. I wasn't asking you out.'

I reddened. 'I know, I . . . '

'Oh my God, you're easy to wind up!'

The blush on my cheeks deepened even further.

'Oh, come on,' she said, relenting. 'Let's go outside. You can tell me which other creeps to look out for.'

As we walked out on to the playground, the curious stares of my classmates were hotter on my back than the warm September sunshine. I felt briefly guilty about Karina – partly because I could already feel my allegiance to her shifting and attaching itself to this strange, alluring girl, and partly because she was going to be so annoyed that I had been the first one to break into the world of the corner house, even if I'd only made a very slight inroad so far. I shook it off, though, as we sat down on a bench, shoving any thoughts of Karina far, far to the back of my mind, and turning to bask in the sun.

Ellen

September 2017

The woman on the other end of the phone is calm with a soothing Yorkshire accent. She takes some details and tells me they will send an officer out to see me within the next hour or so. While I wait, I go through Sasha's things again, trying to work out whether anything is missing. I don't even know what she was wearing yesterday morning. I was still asleep when she left. Her coat isn't here, certainly, but that doesn't tell me anything.

I call Sasha again, hoping against hope that this will be the time she picks up, but voicemail kicks in once more as she smilingly invites me to leave a message. I've already left several, pleading with her to call me, let me know she's OK, but I leave another anyway.

'Sash, it's me again. I'm so worried about you. If ... if I've done anything to upset you, I'm sorry, I didn't mean it. Please come back. I've called the police; they're sending someone out to see me. I don't know if you'll get this but, if you do, well ... I'm going to find you.'

I'm still in her room when the buzzer goes. I hurry into the hall and a woman's voice announces herself as PC Bryant. I buzz her up and stand at the open front door of the flat. I hear footsteps coming up the communal stairs, and then she's here, rounding the corner at the top of the stairwell, walking down the corridor towards me. I try to stretch my face into a facsimile of a smile, although I've never felt less like smiling in my life.

'You must be Ellen,' she says, holding out her hand. 'I'm PC Bryant.' She's a bit older than me, mid-thirties, maybe, small and bird-like with short, dyed red hair and no make-up.

'Come in,' I say, leading her through the small hall into the lounge. 'Would you like a cup of tea?'

'Yes, that would be great. You look like you could use one yourself.' She smiles, and I realise how I must look in yesterday's clothes, make-up smudged under my red-rimmed eyes, hair matted at the back from a night of tossing and turning.

In the kitchen I splash water from the tap on to my face and rake my fingers through my hair, trying to make myself look vaguely presentable. In some sort of weird effort to look efficient and together, I put the mugs on a tray instead of carrying them in my hands. I've put them too close together and they clink against each other as I come back into the lounge, tea slopping out as I place the tray on the coffee table and sit down.

'I know you must be very worried,' Bryant says, reaching out for her cup. 'But if it helps at all, the vast majority

40

of missing persons turn up safe and well within a day or two. It's very likely your friend Sasha will too.'

I take a sip of my tea although it's still too hot. It doesn't help in the slightest. I don't care what happens to other missing persons. We are not talking about other missing persons; we're talking about my best friend.

'Is this her?' Bryant indicates a photo of Sasha on a side table. It was taken at the wedding of our friends Kate and Jonny in the summer, the first of our group to get married. It's a close-up of her face, looking away from the camera, laughing at something someone has said. I remember, though, how she wasn't laughing later, drunk and maudlin, refusing to let me go to bed, making me stay up for hours while she bemoaned Jackson's posses- siveness, droning on and on about how he wasn't the man for her until I felt like shaking her. She was trying to paint herself as some sort of tragic heroine in her own life story, hinting at lost loves, ones who got away, but I was exhausted and drunk, and for once I couldn't be bothered to play her games, to pander to her need for attention. I don't know why she bothered putting on this show for me – I'd been there for all the various boyfriends she'd had over the years, and I was sure she hadn't cared that deeply for any of them.

'Yes,' I say to Bryant. 'Would you like to take it?'

'Yes, please.'

I slide it out of the frame and pass it to her.

'It's great to have this,' Bryant says, 'but can you describe Sasha in your own words?'

'She's—' I break off. I was going to say she's beautiful, because that is the first thing that strikes you when you look at her. She's not just pretty, or attractive. She is properly beautiful, like a movie star. That's not what they want, though. 'She's five foot eight, slim, long blonde hair, blue eyes.' I take a deep breath, trying to dispel the sick, panicky feeling describing her in the language of a TV news report is giving me. 'She has a faint scar on her right cheek, although you can only see it if she's not wearing any make-up. I don't know what she was wearing yesterday. She must have had her coat on, though. It's red – full-length, wool. And her black ankle boots are missing.'

'OK, that's great. I know you've been through this already on the phone, but can you tell me when you last saw Sasha?'

'The day before yesterday, when I went to bed. She was here yesterday morning, though, but she left for work before I got up. Her boyfriend Jackson came over around six last night. He'd been to meet her from work but she'd left at lunchtime. She didn't come home last night. I can't get her on the phone. Jackson's rung around all the hospitals and she's not in any of them, and I've called all the friends I can think of. No one's heard from her.'

'Was it unexpected, that she left work at lunchtime?'

'Yes, she was supposed to be there all day, as far as I know. Jackson certainly thought so. He ... wasn't very happy.'

'Why was that?' Bryant asks in a neutral tone, although her ears have pricked up, a cat sensing its prey.

'He didn't say so, but . . . ' I hesitate, not wanting to drop Jackson in it – he's got nothing to do with this. I mustn't start lying to the police, though, not now. 'He suspected she'd left work early to meet someone else. She hadn't, though. I'd know.'

'We don't always know everything about our friends, even those we're closest to.'

'I would,' I insist. 'She's my best friend, my oldest friend. We tell each other everything.'

'OK,' Bryant says with infuriating calmness. 'How did she seem, on Thursday evening? Was she her usual self?'

'Yes,' I say, because what else can I say? I can't say that she didn't have a usual self, that she was mercurial: charming one minute and a bitchy nightmare the next. Some people couldn't cope. She ripped through friendships like wildfire, leaving her victims scorched and exhausted in her wake; relieved, perhaps, but their lives a little duller for her absence. Not me, though. I would never desert her. She needs me, I suppose, although our other friends would probably be surprised to hear that, would think it the other way around. She's not as tough as she seems, though. Not underneath it all.

'And recently, before that, how has she been? Has anything happened to upset her? Any rows with anyone?'

I think of the way she swept in last Friday. Was it only my choice of music that annoyed her? She hadn't come out of her room all night, and ever since I had sensed a coolness about her, an air of distraction.

43

'No,' I say. Whatever it was about her was so intangible, I couldn't hope to explain it to a police officer. 'She rowed with her boyfriend, but that's not just a recent thing.'

'Did it ever become violent?' she asks.

'Oh no, nothing like that. Will you be speaking to him?' I feel a slight sense of unease at dragging Jackson into this, then chide myself. He'll want to help – he's as worried as I am.

'Yes, of course,' she says. 'Have you looked in her room? Is there anything missing? A suitcase? Clothes?'

'I've been right through her stuff looking for . . .' I tail off, unsure if this is the time to bring up Daniel, or even whether I'm going to mention him at all. 'I don't think anything's missing. Her suitcase is definitely there, and her passport.'

'Is it OK if I come and have a look at her room?'

She follows me down the hall to Sasha's room and looks around in thinly disguised horror at the clothes-strewn floor, the layer of dust on the surfaces, the discarded cups on the bedside table.

'Is it . . . usual for her room to be so untidy?' she asks, deliberately neutral.

'Yes,' I say, kneeling down to look under the bed. 'I clean the rest of the flat but she goes mad if I try to tidy up in here. This is how she likes it.' I push aside a pair of boots that appear to be growing mould, and can make out the shiny pink of her case. 'Her suitcase is under there,' I say, getting to my feet. 'I'm pretty sure nothing is missing from the room, although it's kind of hard to tell.'

'OK,' says Bryant, scanning the room. 'Would you say Sasha was depressed at all? Suicidal?'

'No!' The vehemence of my tone shocks us both. 'Sorry, I didn't mean to shout. No, she's not that type of person.'

'Anyone can suffer from depression. It's not always easy to spot the signs.'

'Yes, I know that. But she's never suffered from mental health problems. She's not depressed.'

'That's good,' she says. 'So you wouldn't describe her as vulnerable in any way?'

'No,' I say quickly, although she is, just not in the way Bryant means. She is strong, resilient. Titanium. I don't know what has happened to her but the one thing I know for sure is she hasn't chucked herself off a bridge. That would be losing, and Sasha always has to be the winner.

'Now, I have to ask this: has Sasha ever been in trouble with the police, or been arrested?'

'No.' Her only contact with the police was the same as mine: eleven years ago, huddled around the Monktons' kitchen table, festive merriment replaced by a thudding headache and a feeling of sick dread.

'Has she ever been the victim of any crime?'

'No.'

'And would you say it's completely out of character for her to disappear like this? Without telling anyone?'

'Yes, totally,' I say without hesitation, but then something flits across my brain and it must be mirrored in my face because her eyes light up.

'She's never done this before?' she asks.

'Well . . . '

'Yes?' She looks at me steadily.

'It was years ago, when we were much younger. It's got nothing to do with this.'

She gives me a look that says she'll be the judge of that. 'Even so,' she says, 'it might help. If she's done something like this before, it might give you, or us, a better idea of where to look this time.'

I look around her bedroom, her possessions as familiar to me as my own, and the fear of losing her pierces me so fiercely I lose my breath.

'It was in 2006.' The words come out in a rush now that I've decided to tell. 'We were seventeen – the summer after lower sixth. We'd been talking about maybe going travelling around Europe together, but we hadn't booked anything, and we needed to earn some money first. I did, anyway.'

'She already had money?' asks Bryant.

'She always seemed to, yeah. I had a Saturday job in the Body Shop, but she never worked. I think Olivia and Tony were quite generous.'

'Olivia and Tony?'

'Her godparents. She came to live with them when she was sixteen.'

'So what happened that summer?'

'Like I said, we'd talked about going away. I'd managed to get some extra hours at the Body Shop and I thought I'd be able to afford to go away for the last few weeks of the holidays, before we went back to school. I popped over to her house to talk to her about it – they only lived down the road – and, well, she wasn't there.'

'How d'you mean?'

'Olivia was the only one in, and she said Sasha was out, she wasn't sure where. So I called her, but the phone was off ...' I am uncomfortably aware of the parallels between this story and the one I've just told her.

'Go on,' says Bryant.

'Olivia said she'd ask Sasha to call me when she got back, but I decided to wait there for her.' Olivia had been guarded, as if she was upset or there was something she wasn't telling me.

'With her godmother? Even though Sasha was out?' says Bryant.

'Yes. We were ... close. I was sort of closer then to Olivia and Tony than I was to my own parents.' Tears are pricking at my eyes and I know my voice is about to break. Although Olivia had seemed distracted, I remember it as a happy afternoon. We had sat at the battered oak table drinking Earl Grey tea and talking about my future. Things had gone a bit wrong for me academically that past year. I'd been caught up in the drama and excitement of life as it was lived at the Monktons', and it had shown in my end of year exam results. But no matter what, I still can't regret those years where I spent more time there than I did at home. Can't regret those evenings around the table when Tony would slip me an illicit glass of wine and I would join in noisy discussions about politics, books, art. If it hadn't been for the Monktons, there's no way I would have taken the path that led me to my dream job, poorly paid and insecure as it is. I probably wouldn't have even gone to university. I would have taken my mum's advice, counted myself lucky to be earning, ended up working full-time in the Body Shop, resenting the university students who swanned in and worked for a few weeks in the holidays, looking down their noses at the full-time staff, pitying them for their little lives. That's what I would have had without Olivia and Tony – a little life.

'What happened?' asks Bryant, dragging me back to the cold reality of Sasha's empty bedroom.

'She didn't come back. I went over to the Monktons' around three o'clock in the afternoon. I sat there with Olivia till about six, but Sasha still wasn't home, so I left. I'd told my mum I'd be back for dinner.' I remember that, because we'd had a row about it, me and Mum. She'd accused me of spending more time at the Monktons' than I did at home. I flinch inwardly now as I think of how I asked her why she even cared. Tony and Olivia had never said a bad word about my mum and dad, but I knew how suburban, how comically lower middle class they thought people like them were. It wasn't about money – they never seemed to have much themselves, to the point where it was a source of pride for them; no, it was subtler than that, a sort of intellectual, artistic snobbery, I suppose, although I never saw it as that. I just thought they were right, and said as little about my home life as possible in case I gave myself away.

'Olivia called me about ten o'clock that night,' I go on. 'She was worried. Sasha still hadn't come back, and she hadn't called, either. Her phone was switched off, and none of the friends Olivia had called knew where she was either.'

'Did she call the police?' asks Bryant.

'No, she ...' I remember being surprised at the time that she didn't. I don't know why, but I don't want to tell Bryant that. 'I think she thought Sasha had gone out and lost track of time, or something.' It sounds lame even to my ears.

'Was that something she often did?'

'No,' I say, bristling. 'But we were seventeen, not twelve. Sasha came and went as she pleased. Anyway, she didn't come back that night. Olivia called me again in the morning, and I think she was going to call the police, but then Sasha did phone her, mid-morning I think it was.'

'Where had she been?' Bryant says.

'She was in France.'

'In France? What was she doing there?' She speaks in the tone of someone who can't imagine choosing to visit France.

I decide to give her the official version. It doesn't make any difference to what's happened now, and I don't want her to assume Sasha's had a row with someone again and decided to take off. I need the police to look for her.

'She'd bumped into some old friends, a couple she

knew from before she came to live with the Monktons. They were going to France to work in a vineyard, and she'd decided on the spur of the moment to go with them. There was no one home when she came to get her passport and pick up her things, and she'd got caught up in the adventure and forgotten to let them know she wouldn't be home.'

When it happened, all I could think about was how she could do this to me: disappear off to France without me, leaving me selling White Musk in the Body Shop, when we'd had all these plans. I was crushed, devastated. I hadn't given a thought to the likelihood or otherwise of her story.

'How long was she gone for?'

'The rest of the summer. Just over four weeks.'

Time had stretched out like elastic. Karina kept pestering me to go round to the Monktons' with her and ask Nicholas and Daniel to come out with us, but I felt funny about going there without Sasha. There was that one, rather strange, party, but other than that I'd hardly seen the Monktons. There had been something in Olivia's voice, when she called to tell me Sasha had been in touch, something I'd never heard before. She was angry with Sasha, of course, understandably so – Olivia had had a sleepless night and been on the verge of calling the police. But there was more. Before, she had always spoken of Sasha with compassion and I had sensed that as a mother of sons, she'd been delighted to be given a quasi-daughter. But that day on the phone, there was a coolness I'd never heard before. A distance, as if she was talking about someone she hardly knew.

Sasha had barely contacted me at all. She'd sent the odd text, as if to say she hadn't forgotten me entirely, to which I replied, because I didn't want her to know how much she had hurt me. When she came back, the thread between us was stretched out, thinner than it had ever been. It might have been in danger of snapping altogether, but I refused to let her go. If I hadn't held on so tightly, maybe we would have simply drifted apart, and everything would have been different.

'So,' says Bryant in a tone that tells me I'm not going to like what's coming next, 'it's not completely out of character for Sasha to disappear off like this, without telling anyone?'

'That was eleven years ago! We were seventeen! People do all sorts of crazy things when they're that age. This is different. She always calls me if she's not coming back.' My God, she doesn't believe me. Is she not going to look for her?

'I know this is difficult,' she says, laying a hand on my arm, which I shake off. 'But adults are allowed to go missing. It doesn't sound as though Sasha is vulnerable, or likely to commit suicide or cause any harm to the public, so at the moment we would grade her disappearance as low risk.' She raises a hand against my protest. 'That doesn't mean we will do nothing, Ellen. Does Sasha have a car?'

'No. I've got one; I take her anywhere she needs to go

by car. There's not much point her having one too, not in London.'

'All right. What I need you to do is give me all the information you can – phone number and provider, social media accounts, bank accounts, GP details. We'll sit and go through it all now. Then we'll share Sasha's details with missing persons agencies, we'll run her name through our database to see whether she's been in contact with the police at all, and check the hospitals. I know you said her boyfriend has already done that,' she touches my arm again, 'but just to be on the safe side – in case he missed any. I'll also need the contact details for her boyfriend, her work, as well as family, friends and other associates. Anyone who might have seen or spoken to her recently.'

Her family. Is there any point them contacting the Monktons when I know for a fact Sasha hasn't seen them for years? As for her mother, she never talks about her any more, and I never ask, aware that it's a taboo subject, although I've never understood why. I reluctantly give Bryant the Monktons' address, and Sasha's mother's name, explaining that I don't have any contact details for her, that Sasha wasn't in touch with her herself. Bryant says she'll look into it.

'So,' she goes on, 'this is the address for Tony and Olivia Monkton, Sasha's godparents. Does Sasha have any other family – brothers or sisters?'

Here we go. 'Not brothers and sisters, no.'

'But?'

'It's ... it might be nothing, but ...'

'Go on. Anything you can tell me might help us find her.'

Oh God. 'When we were younger, the Monktons' older son, Daniel, he raped one of our friends at a party. Sasha and I testified against him at the trial. He was ... angry with us. He blamed us, partly at least.'

'Why?'

'He accused us of lying at the trial. He was delusional. All we did was tell the truth. He was the one who lied.'

'He was convicted?'

'Yes. He was sentenced to ten years, of which he served five in prison. He got out five years ago.'

'So his probation has ended recently?'

'I think so. I don't know exactly. He was living in Scotland, I think, but ... my mum still lives near the Monktons and she thought she might have seen him the other day, on their street. Going into their house.'

'You said he was angry with you?'

'Yes, he wrote to us. Once just before he was sentenced, and a few times after he came out of prison.'

'Did he threaten you?'

'He said ... he would make us pay for what we did.'

'Do you have those letters?' She looks alert now, sitting up slightly straighter.

'No. Sasha had them. I've looked all through her room but I can't find them.'

'Might she have destroyed them?'

'Yes, it's possible.'

'Did you ever go to the police with them?'

'No. Sasha said there was no point.' She said they wouldn't do anything, and worse, it might get them thinking there was something in it, that we had lied. She said we weren't in any real danger. She was right, there were never any explicit threats, not since that first letter. *You will pay for this one day.*

'What do you think? Do you think Daniel has something to do with where Sasha is now?'

'Maybe. I don't know.' I think of the sustained and secret abuse he subjected Karina to, while presenting innocence to the world; the look on his face as he was led away from the dock and into the back of a police van; the days I have lived in fear, every day since he was released. 'Can you ... I don't know, check up on him?'

'We can certainly try and talk to him. We'll definitely be speaking to his parents, so we can verify if they have indeed seen Daniel recently.'

Once I have given her all the information I can, she leaves, pressing her card on me and urging me to contact her if I hear from Sasha, or if I have any further cause for concern. Any further cause for concern? She's missing – what more cause could there be?

I sit alone on Sasha's bed, staring blankly at myself in the long mirror on the wall. My face is pale and there are dark smudges under my eyes, a mix of yesterday's mascara and sheer exhaustion. What if she never comes back? What if I never see or hear from her again? My fear is mostly for her: about what has happened to her, if she is frightened, or in pain, or dead. But I'm also frightened about what I have to do next. PC Bryant said she'll need to talk to the Monktons. I can't bear for my first contact with Olivia in over ten years to be via the police. I need to get to her before they do.

Olivia

July 2007

So here we are. Here she is, demure and contained in her neat little grey skirt suit and court shoes, looking younger than her eighteen years. Apparently she could have asked the court for special protection on grounds of intimidation and fear of testifying, even providing her evidence via live video link. However, she has chosen, or been persuaded, not to. I can only suppose the prosecution team think that her obvious youth and timidity will work in her favour.

Everyone else gets a break; everyone else will get to come up and give their evidence, then be whisked off to a comfortable room where somebody will bring them a cup of tea. But my boy has to sit up there behind a glass screen like an animal, hour after hour, listening to every painful minute of it. I try to focus on what I know to be true about him: his kindness, his cleverness, his ability to interpret and play a familiar piece of piano music to the point where I feel as though I've never heard it before. I try to hold on to these things to drown out the other voice in my head, the one that is allowing in doubt.

The prosecution barrister is straight out of central casting, like the judge. He is elegant – smooth-skinned and high-cheekboned, his hair, which is somewhere between ash blond and grey, swept back from his face, a young Michael Heseltine. I can imagine him passing round the port after the ladies have gone to the other room. Is this a deliberate choice? Would choosing a young woman, like Daniel's barrister, have given the jury the impression that this was some sort of feminist, 'all men are rapists' crusade? Will the jury think if even this right-wing, misogynistic dinosaur believes Daniel is guilty, then he must be?

Karina puts a trembling hand on the Bible and half-whispers the oath.

'Could you speak up a bit, Miss Barton?' says the judge, with what I suppose he hopes is a kindly, avuncular smile. 'Some of us don't have the sharp hearing we once did.'

'Sorry,' she says more loudly, her eyes lowered.

When she has finished, the prosecution barrister stands and leaves a beat of silence, giving the jury a little more time to observe the sweet, nervous young woman before them.

'Miss Barton,' he begins. 'I'm going to take you through the events of the evening of the thirty-first of December 2006. If at any time you wish to stop and take a break, you must let me know.'

She nods, still looking at the floor.

'There was a party at the house of your friend, Sasha North, at number 112 Stirling Road, is that correct?'

'Yes.' Her eyes dart from him to the jury. I've been looking it up – she will have been told to direct her answers to the jury, but that bank of twelve pairs of eyes boring into her, judging her, must be hard to face down.

'At what time did you arrive at the party?'

'Around eight o'clock.' She puts a hand on the rail in front of her, as if to steady herself.

I remember hearing her nervous laughter, wondering if I ought to go and rescue her from that ghastly Roland Wiltshire who had answered the door. He and Amelia had been the first to arrive, and Roland kept letting people in while Tony and I were busy putting out food and making sure there were enough glasses. For that first hour, all I heard was women and girls uneasily trying to get away from him at the door.

'Did you see Daniel Monkton when you arrived?'

'No. I went into the living room and chatted to some friends, then I went up to Sasha's bedroom.'

'Sasha is your friend, and goddaughter to Mr and Mrs Monkton, Daniel's parents, is that right?'

She nods.

'Can you speak your answer please, Miss Barton?' says the judge.

'Sorry.' She looks from him to the barrister. 'Yes, that's right.'

She's on the verge of tears already and we haven't even

got to the hard part. I force steel into my heart; I cannot afford to start feeling sorry for her.

'Who else was in Sasha's bedroom?'

'Just me and her, and Ellen Mackinnon. Another friend of ours.'

'And how long did you stay in there?'

'About five minutes. Then I went downstairs to get a drink.'

'Were you drinking alcohol?'

'Yes. It was a party. New Year's Eve.'

'Of course, Miss Barton. You are not being judged on that. You were no different to any other group of young people enjoying a New Year's Eve party, in a friend's home.'

'Yes,' she says, a little more strongly. 'I thought I was safe there.'

Blood rushes to my cheeks and I have to look away from her flushed, serious face. She *was* safe. She was in my home, with my son. It was he that was not safe; he was not safe from these false accusations, accusations that have not only ruined him, but me too. I've felt the stares in the corner shop, caught someone looking at me on the train into central London. There she is: the rapist's mother. What did she do to him, to make him turn out like that? How can she defend him, knowing what he's done? These questions trail after me all the time, a bad smell that I cannot get rid of no matter how much I scrub myself.

'At what time did you first see Daniel Monkton?'

'When I came down from Sasha's bedroom, I guess it was around twenty past eight.' She sounds more confident now, and I can tell she has rehearsed this, over and over. 'I went into the kitchen with Daniel's brother, Nicholas, to get a drink. Daniel was in there with some of his friends, getting beer from the fridge.'

'Did you speak to him?'

'Yes. I said hello. Happy new year.'

'And did he say anything to you?'

'Nothing much. Hello, how are you, that sort of thing. I went into the front room for a while, then I was back and forth from there to the kitchen for the next hour or so.'

'And when was the next time you saw Daniel Monkton?'

'Around nine-thirty, I think. I bumped into him in the hall and we started talking.'

'Was anyone else there with you?'

'No, it was just Daniel and me. People walked past, of course. I think Sasha and Ellen were in the kitchen.'

The splinter of steel that I've inserted into my heart twists a little further at the thought of Sasha and Ellen, and what I will have to watch them do from up here.

'Can you tell us in your own words what happened next?'

'We talked for ages, just the two of us. At around ten o'clock we . . . ' She falters, then draws a deep breath and continues. 'We started to kiss. There's a little lobby by the front door where they hang the coats, so we went in there. We were leaning up against the coats and kissing, and then he asked me if I wanted to go to his bedroom.'

'And what did you say?' asks the barrister gently.

'I said yes.' She presses her lips together. 'But it didn't mean ... I didn't say ... '

'It's all right, Miss Barton, take your time.'

She's good, I have to give her that. I look along the row to where Karina's mother, Dilys, sits. She has positioned herself as far away from me as possible, her bulk squeezed into the end seat. She is silently crying, mopping her face with an old-fashioned handkerchief embroidered with purple flowers.

'We went up to his room.' Karina has composed herself, hands clinging to the rail again. 'He had some beer bottles in there and we had a drink from them, and talked for quite a long time. Then we started kissing again. We lay down on the bed. He started to pull my skirt up. I told him to stop but he carried on.'

'Did he say anything to you at this point?'

'He said: "This ... "' Her voice cracks, but she sniffs and tries again. 'He said: "This is what you want, isn't it?"'

I dig my nails into my palms as hard as I can and try to think about something, anything, else. I will be here in body every day, but I cannot always be fully present. It is simply not possible.

'And what did you say?' asks the barrister.

'I said no.' Her voice is strong, and for the first time she addresses the jury directly. I can't look at Daniel. I daren't see the expression on his face.

'And did Mr Monkton stop?'

'No.' She's whispering again. 'I pushed his hand away. I pulled my skirt down, but he pulled it up again. I managed to wriggle out from under him and I tried to get out of the room, but he pulled me back and pushed me down on the bed. He smashed his beer bottle, and he held the broken edge against my . . . my private parts. He threatened to cut me . . . inside.'

My legs want to propel me upwards, out of here. I can't listen to any more of this. I grip the edge of my seat. I mustn't make a scene. It will be over soon. I keep repeating to myself: *she's lying, she's lying,* but there's something about it that sounds true. I can't help it, I have to look at him, to see what effect this is having on him. When I do, though, I wish I hadn't. His anguished eyes are fixed on me, and I am terrified that he has seen the doubt in mine.

'What happened next, Miss Barton?'

She twists her hands around and around, licking her lips and trying to control her breathing.

'I'm sorry, I know this is distressing for you.'

'It's OK,' she manages. 'He forced himself on me. He raped me. And then he said if I told anyone, he'd really hurt me. He put a T-shirt under me and cut my thighs with the bottle. He said it was a reminder. Not to tell. That if I told, he'd do something worse next time. When he'd finished, he got up and went to the bathroom. He said he'd see me downstairs in a bit. I couldn't get up. I just lay there for a while, I don't know how long, and then eventually I managed to get up off the bed and stagger out on to the landing. There was no one around. I didn't know what I was doing, but I felt hot so I thought I'd go outside. I went into the garden. I suppose it was freezing out there, but to me it was a relief. I sat down under the mulberry tree. That was where Ellen found me.'

'Thank you, Miss Barton,' says the barrister. 'I appreciate this is difficult. Now, you said that Mr Monkton threatened you with worse injuries if you told anyone what he had done. How did you feel when he said that?'

'I was frightened. I believed he would hurt me badly.'

'Can you tell us why you believed that?'

'Me and Daniel had been in a sort of ... relationship. For about three months.'

I thought we had got to the worst of it, that I had known what the worst of it was, but I was wrong. I sense a movement from the dock and I realise that Daniel's head has whipped round to look at her, an expression of horror on his face. I can't see his barrister's face from here, but I can tell from the set of her back that she is shocked, her pen poised over the papers in front of her.

'Can you tell us what type of relationship, Miss Barton?'

She hangs her head. 'A ... sexual relationship.'

My heart is racing. All those times she was in my house. I would have known, surely? I found out quickly enough about ... the other thing. Is she saying this was going on at the same time?

'During the course of this relationship, can you please tell us how Mr Monkton treated you?'

'He was violent towards me.' She's more defiant now. 'He hit me on several occasions. Once he stubbed a cigarette out on my back.'

Daniel can't tear his eyes away from her. I am horrified

to find myself wondering if he's shocked because she's making it up, or because she's telling the truth.

'He was also . . . ' She presses her lips together, then gathers herself. 'He was violent in the bedroom. He didn't rape me, exactly, but . . . he was violent.'

The barrister regards her solemnly. 'Can you explain what you mean by that?'

'There were times . . . when I didn't really want to do it, to have sex, or it was hurting me, but I didn't say. I didn't say no. But I think he knew. I think he knew I didn't want to, and he . . . he liked that.'

My hands clutch the bench tighter and tighter. One of the screws that hold the seat to the legs is coming loose and the sharp edge of it digs into my palm, but I welcome the pain, increasing the pressure until I feel the wetness of blood, because it dulls the voice in my head: the one that tells me that Karina is speaking the truth, and even worse, that this is all my fault.

Ellen

September 2017

It's years since I was this close to the Monktons' house on foot. I drive past it all the time on my way to visit my parents, but I never walk this way any more. It's smaller than I remember, as things from the past usually are. I try not to look at Karina's old house opposite.

I need to be at the studio at 6 p.m., so I've only got an hour or so. I suppose there's a possibility Olivia won't talk to me at all, a thought that gives me a little stab of pain.

I haven't been able to stop myself keeping an eye on the Monktons over the years, although I've kept my association with them a secret in the industry. If any of the editors I've worked for, or my boss at the radio station, knew I had a personal connection to the elusive Olivia Monkton, they'd never stop hassling me to get an interview. There are often articles written about her, but it's very rare for her to actually speak to a journalist. I can only think of one interview that appeared in the online magazine *Opera Today* a couple of years ago. She was appearing in a touring production of *The Marriage of Figaro*, and they must have pressured her into doing some press. The journalist had obviously been briefed not to ask about her children, but he did manage to slip in a question about how she had been able to balance family life and career. She glossed over it, talked about how supportive Tony was, how the arts could be more flexible than you might think, but I could feel the strain beneath her stock answers; I could hear the real story.

There's less to find online about Tony, but I suppose it was always Olivia who was the star. Even the music press isn't particularly interested in a second bassoon. Nicholas is on LinkedIn, he's a business development manager for a software company, but there's very little information about him. He doesn't seem to be on any other social media sites, or to have done anything news-worthy. There's lots to read about Daniel from around the time of the trial, of course, but nothing recent.

I steel myself as I walk up the path. Nothing much about the outside of the house has changed, it's all just a little shabbier. The front door hasn't seen a coat of paint since I was last inside, the windowsills are chipped, and a couple of tiles hang precariously from the edge of the roof. To the right of the house, the old garage, which was never used to house the car, is even closer to falling down than it was eleven years ago.

The doorbell chimes as it always did, *bing bong, bing bong*, like Big Ben. My stomach dances as I hear foot-steps and a shape looms through the coloured glass panels. There's a brief second of incomprehension on her face, and I think I'm going to have to tell her who I am, but then recognition dawns and she gives a sharp intake of breath, her hand flying to the butterfly necklace she's wearing. I remember that necklace. The butterfly's wings are made of dark amber, threaded with golden, spidery swirls. She twists it in her fingers, the skin on her hands loose and dry.

'Oh!' It's more of a primitive sound, an exhalation, than a word. She doesn't greet me, and continues to stare in what I hope isn't horror, but shock.

'Hello, Olivia.' It comes out smaller than I intended and I clear my throat. I drink in her appearance, taking in her hair, which is almost completely grey now, the collar-bone that protrudes where there used to be a comfortable plumpness, the lines on her face. I wonder if she's as struck by the change in my appearance.

'Ellen.' One thing that hasn't changed is her voice: the melodious, warm richness of it. 'What . . . what are you doing here?'

'I'm sorry, I would have phoned but . . . I needed to see you in person. To talk. It's Sasha.'

A shadow falls over her face. 'Sasha? What do you mean? I haven't seen her since . . . well, I haven't seen her.'

'I know. Can I come in? Please? I need to talk to you.'

'Of course.' She gives herself a mental shake and the old Olivia kicks in: the hostess, the heart of the home, the one who liked to have everybody gathered around her kitchen table. 'Come in.'

Inside, again everything is the same. I don't think they've decorated, and through the door I can see that the piano room is still festooned with piles of books and old newspapers. Even the telephone, on its dusty elephant table in the hall, looks the same, the yellowing handset unbelievably still attached to the cradle by a twisted cord. She leads me past the huge oak bookcase into the kitchen, and I automatically sit down at the table, in what my body obviously still considers to be 'my' chair, the one on the other side of the Aga. I can see through the window, which looks to be as painted shut as it was eleven years ago, into the garden. The grass is overgrown and I'm reminded of that long-ago day when Karina and I explored it, years before the Monktons moved in.

Olivia fills the kettle and places it on the Aga to boil before sitting down opposite me.

'I'm sorry I seemed so shocked. It's lovely to see you, Ellen. It's just ... it's been so long, and what with everything ... '

'I know,' I say quickly. 'It's good to see you too. I've wanted to come before, but I wasn't sure ... '

It's true – there have been many times I've wanted to see her. So many times I longed to tell her what I do for a job. I'm longing to tell her now, even when there are so many more pressing things I need to say. Part of me is wondering, breathlessly, if she is going to ask me that most mundane of dinner party questions: what I do for a living. My parents are immensely proud of me, of course, although I'm sure they wish I had chosen something more reliable as a profession than freelance classical music journalist. Nonetheless they are proud that I am managing to scrape a living from the thing I love, however precarious and meagre. I've always thought it would have really meant something to Olivia, though, to know how much she had inspired me.

'I wish you had come,' she says. 'I would have loved to have seen you. I've seen some of your work, over the years.'

Oh. So she knows, has always known, and yet never got in touch to say ... Well, what could she say, really? The gap between us was too wide for ordinary communication. It was always going to be something like this, some cataclysmic event that drew us back together.

'I didn't think you'd want to see me,' I say. 'I thought if you didn't want to see Sasha, you certainly wouldn't want to see me.'

'It wasn't that I didn't want to see her, exactly,' says Olivia, the crease between her eyebrows deepening. 'But ... she could hardly live here before the trial ...' With a potential rapist, against whom she was testifying. The words she doesn't say rattle around in the silence between us. 'And afterwards ... she went off to university and that was that, we never saw her again. I tried, Ellen, I honestly did. She wouldn't take my calls, though, so what could I do?'

'She wanted to see you really, I'm sure,' I say, although I am nothing of the sort.

69

'I don't know, Ellen,' she says. 'Things were never the same, after she got back from France.'

'Because of the money?' I say, tentatively. I've never discussed this with her.

'What do you mean? What money?'

'The money that went missing from your purse. She said you argued about it, so when she bumped into those old friends of hers and they said they were going to France, she just took off.' I remember the night she finally told me the truth about that summer. It wasn't long after we'd moved in together in London, after university. We'd sat up late one night, working our way through bottle after bottle of wine, and it had all come spilling out. The accusations, Olivia's refusal to believe that Sasha was telling the truth.

'That wasn't ... no, it didn't happen like that. That wasn't it at all.' The kettle is whistling and she gets up, busying herself with mugs, teabags, milk, keeping her back to me.

'What was it then?' I ask.

She puts my tea down in front of me. She has made me Earl Grey without asking; not too much milk, exactly how I like it. Why would Sasha have lied to me? Or is Olivia lying to me now?

'It's all so long ago,' she says. 'I honestly can't remember. I'm sure we did argue about something. Anyway, you said you were here to talk about her?'

'Yes.' I pull my focus back. 'She's gone missing. I've spoken to the police, and they're going to want to talk

70

to you. I wanted to let you know that, and ... also I thought you might know something, or ... I don't know, be able to help.'

'Sasha's missing?' I can see the blusher on her cheeks where her skin has paled beneath it.

'Yes, she didn't come home from work yesterday and no one's seen her since. I called the police today, but they say she's not vulnerable, or a danger to other people, so she's classed as low risk, at the moment, anyway.'

Something passes over Olivia's face, either at the word vulnerable, or possibly at the idea of Sasha being a danger to others, but it's gone so quickly I can't identify it. Her face closes down.

'I'm sorry, Ellen. As I said, I haven't seen her for more than ten years. I haven't even heard from her since she left for university. I certainly won't be able to help the police. Do you and she live together then?'

'Yes, we've shared a flat since we left university.'

'In London?'

'Yes.'

There's a twist of pain in her face, and I feel suddenly guilty. Why did I take what Sasha said at face value? But then why wouldn't I? She had no reason to lie. I assumed if she felt such anger towards Olivia, she must have had good reason.

'I'm not entirely sure why you came,' she says, and there's a slight edge that wasn't there before, a coolness. 'I'm the last person who would know where she is. As for calling the police ... let's face it, it's not exactly unknown

71

for her to disappear without warning, is it? Sounds as though she's done another of her flits. She'll be back.'

'She's different now,' I say. I can't bear this. I know Olivia hasn't seen Sasha in years, but surely it's obvious something isn't right here? 'Something's happened to her, I'm sure of it. She always lets me know where she is. We've been living together for seven years, and in all that time, she's never done this. I'm scared, Olivia.'

Her face softens a little at this, but she won't be moved.

'I'm sorry this is happening to you, Ellen. I know how much you loved her, and I can see you still do.' She says it as though it's weird, like I shouldn't still love her, and I go to speak, but she cuts me off.

'This is what she does, I'm afraid. I know you want to see the best in her, but ... ' She stands up and puts our mugs on the side by the sink, although neither of us have had more than a few sips. I stand up too, close to being defeated, but there is one more thing I need to ask.

'Olivia, there's something else. It's ... it's about Daniel.' It feels as though there is a small bird trapped in my chest, fluttering its wings in a mad attempt to escape.

She has her back to me at the sink so I can't see the expression on her face, but I detect a tightening of her frame, a barely perceptible drawing in. She starts to wash the mugs, squirting a great jet of washing up liquid into one and scrubbing at it with a brush.

'Yes, what?' she says, still with her back to me.

'Is he ... He is still in Scotland, isn't he?'

'As far as I know,' she says lightly, as if she's talking about a mere acquaintance.

'You don't actually know?' I say, my fingers curling into my palms, nails digging in.

She swings round, the brush dripping soapy water on to the terracotta floor tiles.

'Ellen, I hope to God you never have to go through anything close to what I've been through.' For the first time today I see the real her, the woman who had her whole life turned upside down eleven years ago. 'But if you do, maybe you'll understand. I had to hear things no mother should have to hear. I have had to try to make my peace with the man my son is. The only way I can do that is by pretending he doesn't exist. If you think that makes me a monster, then so be it.'

She places the cup upside down on the draining board and wipes her hands on a tea towel.

'It's been lovely seeing you, Ellen, but I've got things to do,' she says, slipping smoothly back into her public persona.

'But my mum ...' Dare I broach this? Mum wasn't sure, after all. I think of Sasha and harden my resolve. 'Mum said she thought she saw Daniel coming here, into this house, last weekend.'

'She was mistaken,' Olivia says sharply. 'Did you not hear a word of what I just said?' She walks into the hall and I have no choice but to follow.

'What about Tony?' I ask in desperation to her retreating back. 'Could Daniel have been here to see him?'

73

'No!' She spins to face me. 'Please, Ellen. It's time you went.'

'Will you at least take my number, in case you think of anything?' I ask.

She agrees reluctantly and taps it into her phone. She opens the front door for me and I almost miss it because I'm looking around, drinking in the details for what I suspect will be the last time, but I just catch the end of a glance Olivia throws up the stairs. I follow her gaze and she immediately launches into chatter, telling me what she's got to do that afternoon, a meeting with a director she's worked with before. In the doorway, I hesitate, wanting to embrace her, to relax into her arms, into the once-familiar smell and feel of her, but she steps back, folding her arms.

'Goodbye, Ellen.'

I blink back the tears that threaten, and walk quickly down the street. When I reach the last point where I can see the house before the road bends away, I take a quick look back. At the window that used to be Sasha's, I catch the tail end of a quick movement, the curtains quivering as if they've just been dropped back into place. Is it Olivia, taking a final look at me, the girl she was once so close to?

Or is there someone else in the house?

Ellen

October 2005

I didn't tell Karina that Sasha had invited me to the party. I knew she would make me ask Sasha if she could come too, and I wanted her all for myself. There was a risk Karina would see me going in, but it was one I was prepared to take. What could she say, after all? I was allowed to have other friends, wasn't I? Even as I justified it to myself, I knew I was being disingenuous. The fact was I knew Karina would be upset and I did it anyway.

Mum seemed pleased I'd found a new friend. She'd always been a bit concerned about my reliance on Karina. Not that she thought there was anything wrong with her – in fact, she and Karina's mum were friends, sort of – but she worried I was too dependent on her, with no other friends to fall back on if things went wrong. She hadn't even said anything when she saw me ready to go to the party in a very short skirt I'd bought specially.

I wanted to linger for a moment outside the house, to compose myself, but the longer I did, the more chance there was Karina would look out and see me, so I hurried through the gate and up the short path to the front door with its stained-glass panel. Goosebumps bloomed on my arms as I stood in the shadow of the corner house, so much larger than any of the others on our street, waiting for someone to let me in. When I heard footsteps inside, I risked a brief look behind me; it might have been my imagination, or a trick of the light, or maybe I really did see a swift movement at Karina's window, someone drawing back into the shadows. Whichever it was, I turned quickly back to the door, where Sasha was standing, luminous in a silver, sequinned dress that winked at me where it caught the light from the streetlamp.

The hall was decorated with hundreds of tiny fairy lights, and a buzz of conversation spilled from the kitchen. On the wall hung a huge picture of a loosely drawn, naked woman's body, the dark lines sweeping languorously across the canvas. To my left there was a low telephone table; its surface was dusty and underneath, instead of legs, an intricately carved elephant held up the tabletop. Through a partially open door to my left I glimpsed a room with floor-to-ceiling shelves, full of books. There was a wood-burning stove, with logs stacked either side of it, and in the corner, the grand piano Karina and I had watched being delivered back in the summer.

'Come on, let's go upstairs.' Sasha grabbed my arm and pulled me towards a wide staircase in the centre of the hall. To the left, behind the stairs, there was a door to what I took to be the kitchen, with a huge oak bookcase next to it containing yet more books. As we were starting up the stairs, the dad came out of the kitchen singing to himself operatically. He had the paisley scarf thing around his neck again and a glass of red wine in his hand.

'Hello there!' he said to me.

'Hello,' I said, blushing, remembering what Karina had said about him that first day. She was right: he was good-looking. For a dad, obviously.

'Why don't you two come into the kitchen and meet some people?'

'Maybe later,' said Sasha. 'Come on, Ellen.'

'OK. Have fun,' he said, wandering off, still singing.

In Sasha's room, the one Karina and I had seen her looking out of that first day, she sank down on the bed.

'Thank God you're here.'

I glowed with pride, although I had no idea why it was so good that I was there. I didn't really care. No one had ever made me feel indispensable before, especially not someone so glamorous, someone who seemed as though they ought to be in the cool girls' gang.

'All these people here supposedly for me,' she went on. 'None of them gives a shit; most of them have never even spoken to me. It's all their friends.'

'Whose friends?' I said, confused. Sasha hadn't told me the party was for her, she'd just said there was going to be one, and asked me to come. That had been a couple of days before, and I hadn't seen her around school to ask her any more. We weren't doing any of the same subjects for A level, and also Karina was back at school and for reasons I couldn't fully identify, I didn't want her to find out I'd got to know Sasha.

'Olivia and Tony's.'

'You call your parents by their first names?' I'd heard of hippies and alternative types who did this, but never met anyone who did it in real life.

'They're not my parents.'

'Oh. So who . . . ?'

'Olivia and Tony are my godparents. My mum's a model, she works all over the world, but she's mostly based in America.' Sasha sounded as if she was reciting something pre-planned, lines in a play. 'She used to take me around with her, but now she thinks I need to be in one place, for my education. She wanted me to finish my studies in the UK, so she sent me to live with Olivia and Tony. They've always been close to my mum.'

'So . . . did you know them, before you came to live with them?' I tried not to sound shocked.

'A bit,' she said. 'I'd met them a few times, when we were visiting.' She slung a quick glance at me. 'It's fine,' she said, laughing. 'Don't look so horrified. Olivia and Tony are great. I'm sixteen, not five.'

'So those boys . . . ?' I thought of their dark heads bent together as they went into the house the day they moved in, Sasha following behind, all alone.

'Their sons, yeah.'

'How old are they? I haven't seen them around school.' Karina hadn't stopped going on about it, in fact: where are those boys?

'Nick's sixteen, he's got a scholarship to Dulwich College, and Daniel's eighteen. He's recently started at the Royal College of Music.' I sensed a subtle sneer there, millimetres below the surface.

'Blimey, he must be dead talented.' Even I'd heard of the Royal College of Music.

'Yeah,' she said. 'He plays the piano. They're all musical. Olivia's an opera singer, quite a famous one, and Tony plays the bassoon in the London Symphony Orchestra.'

'Wow! Really?' My uncle Tim would get his electric guitar out at parties sometimes and play 'Stairway to Heaven', but as far as I knew I'd never met a classical musician. Sasha shrugged, clearly unimpressed. I was about to ask more when there was a tap at the door.

'Sasha, darling, are you in there?' The tone was plummy, rich; nothing like my own mum's reedy tones.

'Come in,' Sasha called, and the door opened. Olivia was both taller and wider than she'd seemed from Karina's window. She was dressed in a long, deep-red tunic over flared black trousers, a tangle of mismatched glass beads hanging from her neck over her voluptuous bust and down to her waist. Her dark hair, spidered with a few silver strands, was piled in a messy bun on top of her head, secured with what looked like chopsticks.

'Oh, hello!' A huge smile spread across her whole face when she saw me. 'You must be Ellen, the friend from school! Sasha said you might be coming!'

'Hello, Mrs . . . ' I blushed, realising I had no idea what her surname was.

'It's Monkton, but call me Olivia, please. Mrs Monkton is Tony's mother to me, and God knows I don't want anyone confusing me with that old bag.' She smiled conspiratorially and I couldn't help warming to her. 'Are you girls all right up here, or do you want anything? There's some Cokes and stuff in the fridge.'

'We're fine, thanks,' said Sasha, more coolly than I was expecting, given her professed happiness with her living situation.

'OK, I'll leave you to it,' she said, her smile still firmly in place, although I could sense disappointment. 'Let me know if you want anything.'

As she closed the door behind her, Sasha slumped back on the bed.

'Coke! What does she think we are, little kids? I'll go down in a bit when they're all pissed and get some proper drinks.'

'Great.' I tried to sound enthusiastic, but I'd never had more than a sip of my dad's beer when we were on holiday, and a couple of alcopops at Tamara Gregg's party last summer. My mum and dad didn't drink at home so there was never any alcohol in the house, apart from an ancient bottle of brandy languishing at the back of the cupboard that my mum bought in a failed attempt to make mince pies one year.

Just then there was a jostling sound on the landing outside. The door opened again and the two brothers tumbled in. They were very alike with their thick, dark hair and long, straight noses. What I assumed to be the younger one was a touch shorter and less broad, with a sprinkling of acne across his forehead and cheeks.

'You could knock, you know!' said Sasha, sitting up.

I tugged uselessly at my skirt, pressing my thighs together. It felt much shorter than it had when I'd left my house.

'Sorry,' drawled the older brother, openly eyeing my legs. 'Bit pissed.'

'A bit!' said the younger one. 'You've been drinking all afternoon. Sorry,' he said to us. 'We'll leave you to it.'

'You're new,' said the older one, swinging his eyes up from my legs to my face, as if he'd only just realised I was someone unknown. 'I'm Daniel.' He plonked himself down next to me on the bed. I shifted away from him slightly, and his brother laughed.

'Look, Dan, she's trying to get away from you! Leave the poor girl alone.'

'Fuck's sake, Nicky! I'm being friendly. Like a normal person. Just because you can't talk to girls without embarrassing yourself.'

The younger brother blushed. Daniel shook my hand in an exaggerated fashion. 'Very nice to meet you ...'

'Ellen.'

'Ellen, of course. Heard all about you.'

I didn't know if he was saying it to be polite, but that was the second person now who claimed to have heard of me, and it warmed me inside a little. Had Sasha really mentioned me? I wasn't used to being talked about.

'Seeing as you're here, you can make yourself useful

and go and find me and Ellen something proper to drink,' said Sasha coldly.

Daniel stood up unsteadily and bowed elaborately.

'Your wish is my command, Lady Sasha.'

His brother nudged him, and I got the impression that this was a nickname they usually only used behind her back.

'It's all right, Nick,' Sasha said. 'I know that's what you call me.' Nicholas, whose face had only just returned to its normal colour following Daniel's earlier remarks, blushed again. 'Just go and get us a bloody drink, OK?'

'Sorry,' Nicholas muttered to Sasha, and the two of them shuffled out of the room.

Five minutes later, Nicholas reappeared, plonked a half-full bottle of wine and a couple of tea-stained mugs from the kitchen down on Sasha's bedside table, and left us to it. I winced at the first sip, but once I'd forced a mug of it down I stopped noticing the sour taste. Emboldened by the wine, I pressed her again.

'So, how are you finding it so far? Living here, with them?'

'It's fine,' she said. 'I'm pretty self-sufficient anyway. Used to looking after myself, I mean. I don't need to feel ... part of the family. I'm happy doing my own thing.'

'I don't always feel like part of my family,' I confessed. I'd never voiced this thought before, but as I said it, I realised it had been there, lurking in the corner of my brain, for quite some time. 'Sometimes I feel like I'm a changeling child, you know like in one of those fairy tales? I like books and art, I'm interested in what's going on in the world. My mum and dad are only interested in what's happening in *EastEnders*, or the football results, or John and Linda's new conservatory.'

'They sound nice,' said Sasha. 'Nothing wrong with being a bit boring.'

'I know. It's just that . . . well, something like this would never happen at my house.' I waved a hand towards the door. Downstairs, someone was playing the piano and a man was singing an opera song. A heady babble of conversation, laughter and music drifted up the stairs. As it had in the classroom that first day, Sasha's hand stole to her cheek, where I could still see a faint scar through her expertly applied foundation. I took another gulp of wine.

'How did you do that, to your face? If . . . if you don't mind me asking?'

'Why should I mind?' She dropped her hand. 'I got locked out once, at my old house. Forgot my keys. My mum wasn't due back for hours, so I had to break a window to get in. Stupid, really. Thank God for make-up!' Sasha drained her mug and picked up the bottle, but it was empty.

'We need some more booze. Come on.'

I stood up to follow her, swaying a little and privately thinking I'd better not have any more. At the bottom of the stairs, Sasha headed for the kitchen in search of wine, but instead of going with her, I was drawn across the hall to the front room, the one with the piano and the books piled everywhere. From the doorway, I could see Daniel seated at the piano. He made to get up, but Olivia, sitting on the sofa by the window, called out to him.

'Oh no, Dan, play something else. What about that Schubert?'

'I think everyone's heard enough, Mum,' he said, glancing around the room.

'Oh no, it's *wonderful*,' gushed a thin, olive-skinned woman in a canary-yellow trouser suit. 'I'd love to hear more.'

'OK.' He stood up and lifted the seat of the piano stool, searching for the piece.

'Oh, if I *must*.' I looked to my left, unsure as to whether I had heard the muttered words correctly. Nicholas was standing in the corner of the room. He grinned at me and rolled his eyes. 'My brother, the musical prodigy,' he said. 'I think I've heard enough, even if Mum hasn't.'

As he passed me and left the room, my attention was drawn back to Olivia, who was watching Daniel as his hands started to move across the keys again. She was mesmerised, lost in the music, and I thought I saw tears glistening in her eyes. Daniel too was swept up in the notes that tumbled effortlessly from his fingers, filling the room, silencing the chatter. He hardly seemed to need the sheet music in front of him, and for a few disconcerting seconds I thought it was me he was looking at, a peculiar, unreadable expression on his face – hatred, maybe, or longing. Or perhaps both. Then I realised that it wasn't me he was looking at, at all. His eyes were focused just to the right of my face, over my shoulder. I turned and saw Sasha standing behind me with a bottle in her hand, her face in shadow, bright hair silhouetted like a halo by the hall lamp behind her. She stepped forward to pour some wine into the empty mug in my hand, and as she did so, I caught the tail end of a secret little smile that wasn't meant for me.

Ellen

September 2017

At the studio, preparing for the show, my earlier encounter with Olivia hangs around me like a cloak. There have been so many times over the years that I've dreamed of being reunited with her, but I always imagined it would be my professional life that would bring us back together. I never thought it would be Sasha. In my daydreams, Olivia welcomed me with open arms, delighted beyond measure to discover she had inspired a lifelong love of classical music in me. Finding out that she has always known about my work is a kick in the teeth, the casual way she mentioned it making me wince every time I think of it.

I wonder if PC Bryant has got anywhere, or whether she's even looking for my low-risk, un-vulnerable, non-dangerous friend. I think of all the things Bryant asked me. One of them was about Sasha's social media accounts, and it occurs to me that I haven't checked them. I grab my phone and open Twitter. Sasha does have an account but I don't think she uses it much. I only use mine for work stuff, to keep up with the classical music world and attempt to promote the station, or my articles. She hasn't tweeted for nine months, and that was only to retweet a newspaper article about domestic violence. I switch to Facebook. I rarely check my account, and post even more infrequently, but I know she's a bit more active on there. Her most recent update is from the weekend before last. It's a photo of her and Rachel on the Southbank as evening falls, the London skyline visible behind them. *Out on the town in the best city in the world* reads the caption. Sasha looks right into the camera, half-laughing at a joke we are not privy to. I remember her saying she was going out with Rachel and some of her other university friends. I always work the Saturday evening shift at the station – I offered when I first started, eager to impress, and now I'm stuck with it, otherwise I would have joined them. It's not the first time my work has got in the way of my social life, but I've never minded. I still feel so lucky to do what I do, to make a living from the thing I love. I think Sasha minds a bit, making occasional digs about how I'm too busy to spend time with my friends. She'll send me photos of her and Rachel out on a Saturday night – two cocktails on a table, or a selfie of the two of them smudged up together, cheek to cheek, shining with joie de vivre. *Look what you're missing.*

I click on the 'likes', checking I didn't forget anyone when I gave Bryant the list of her friends. I know them all, by name at least. Work colleagues, old university friends, the odd ex-boyfriend she's stayed friendly with. A name catches my eye and my hand freezes over the screen, my breath suddenly very loud in the silence: Leo Smith. He hasn't just liked the photo, he's 'loved' it with a little red heart. I knew she was friends with him on Facebook – I am too, have been since we were at school – but he never likes or comments on my photos. I didn't know she'd had any contact with him, or heard from him in years. An old, buried jealousy shifts within me, a tiny flame I thought was extinguished long ago. I scroll through her newsfeed, checking each photo and status update for Leo's name. It doesn't appear often, but every now and then he 'loves' a photo of her, even doing the heart eyes emoji on a particularly pouty one, and very occasionally commenting. *See you there*, he has written on one where she says she's on her way to a party. See you there? Where? It was about a month ago, but I can't remember her saying she was going to a party. It was a Saturday, so I would have been working. Why didn't she tell me she'd seen Leo? She knows I'd want to know, to hear about him. My thoughts tumble ahead, seeing them entwined together, as I did so many times in my imagination as a teenager. I know he fancied her when she first moved in with the Monktons, but she swore she wasn't interested in him. And when he and I finally got together, that long, hot summer without her, I had done my best to put it to the back of my mind. He was with me, and that was enough. It was nothing to do with her, how it ended. If it hadn't been for the New Year's Eve party and all that followed, maybe we would still be together now. Instantly I chide myself for my stupidity. Who ends up with their high school boyfriend? We would have fallen apart somehow or other in the end.

That doesn't matter now, anyway. What matters is finding Sasha, and if Leo knows anything that might help, I need to swallow my pride and my ridiculous, decade-old jealousy and get in touch. I message him on Facebook, explaining that Sasha is missing and I need to see him. I can't risk him not replying, I need him to understand the seriousness of the situation.

He messages back straight away: What do you mean, missing? Are you sure she hasn't done one of her disappearing acts? P.S. Nice to hear from you, hope you're well. x

No, she would have told me, I type. Looks from her FB page like you have seen her recently. Can we meet up? I am really worried about her.

OK, when?

I'm working tonight, but could meet for a coffee tomorrow morning? Wherever you like.

He suggests a coffee shop in Soho, and we arrange to meet there at eleven.

My show passes in a blur and when I hand over to Matthew for the night shift, I realise I hardly know what music I've played.

'You OK?' says Matthew, once he's got his first piece of music on, shifting his headphones back off one ear.

'You seemed a bit distracted on air. I was listening on my way in.'

'Oh God, really?' I thought I'd done a reasonable job of hiding my state of mind. 'I hope Anna wasn't listening.' Anna is our boss, by turns charming and terrifying, and we live in fear of disappointing her.

'On a Saturday night? Nah, she'll be out gallivanting.' Despite being in his thirties, Matthew's vocabulary is that of an elderly man, a war veteran. 'How's the fragrant Sasha?' Matthew met Sasha once, a few months ago, when she came to meet me after a shift, and has never forgotten her. He's married, so I assume (well, I hope) his interest in her is merely aesthetic, that he appreciates her the way one might a painting or a particularly lovely view.

'She's . . . I don't know, actually. She didn't come home last night, she . . . ' I dissolve into tears.

'Hey, come on.' Matthew pats me awkwardly on the shoulder and looks furtively at the computer screen to see how much time there is left on this piece.

'Sorry,' I say, standing up. 'You've got your show to do. I shouldn't have said anything. I'll see you soon.' I hurry out of the studio, leaving him looking perplexed and somewhat relieved.

Out on the street, I take in a lungful of the cool night air and start walking to the tube station. If I worked on Classic FM I'd be in Leicester Square right now, threading my way through street performers and tourists and hen parties up in town for a big night out. As it is, I'm hurrying along the Wandsworth Road, my coat pulled closely around me. A group of young men spill out of a pub as I pass, debating the merits of going on to a club. One of them stumbles and knocks into me, and I shrink back in alarm.

'Sorry,' he says, holding his hands up in exaggerated apology.

I hurry on, more shaken than the incident merits. The street is getting quieter, pubs and chicken shops giving way to residential buildings. I look over my shoulder, walking faster and faster. Matthew usually gets a taxi home when he does a late shift, but his wife has some high-powered job in the City, so unlike me he can afford to blow half his wages on cab fares. I'm not far from the station now, but my sense of unease is growing, along with a feeling that someone is following me. I haven't seen or heard anyone, but I have developed a sixth sense for these things, as all women have since the first time we walked home alone with our keys clasped in our knuckles, our bodies flooded with adrenaline, poised for fight or flight. I force myself to keep walking steadily, although the clip of my heels is getting faster and faster. I steal another look behind me but there's no one there. I can see the lights of the station up ahead and can bear it no longer. Gripping my bag with one hand, I break into a run, my breath coming in short gasps, my shoes slapping on the pavement, and finally I'm there, the bright lights enveloping me. I stand for a moment in the ticket hall, allowing my breathing to return to normal, pretending to look through my bag for my ticket.

I am safe. I probably always was safe. Unless . . . unless I have never been safe. Maybe security has been an illusion, a ten-year masquerade that is only now approaching its final act.

Ellen

September 2017

I see Leo before he sees me. He's sitting in the window, on a high stool, looking the other way up the street. He looks the same, as I suppose he would. A little worn around the edges, perhaps, his golden syrup hair a touch darker. I stand there on the street for a minute, the rain flattening my carefully blow-dried hair. I have an urge to turn and run, to choose not to face him, this, whatever it is. Then I think of Sasha, and I know I have no choice. No one else is looking for her. It doesn't matter what she's done. She needs me, as she always has. I push the door open and he turns at the tinkling of the bell, his face breaking into a wide grin at the sight of me.

'Ellen!' He stands up and kisses me on both cheeks. He was always confident, but time has added a certain polish. 'Can I get you a coffee?'

'Yes, please.' I welcome the chance for a couple of minutes to get a handle on my feelings, how I'm going to play this.

He comes back with my coffee and sits next to me. 'Still no word from her?' he says.

'No.'

'God, that's worrying. When did you last see her?'

'Thursday night, but she was at work Friday morning. I was still asleep when she left – we share a flat.'

'I know.' He looks at me oddly. 'Did she not tell you she'd been seeing me?'

'Seeing you?' I put my cup down on the table too hard and coffee slops on to my fingers.

'Sorry, I don't mean … seeing me, like going out with me. I mean we'd seen a bit of each other. As friends.'

My heartbeat slows again.

'No, she didn't mention it. When did … How did you get back in touch?'

'We've always been Facebook friends – like you and I. Then I bumped into her in the pub randomly, a couple of months ago, I guess. It turned out we had a couple of friends in common, and had both been invited to the same party a few weeks later.'

See you there.

'We've met for a drink a couple more times since. With other people too,' he adds hastily. 'It was good to catch up. Her boyfriend was there one of the times – Jack, is it?'

'Jackson.' He never mentioned it, but maybe he doesn't know I know Leo too. I wonder if he was jealous of Leo, suspicious of this re-kindling of an old friendship. He was jealous of pretty much everyone else she talked to.

'Have you called the police?'

'Yes. They weren't much use, though. They've classed her as low-risk. They said she's not vulnerable.'

'Ha. They're not wrong.'

'What do you mean?' My hackles rise.

'You know what I mean. Sasha – she's tough as old boots.'

Is she?

'You don't know her like I do.' I try to speak emphatically but I can't quell the note of uncertainty that creeps in.

'No, I know, but I remember her from the old days. Nothing fazes her.'

Not nothing.

'The thing is, I was at my mum's yesterday, and she said she'd seen ... well, she thought she might have seen Daniel. On our road.'

'Daniel Monkton?' Leo looks horrified, and I remember how badly he had been affected at the time. He was closer to Nicholas, but he'd still considered Daniel a mate. Leo withdrew, went into himself after the New Year's Eve party. We'd tried to keep things going between us, but it was too hard, for both of us, and eventually he'd brought our relationship to a limping close.

'She might have been mistaken, I guess. It could have been Nicholas – they were pretty alike, although I don't really know what either of them look like now.'

'No, me neither,' said Leo, drumming his fingers on the table.

'She didn't mention them, did she? The Monktons? When you saw her?'

'God, no, we didn't get into any of that. Did . . . Do you and her talk about it?'

'Not really.' It's the great unspoken truth that lies between us, keeping us apart yet glueing us together.

'Can you think of anything she did say that might give a clue as to where she is now? Anything at all?'

'No, sorry. We didn't have any deep conversations. It was all . . . light, you know. Nothing serious.'

I take a sip of my coffee. This is getting me nowhere. I shouldn't have come. My phone trills in my bag and I get to it just in time, almost cutting the call off in my haste to swipe and put the phone to my ear in one swift movement.

'Hello?'

'Is that Ellen Mackinnon?' I recognise PC Bryant's voice and everything goes into slow motion. What is she phoning for? Images flash through my brain.

'Yes, speaking,' I manage.

'Don't worry, it's not bad news,' she says, as if she can read my thoughts. 'We called all the hospitals and she's not been taken in to any of them, and she's not coming up on the police database.'

Is this what she calls good news?

'I've also been able to gain access to Sasha's mobile phone records and her bank account. Her phone hasn't been used since Friday morning, and appears to have been switched off ever since. We can investigate further in due course if necessary.'

If necessary? What does that mean? Something must have happened on Friday morning to cause her to walk out of her life.

'And her bank account?'

'Yes, I wanted to ask you about that,' she says, and something tells me I'm not going to like what she's going to say.

'There was a large withdrawal in cash from Sasha's account last week.'

'How large?'

'She pretty much cleared out the account. There was around twenty thousand pounds in there. Do you have any idea why Sasha might have done that?'

My stomach has dropped away, as if I'm on a rollercoaster that's just plunged down from its teetering heights.

'No,' I say. 'No idea at all.'

'I know when we spoke last time,' she goes on carefully, 'you thought it was unlikely Sasha had decided to take some time out.'

'Yes.' I know where she is going with this, but Sasha wouldn't take off without telling me.

Wouldn't she? says the voice in my head.

'The fact that she's made this withdrawal does perhaps indicate that she was planning to go away,' says Bryant.

'But her passport – she didn't take her passport,' I say in desperation.

'Maybe she hasn't gone abroad,' says Bryant gently.

I can tell she thinks I'm clutching at straws, and

perhaps I am. Perhaps I have been walking around blind-folded for the last twelve years.

'There's something else,' she says. 'We spoke to Sasha's boyfriend, Jackson Pike.'

'Yes?'

'He said they'd argued a couple of days before she disappeared.'

'They argue all the time. That doesn't mean anything.' Leo is watching me intently. *The police*, I mouth to him.

'Yes, I got that impression,' says Bryant. 'However, Jackson said he suspected she was seeing someone else, and that during the argument, Sasha said she needed a break, wanted to get away. That she'd had enough of all this.'

'That doesn't mean anything. He always thought she was seeing someone else. He was jealous, the jealous type. And as for her saying she wanted to get away – it's exactly the sort of thing she'd say without meaning it, a throwaway remark.'

'Please understand, Ellen, we're not closing the case. But what Jackson has told us, along with the fact that she has disappeared in the past without explanation, plus the withdrawal from her bank account, means we are not able to treat this as a high-risk case. We'd love to be able to leave no stone unturned looking for every missing person, but we do have to prioritise. We'll keep looking, keep talking to people, we're going to check CCTV footage, but I'm not able to escalate the investigation any further than that at this stage. As I said before, do keep in touch, let me know if anything happens that might change things, or of course if you hear from Sasha herself.'

I agree that I will, but I know I'm not going to hear from Sasha. Either something has happened to her, and I'll never hear from her again, or ... or something else is going on.

'What about Daniel?' I ask. 'Did you run him through the computer?'

'Yes, I did. Obviously he's on record, due to the conviction in 2007, but there's nothing since then. He certainly hasn't crossed the police's path since his release in 2012. His probation ended recently, and I haven't yet been able to ascertain where he's living. His parents say they haven't heard from him in years. There's not a great deal more I can do, I'm afraid, in the absence of any specific threat.'

We say goodbye, and I take Leo through what Bryant told me. He listens and expresses concern, but I'm aware that he's not invested in this, not like I am. If something bad has happened to her, it feels like I'm the only one who can find her, the only one who's properly looking for her. And if something else is going on here, I need to know what it is.

I feel like I'm walking up a mountain through cloud, murky and damp against my skin. Perhaps Sasha is somewhere up there at the top, in the sunshine above the clouds, throwing back her head and laughing, her golden hair tossed by the wind.

I just hope she's not laughing at me.

Ellen

September 2017

The text pings in at 6 p.m. on Sunday evening. Sasha has
been gone for more than forty-eight hours.

Can I come over? Need to talk.

Oh God. Jackson. What does he want? I'd be tempted
to ignore him if I didn't know he'd come over anyway. I
consider making an excuse, but I can't keep him away for
ever. And actually, I should speak to him again, in case
he knows something. I don't think he's got anything to
do with Sasha's disappearance. He's besotted with her,
although sometimes he has a funny way of showing it.
But he might be able to shed some light.

By the time the buzzer goes, I'm a third of the way
down a bottle of wine. Usually that would be enough
to blur the edges, but tonight I'm razor sharp. I don't go
to the door straight away. Instead I carry on standing in
the kitchen, looking at a photo of Sasha and me on the
fridge. It was taken on a night out a couple of years ago –
Rachel's birthday, I think it was. Sasha's wearing a black

catsuit and her cheeks are highlighted in silver, sparkly face paint. She looks otherworldly, like a unicorn or a dryad. She's smiling straight into the camera; I'm looking up at her adoringly.

The buzzer goes again and I'm jolted out of my introspection. I buzz him up and then peer through the peephole until he appears, pushing his dark hair back impatiently, looking up and down the corridor. I open up and he comes straight in without being asked. There are dark hollows under his eyes, and he carries with him the faint scent of rolling tobacco and stale smoke.

'Do you want a drink?' I ask his retreating back as he strides into the lounge.

'Yeah, glass of wine, please,' he throws back over his shoulder.

When I come in with his drink and my own replenished, he is sprawled on the sofa, legs apart, one knee jiggling up and down frenetically.

'What's going on, Ellen?' he says. 'Where is she?'

'I don't know.' I sit down primly in the armchair – Sasha's chair, the one she always sits in, to the point where I can feel the imprint of her beneath me. 'If I knew that I wouldn't have called the police, would I?' Who does he think he is, barging in here without even saying hello or asking me how I am?

'What did the police say to you?' he asks, leaning forward. His elbow comes to rest on his knee and the jiggling stops abruptly.

'They won't do anything much. They say she's not

vulnerable, not high risk. And also . . . ' I am unwilling, for some unidentifiable reason, to tell him about the money.

'What? What is it?'

Shit, why couldn't I have kept my mouth shut? I try to make something up but my mind is slow, my thoughts sticking to me like thick, black treacle. Anyway, I suppose he might know something about the money, something that might help.

'She cleared out her bank account last week. Took the lot – twenty thousand pounds.'

'What? Why?'

'I don't know. I thought maybe you might?'

'No.' He looks genuinely bewildered, raking his fingers through his hair till it stands up on end.

'She hadn't mentioned anything, or . . . I don't know . . . been anywhere?' It's a stab in the dark, but he frowns and starts nodding.

'There've been a few times when she wasn't where she said she would be.'

'What do you mean?'

'I called her at work one afternoon and she wasn't there. Her work phone kept going to voicemail and her mobile was off, so I called reception and they said she was on annual leave. When I asked her about it later, she said she'd gone out to a meeting, that the receptionist must have got it wrong.'

'When was this?' A sick feeling creeps into me, as it has every time someone has said something about her that doesn't make sense, something I can't understand.

'A couple of weeks ago? I thought . . . '

I know what he thought. I would have thought the same under the circumstances.

'She wasn't cheating on you, Jackson. I'm sure of that.' I'm not sure of it, or indeed of anything, but loyalty to Sasha compels me to keep on playing my part. I wonder again about the Friday before she disappeared, what had put her in such a strange mood. 'The police told me that you'd argued, a couple of days before she disappeared.'

'I wish I'd never said anything!' He jumps up and goes over to the window, staring out wildly. 'I was trying to be honest, thought it was best to tell them anything that might help. What if they think I had something to do with it?'

I'm not quick enough to reply and he whirls round furiously. 'Not got anything to say to that? Maybe you think I've done something to her too?'

'No! I don't, Jackson. Honestly.' I am tempted to tell him my fears about Daniel, but I don't know how much Sasha has told him about what happened back then, so I hold back.

'No, she's taken off,' he says. 'I'm getting more and more sure of it. She was definitely up to something.'

'Why are you so sure she's to blame?' Unexpected anger explodes within me like a rocket that whines slowly up and then bursts into scattering, incandescent sparks of burning light. 'Why are you so quick to assume she's in the wrong? You came barging in here on Friday, demanding to know where she was, and now you're implying that she was up to something dodgy, that she's run off with someone or something. Can you not step outside your stupid, selfish head for one minute and admit the possibility that something's happened to her? That someone has hurt her, or taken her? Don't you even care?'

'Yes, of course I care.' His eyes blaze. 'What do you think I'm doing here?'

'I think you're trying to insinuate horrible things about her ... That she was cheating on you. How dare you—'

'Oh, for fuck's sake, Ellen, she's not perfect. In fact, she can be a total bitch when she puts her mind to it. What is it with you and her? Why are you still sticking up for her? It looks as though she's pissed off without even bothering to tell you where she's going and you're still defending her.'

I try to take a breath but there's nothing there. His words have knocked it out of me. He stands up and walks to the door, taking one last shot at me before he goes.

'I think you're protesting too much. You know what I'm saying is true, you just don't want to admit it. You know as well as I do what she's really like. See you, Ellen.'

With that he is gone, leaving a bitter, dark cloud in his wake. Every time I try to breathe in, it's as if I'm inhaling his vicious words. They echo through my mind, running through my bloodstream, faster and faster, until I'm close to passing out. It's the grain of truth in them that is the worst part, the part that really hurts.

I need to do something to drown out his voice in my

head. Something practical, to help Sasha. I think about what Olivia said about Daniel. I can understand why she's had to shut it out, what he did. God knows, I've tried to do it myself over the years. I guess Sasha did too because we rarely spoke about it. For the five years he was in prison, I could breathe, but everything changed when he was released. We had been told at the time to expect his custodial sentence to be around five years, so it shouldn't have come as a complete shock, but it did. I had almost managed to convince myself that it was never going to happen, that he had magically disappeared and I'd never have to think about him again. It was the first time we'd heard anything from Karina since the trial. She didn't contact us directly, but she asked her mum to tell my mum. They were legally required to let Karina know he was coming out. We'd have realised anyway, because it wasn't long after that the letters started.

I google him periodically, of course. I can't help myself. There's never anything new, but adrenaline buzzes through me nonetheless as I open my laptop, feeling the warmth of it on my crossed legs. I type 'Daniel Monkton' into Google. I am quite au fait with the other Daniel Monktons. One of them is a magician in America, with a good line in children's parties; another enjoys posting racist memes on Twitter. The ones that do relate to him are all old articles about the trial that I've read before. I do my usual round of searches – Facebook, Twitter, Instagram, LinkedIn.

Nothing. His present-day digital footprint is non-existent – no mean feat in this day and age. It's as if he simply doesn't exist.

I drum my fingers on my laptop, unable to stop my thoughts straying to one person – a person who, in a way, is the last who would know anything, the last person who would want to see him. She won't want to see me either. But Sasha and I, we went out on a limb for Karina. We testified in court against Daniel. I've always secretly felt that she should have been more grateful than she was, but I suppose given what she'd been through, it was unreasonable of me to have expected anything of her at all. But I wonder now if she knows anything – after all, she was told when he was released from prison. Maybe they keep her informed of his whereabouts? And if they don't, then don't I have a duty to warn her? If Daniel has done something to Sasha, Karina is in danger too. As am I, but I am trying to keep that particular thought firmly at bay. Sasha needs me to be functioning. I mustn't let her down.

I've looked for Karina on Facebook before, but she doesn't seem to be on there. I try again though, scanning down the list, but as ever, none of them are her. I suppose she might have got married, or changed her name for other, murkier reasons. I google her, but I can only find other Karina Bartons, ones who are doing charity runs or posting on Instagram or offering aromatherapy services. I check them all out, just in case.

My fingers dance over the phone's keypad without me

having to think about it at all, and after a couple of rings she answers.

'Hello?'

'Hi, Mum, it's me. Is … is everything OK?' Even though I know she always answers the phone sounding as if some terrible disaster has befallen her, I still have that moment's fear, every time, that this time, something actually has.

'Yes, I'm fine. Have you heard from Sasha?'

'No, that's why I'm calling. The police won't do anything, not yet, anyway, so I'm trying to speak to anyone who might have an idea where she is. I thought … I might speak to Karina?' I sense waves of concern rippling down the telephone wire. I go on, not giving her a chance to voice them. 'I wondered if you had a telephone number or address for her mum? Obviously I know they moved, but I wasn't sure where to.'

'Is that a good idea?' she says, careful to keep any judgement from her voice.

'I don't know, Mum!' Frustration bubbles up. 'Did you not hear what I said? Sasha has disappeared. I'll do anything, talk to anyone.'

'Is it a good idea to go digging all that up, though? Are you sure Sasha's not taken herself off somewhere? You know what she's like.'

I thought I did, but I can still hear Jackson's words, still feel them.

'Please, Mum, I need to know what's happened. Do you know where Karina's mum lives?'

She sighs and I can hear rustling as she flips through the pages of her address book, an ancient tome in which the dead are crossed through with a black magic marker.

'I've got an address,' she says. 'Dilys gave it to me when they moved. She said she'd get in touch when they got a telephone number sorted, but she never did. I didn't expect it, really. She did write to me when Daniel was released from prison, but she still never gave me her number.'

She gives me the address, a street I know in Forest Hill, ten minutes or so from where they used to live.

'They didn't go far, then,' I say.

'No. Dilys's life was around here, wasn't it? She just couldn't stand living opposite . . . well, you know.'

Opposite the family of the boy who had ruined her daughter's life as it was just beginning. I extricate myself from the conversation as soon as I can, and sit staring at the scrap of paper on which I've written the address, my mind a jumble of conflicting thoughts.

I am wired when I get into bed, with no chance of sleep. Yes, I'm worrying about Sasha, I'm thinking about Karina, plus the argument with Jackson still reverberates through me. It's not only that, though. After a few minutes of lying there, every muscle in my body tensed, I realise what it is: I'm listening. I'm alone in the flat, and the only person with a key is the one person I want to see more than anyone in the world. And yet I am listening and, more than that,

I am waiting. Waiting for the creak of a floorboard, the tinkling of glass; for a sign that the day I have been awaiting for five years is here. The day Daniel Monkton makes me pay.

Olivia
July 2007

I am desperate for the loo, but Dilys is sitting in my path, at the end of my row. We've got an hour for lunch and I assumed she would be getting up to leave, but she looks rooted to her seat. I'll either have to ask her to move or squeeze past her, feeling the warmth of her skin, hatred oozing from every pore. I consider waiting, but I can't, those two cups of coffee I had to sustain me before I came in pressing urgently on my bladder. I briefly consider climbing over the bench in front and going along the next row, but I'll look ridiculous, plus I'll attract her attention anyway doing that. I stand up and move along our row until I get to her.

'Excuse me, please.'

She doesn't look up; doesn't acknowledge me.

'Dilys, please.'

'Don't use my name,' she hisses, still not looking at me. 'Don't you dare speak my name.'

'I'm sorry,' I say, unsure exactly what I am apologising

for. Using her name? Making her move out of her seat? Raising a depraved sexual predator of a son? 'I need to go to the lavatory.' I curse myself for using such a ridiculous, upper class word. I haven't said 'lavatory' since I was a little girl and my mother told me that 'toilet' was vulgar.

'Oh, I'm sorry, you need to go to the *lavatory*?' She elongates the word, putting on an absurdly posh accent. 'Why on earth didn't you say?' She stands up so I can get past, and I am nearly out of the door that leads down to the loos, but she hasn't finished with me.

'Why couldn't you have stayed away from her?' I get the sense that these are words she has been trying to keep in, words she wanted but also didn't want to say, that are now spilling out of her in a torrent of bile. 'With your music, and your pictures, and all those books? Staring out of that window all summer. She thought I didn't notice but it was all she could talk about. She was perfectly happy before you came on the scene.'

'I'm sorry,' I say again, weakly.

'It's a bit late for that, isn't it? Much too late.' We stare for a few seconds, eyes locked, until I drop mine.

'I must ...' I mutter, and escape through the door, running down the stairs, my heart thudding in my chest. My instincts are screaming at me to run out of the courthouse and keep running, to get as far away from Dilys as I possibly can. I won't, though. I can't. I have other, stronger impulses that bind me to this place, until it is finished, one way or the other.

I avoid her when I get back, sitting in the last row

with my back to the wall, but she ignores me anyway, completely focused on Karina as she re-takes her place on the stand, looking more nervous than ever.

Daniel's barrister stands up and I notice for the first time how small and slight she is. Her dark hair is tied back in a glossy ponytail under her wig.

'Miss Barton,' she begins. 'On the evening of the thirty-first of December 2006, did Daniel Monkton hurt you in any other way, other than the wounds to your thigh? Were there any other physical signs that you had been forced into sexual intercourse?'

'No.' She sounds unsure, and again I am torn between my natural female impulse to believe her, and my opposite maternal protective instinct.

'There are witnesses that say you were ... let's say ... *interested* in the Monkton family before you had even met them. That you observed them moving into the house opposite yours in the summer of 2005, and that you subsequently spent many hours watching them from your window. That your interest verged on obsession. Would you say that was true?'

'No,' she says, back on surer ground. 'Of course I saw them moving in: they live right opposite. I became friends with Sasha when she started at our school. But I wouldn't say I was obsessed with them. Not at all.' She's lying now, I'm sure of it. I had seen the hunger in her face, but stupidly thought it harmless. In fact, more than that: I was flattered. I loved how she had cast me as the welcoming head of this bohemian, musical family, a family so much

112

more interesting than her own. I thought I was broadening her horizons, showing her what life could be. What ridiculous vanity that seems now. But I was distracted, wasn't I? I was looking the other way; I thought danger lay in another direction. I was so busy taking care of the other situation, I completely missed this one.

'OK,' says the barrister thoughtfully. 'This relationship that you say you had with Daniel Monkton in the three months preceding New Year's Eve 2006 – did anybody know about it?'

'No, not as far as I knew at the time.'

'You didn't tell any of your friends?'

'No. He wanted us to keep it a secret. He didn't want anyone to know.'

'None of your family or friends ever questioned where you were going when you went to meet him?'

'No. We ... we didn't see each other all that often. He was ... busy.' There's a vestige of shame at having to admit to how little she'd been prepared to accept. Something shifts inside me, as it does every time she says something that sounds true.

'And there were no communications between you – no texts, emails, phone calls?'

'He didn't want us to call or text or anything. We would arrange each time when was the next time we would see each other. Usually it would be times when he knew there wouldn't be anyone in at his house. It didn't matter because if I turned up and there was someone there, I could pretend I'd come to see Sasha.'

I try to remember if there were times when she came to the door and looked surprised to see me, but it's hopeless. She and Ellen spent so much time at the house it's impossible to pick out any particular occasion.

'So there is no evidence whatsoever that this three-month relationship actually happened?'

'No, but that was because—'

'I put it to you,' she interrupts smoothly, 'that no such relationship existed. That on the night of the thirty-first of December 2006, you engaged in consensual sex with Daniel Monkton. Then, for reasons I can only guess at, you took his beer bottle, broke it and used it to cut your own thighs, and you falsely accused him of raping you.'

'No, that's not true.' Her knuckles are white on the rail in front of her.

'When you were eleven years old,' the barrister continues, 'did your parents take you to see an educational psychologist?'

Dilys's back goes rigid a few rows in front of me, her head very still. Karina throws a panicked look up at the public gallery.

'Yes.' It sounds more like a question than an answer.

'Can you tell me why that was?'

'It was nothing. I only went a couple of times. The school asked them to ... They were worried about me ...'

'Why were they worried?'

'I was ... making stuff up. About things that were happening at home.'

'What *things*, specifically?' she asks, steely-eyed.

'I told a teacher that my dad had . . . interfered with me.' Her voice has dropped to a whisper. Dilys's head is down.

'And that wasn't true? Your father wasn't sexually abusing you?'

'No,' she says to the floor, two bright spots staining her face.

'And did the psychologist help you to get to the bottom of why you were telling these untruths?'

'She thought . . . ' Karina throws another despairing look up at Dilys. 'She thought I was doing it for attention. Because I was having some trouble settling into secondary school.'

'So at the age of eleven, you levelled some very serious accusations at your father, accusations that could have got him into a great deal of trouble and seen him prosecuted under the law, because you wanted attention?'

'It wasn't like that . . . ' Her words hang helplessly in the air. She knows she has no choice but to answer. The barrister waits, looking at her enquiringly, knowing the same thing. 'Yes,' Karina says, almost under her breath.

I watch her as she steps down from the stand, and a shameful seed of triumph sprouts in me at the defeated slump of her shoulders.

Ellen

October 2005

Karina had seen me, of course. I don't know how I thought she might have missed it, so obsessed was she with the comings and goings at the Monktons'. I knocked for her as usual on the Monday morning to walk to school, but when Dilys answered the door, she looked confused.

'Karina's already left, love. Didn't she tell you?'

'Oh!' I thought quickly. I didn't want her mum to get involved if Karina was going to fall out with me. 'Oh yes, sorry, she did tell me she was going to go in early today. I must have forgotten.'

'You'd forget your head if it wasn't screwed on.' She laughed fondly. She'd always liked me, said I was like one of the family, especially since Karina's dad died.

'I'd better get to school. Sorry about that.' Back on the pavement, I stood for a moment, pretending to rummage in my bag for something. Did I dare to knock for Sasha? We'd had a good time at the party, but in spite of her assertion that Tony and Olivia were great, I could

116

see that she wasn't yet part of the family. Not a cuckoo in the nest, exactly, but still a relative stranger. There'd been an edge in the room when the boys were there, but I wasn't sure if that was because of Sasha, or simply a result of the spiky relationship they had with each other. The party had still been in full flow when I'd bowled home, having promised to be back by 11 p.m., my head whirling not only from the wine but from a heady mix of Sasha's sophistication, the house, the books, the music. She hadn't said anything about when I'd see her next, or mentioned walking to school together. Just as I'd decided to leave it and walk alone, the front door opened and the whole family spilled out on to the path. The two boys were arguing furiously and didn't notice me. They headed off down the street, Daniel walking a few paces ahead, with Nicholas gesticulating in his wake, Olivia shouting last-minute instructions at them before climbing into the passenger seat of their battered Citroën. Tony swung into the driver's seat, calling for Sasha as he did so.

'Sash! Do you want a lift?'

She closed the front door behind her and smiled at me.

'No, thanks, I'll walk.'

She took my arm as we walked down the road. I tried not to think about what Karina would say if she saw us.

'I'm so glad you could come to the party,' Sasha said. 'It would have been even more weird without you.'

'What do you mean?' I said, feeling that same warmth steal over me again at the thought of being the one who made things better for her.

'Oh, you know, what we were talking about, fitting into the family and all that. They're all trying so *hard*. Well, Olivia and Tony are, anyway.'

'Not the boys?' I asked.

'Oh, I don't know, they're ... *boys*. Always thinking about one thing.'

'What, you think they ... fancy you?' I asked, slightly appalled. I knew they weren't her brothers, but still.

'No,' she said. 'Not that. It's just, you know what boys are like.'

I didn't, not really. My entire sexual experience consisted of the kiss at Tamara's party in the summer. I didn't have any boys that I considered friends. They were a race apart as far as I was concerned.

'Don't tell anyone I said so, though, will you?' she said.

'Of course not.' A little thrill went through me at this sign of her trust in me. 'I'm really glad you've come to live here,' I added.

She squeezed my arm. 'Yeah, me too.'

I saw Karina as soon as we walked through the school gates. She was on the far side of the playground talking to Roxanne and Stacey, a couple of girls we hated, and Leo Smith. Karina was flicking her hair around and laughing, her eyes never leaving Leo's face. Although she was hanging from his every word, he was mainly talking to Roxanne and Stacey, hardly even looking at Karina. I was pretty sure he had no interest in her and never would, and I felt a strange kind of pity for her. I wasn't used to feeling sorry for Karina; we'd always been pretty much on an even social footing, part neither of the popular gang, nor of the unfortunates with the thick glasses, or the bad hair, or the oddball parents – the ones who got bullied. But I could see her as I knew Roxanne and Stacey were seeing her, and probably Leo too, if he was thinking about her at all: pathetic; a hanger-on; someone trying too hard to be liked – a failsafe way of making sure the opposite occurred.

She flipped her hair again, and as she did so, she caught my eye. For a second, panic skimmed across her face, and then she smiled. It was brittle, and I wasn't sure what lurked behind it, but it was a smile nonetheless. Maybe she wasn't pissed off with me. Roxanne said something to Leo and she and Stacey flounced off towards the school building. Karina and Leo stood there uneasily for a few seconds, neither of them apparently speaking. Leo said a few words and loped after the girls, leaving Karina twisting her hands together as if she didn't know where to put them.

'I'm just going to go and say hi to Karina,' I said to Sasha.

'I'll come with you.'

'Um, do you mind if you don't? I think she might be in a bit of a mood with me. I should test the water first. If you don't mind, that is,' I added hastily.

'Oh God, is she one of those that gets pissed off with you if you talk to anyone else?' Sasha rolled her eyes. 'What is she, eight? Best friends for ever, cross your heart and hope to die?'

'Yes, something like that,' I said, laughing but feeling

gut-wrenchingly disloyal to the girl who'd come with me to buy my first bra. 'I'll see you later, OK?'

Sasha waved me off, dismissing me from her presence.

As I made my way over to Karina, there was a second when she almost sped off into school, but something stayed her feet, and she looked at me challengingly.

'You left early this morning,' I said, when I realised she was waiting for me to speak first.

'Sorry, I didn't realise we had to do everything together.'

'We don't. But we always walk to school together.'

'We certainly don't do everything together, though, do we?'

'What do you mean?' I knew exactly what she meant, but we had got ourselves into a strange conversational dance, stepping gingerly around each other, confrontation hovering at the borders.

'Oh, for God's sake, you know what I mean, Ellen.' The dance was over.

'Sasha invited me when you were off sick. What was I meant to do – say no?'

'No, of course not. But did you ask her if you could bring me?'

I didn't say anything and she laughed scornfully.

'Exactly.'

'I don't know her that well, Karina. It's a bit weird if I ask to bring my friend. She doesn't even know you.'

'You know how much I wanted to see that house. You know I like the brother, the older one.'

'He's not her brother, actually.'

For a minute her face lit up, eager for details, but then she closed down again, remembering she was still angry with me.

'Whatever. Sorry to have got it wrong. Obviously you know all about them now.'

'Come on, Karina, let's not fall out. If I get invited there again, I'll definitely ask if you can come. OK?'

She hesitated, torn between her desire to get into Sasha's world and her need to punish me. Desire won, as it usually does.

'OK.' She paused, and I knew she was battling with her curiosity. 'Go on, then, what was it like?'

'Exactly what we thought,' I said. 'Dust everywhere, shelves and piles of books, massive pictures on the walls. All the adults got drunk and they were playing the piano and singing opera songs.'

'Oh my God! And what about the boys? Who are they, if they're not her brothers?'

'None of them are her family,' I said, eliciting a satisfying gasp from Karina. 'Her mum is some international model and she decided Sasha needed some stability, so she sent her to live with the Monktons. Olivia and Tony are her godparents. The boys are their sons.'

'And did you meet them?' breathed Karina. 'What are they like?' There was a hunger in her voice, and for the first time I properly understood what this family meant to her. The summer spent staring out of her window had mainly been a distraction for me, something to do on the long, hot days while other girls took exotic holidays. But it was more than that for her. She was . . . invested in them, somehow. No wonder she was so pissed off with me for getting in there first.

'Yeah, I met them. We didn't spend that long with them, though. They're quite . . . competitive. Spent most of the time taking the piss out of each other. I don't think Sasha gets on with them all that well.'

'Maybe they're in love with her,' she said. 'I mean, they're not related, are they? That would be so romantic!'

'I don't think so.' I thought about what Sasha had said on the walk to school today, and also about the way Daniel had looked me up and down on the bed. I decided not to tell Karina about that, pretending to myself that I thought she might be jealous and didn't want to rock the boat now we were getting on again. The truth was I wanted to keep Sasha to myself, wanted to protect our fledgling relationship. I'd never had secrets from Karina before, and although I felt ashamed, part of me revelled in it.

'Why don't we all do something?' I said, prompted by guilt. 'The three of us – you, me and Sasha?'

She was torn again, I could tell, between wanting in on whatever I had going with Sasha and remaining aloof, keeping up the pretence that she didn't care. But by the time we got to the classroom, we'd decided I would ask Sasha to come to the cinema with us at the weekend.

As we walked in, the first thing we saw was Sasha sitting on her desk, legs neatly crossed. Leo Smith was standing a touch too close and talking in low tones. Sasha was doing none of the hair flicking and giggling I'd seen from Karina earlier, and yet Leo was hanging from her every word. Karina's face fell.

'It's not her fault if he likes her,' I said to Karina, sensing that all the work I'd done to get her back on board was crumbling. 'She's not interested in him anyway. She said he was a creep.'

'Really?' said Karina dubiously. 'I suppose she doesn't look that interested.'

She didn't, it was true. Leo was doing all the work. Sasha caught my eye and relief swam across her face. She smiled and beckoned us over. Leo was mid-sentence but she interrupted him.

'See you later, then.'

'Oh, right.' He looked crushed. I'd never seen him anything but brimful of confidence and it was strangely pleasing. He ambled off and sat down at his desk, searching through his bag for something that didn't exist.

'Thank God you two turned up,' Sasha said. 'Thought I was going to die of boredom.'

I felt Karina relax beside me.

'This is Karina,' I said. 'She lives opposite you.'

'Oh yeah, I've seen you,' Sasha said smoothly.

I sensed Karina tense up again, and I knew she was wondering if Sasha had noticed her summer of surveillance.

'Do you fancy coming to the cinema with us at the weekend?' I asked quickly, hoping to distract them both from what they might be thinking about each other.

Sasha threw a look at Karina and back to me.

'Yeah, sure,' she said.

We made a plan to meet on Saturday evening. As Miss Cairns came in and we took our seats, I glanced over at Leo. He'd given up the pretence of looking through his bag and was gazing hungrily at Sasha. I knew I'd seen that expression somewhere before, but it took me a few seconds to place it. I'd gone my whole life without seeing anybody look at someone else like that, but now I'd seen it twice in three days. Leo was looking at Sasha in exactly the same way Daniel had at the party.

Ellen

September 2017

I finished the bottle of wine and made reasonable headway on another after Jackson left last night. Mouth fuzzy and head bleary with lack of sleep, I squeeze into a parking space a few doors down from Karina's house, realising I haven't given much thought as to how I'm going to approach this. I suppose all I can do is be honest, but there's a tremor in my hand that I can't still as I reach for the doorbell. When the door opens, a jolt of adrenaline floods my body. For a confusing second I think the woman at the door is Karina's mum, Dilys, but she looks too young. It takes my mind a few seconds to catch up with the fact that it's not Dilys, miraculously younger: it's Karina herself, ten years older, much larger and wearing thick-rimmed glasses. She has filled out, her hard edges smoothed by the extra flesh she has gained since I saw her last. I know she recognises me straight away because her hand flies to the ends of her mousey hair, twisting them around her fingers, in a gesture so recognisable it almost brings me to tears. She doesn't speak, so I do.

'Hi. Sorry, I know this is a shock.'

She stares at me as if she can make me disappear by merely maintaining eye contact.

'Can I come in?'

She twists her head and looks behind her helplessly.

'No,' she whispers. She takes a step closer. 'Are you here because of him? Or has she said something?'

'What? Who?'

'Karina! Who is it?' calls someone from inside the house. Dilys.

'Oh, no one,' she says unconvincingly over her shoulder, but the stairs creak, someone puffing down them laboriously, and Dilys hoves into view. She too has put on weight, and she looks at me uncomprehendingly, breathing heavily, until realisation dawns and she smiles.

'Ellen! What are you doing here? Not that it isn't nice to see you. She hasn't been on to you with this nonsense, has she?'

'What do you mean? What nonsense?'

'I haven't been on to her about anything,' snaps Karina at Dilys. She turns back to me. 'Have you seen him?' she says under her breath, although there is no one to hear except me and Dilys.

'Seen who?' Why is everyone talking in riddles? 'Karina, I'm here because of Sasha. She's disappeared and I'm frightened. The police won't do anything. I'm sorry if seeing me brings up things you don't want to think about, but I'm desperate. I can't help thinking this might have something to do with ... everything that happened.'

'Sasha's disappeared? When?' Karina says, her fingers stealing back to the ends of her hair. She looks terrified – the only person so far who has had what I consider a sane reaction to this news.

'Friday.'

She nods, and then says three words that chill me to the bone: 'I saw Daniel.'

'What? Where?' My heart skips along frantically. Oh God. Mum was right.

'The week before last. In Forest Hill.'

'But ... I thought he was in Scotland? He lives in Scotland.'

Her face takes on an expression of something close to pity. 'People can move, Ellen. There's been nothing to stop him coming back here for five years.'

'He hasn't, though. Olivia said she hasn't seen him for years, hardly hears from him.'

Thoughts tumble through my brain, trying to catch up with each other.

'You don't know it was him,' says Dilys, her breath still crackling from her lungs.

'It was him, Mum.' There is a hardness in her voice that I don't remember from before.

'You've thought you've seen him before, though, haven't you?' She looks at me. 'She used to see him everywhere she went at first, and that was when he was

127

in prison.' Dilys sounds triumphant. 'You need to forget him and concentrate on you,' she says to Karina. 'Start living again. Ellen's here, look – it's a sign!'

'That was different, Mum,' says Karina quietly. 'That was right after ... I wasn't thinking straight.' She looks back at me. 'I saw him. I know I did.'

'Did he see you?' I ask.

'No.'

We share a look, and I don't know if it's guilt, or complicity, or fear.

'What d'you think he's doing back here?' I take a step closer to her, a muscle memory of our former friendship kicking in as I do so. I remember what it was like to hug her, link arms with her, sleep top to tail in a single bed with her. I remember how it felt to make her laugh till she cried. I can't imagine this woman laughing, though, with her puffy, lined face and bitten-down fingernails. I imagine how she must see me – thin, pale, dark circles under my eyes. This is what he did to us, both of us. Look what he has made us.

Karina weighs something up internally. 'I don't know,' she says, and this time it's definitely fear that flits across her face.

'Karina,' I say urgently, putting my hand on her arm. 'What is it?'

She pulls her arm back as if my touch has scalded her. 'Nothing.'

'Can you think of anything I can try, to find Sasha?' I say, thirsty for any drop of information. 'Have you heard from Daniel at all since he came out of prison? Do you know where in Scotland he was living?'

The shutters come down on her face and she shakes her head. 'I don't know anything, Ellen.'

'Sasha and I . . . we had a few letters from him, after he came out of prison. Saying we lied, that it was our fault he went to prison. Did you . . . ?'

'I haven't heard from him and I don't want to. All I know is, he's back in London.' She takes a step closer. 'If you do see him, don't you dare tell him where I live.'

'Of course I won't. But if you see him again, will you tell me? Please?'

She shrugs, which I take as tacit acceptance, and I scribble down my number on a bit of paper. She takes it reluctantly. Dilys has been watching our exchange with the air of someone waiting to say their piece.

'You should invite Ellen,' she says to Karina as I put the pen back in my bag.

'What? No, don't be silly, Mum,' Karina says, blushing.

I look from one to the other. I have no desire to be invited to anything, but I can't simply act as though Dilys hasn't spoken.

'What's this?' I ask.

'It's Karina's birthday this week. We're having a little party for her on Friday night, here at the house. Family, mostly, but it'd be lovely if you came.'

Dilys's face is filled with naked desire for it not to be too late for Karina to have a normal life, a friend. I try to think of a convincing excuse, but then I look at Karina and, underneath the shame, I can see hope: she wants me to come too. I won't ever regret my friendship with Sasha, but I can't help wondering what Karina's life would look like now, and even mine, if Sasha had never come to live with the Monktons.

'Yes, that'd be lovely,' I say weakly. 'See you then.'

As I drive back round the South Circular, Karina's party is the least of my worries. Although Scotland is hardly the other side of the world, it felt far enough away for me not to have to look for him around every street corner. But here, in London? When it was only Mum who thought she'd seen him, I could dismiss it, but it's not so easy now, not now I've seen the look on Karina's face. Dilys says she imagined it, but I don't think so. I saw her fear, echoing that long ago day in the courtroom, dust motes dancing in the sunlight that streamed through the high windows. A sob forms in my throat as I think about what this means for Sasha. Oh God, where is she? What the hell has he done to her? And under these thoughts, a silky, sinuous voice whispers another question in my ear: is he coming for me next?

Olivia

July 2007

In some ways I've been dreading this day more than the others. I want to say Sasha is like a daughter to me, but I simply can't. There's always been a barrier, a wall around her. I understand why, of course I do, but I thought I was going to be able to break it down, to reach her. Until I found out what was really going on. Everything changed then. We never recovered from it, even before the New Year's Eve party.

No, it was Ellen who was like a daughter to me, more so than Sasha could ever hope to be. The poor thing doesn't get much in the way of culture or intelligent conversation at home, and it was wonderful to watch her blossoming the more time she spent with us. I've missed her more than anyone since this whole terrible business blew our lives apart.

Sasha moved in with Ellen's family after Daniel was arrested. I've hardly spoken to either of them in six months. The house has been largely silent since she left.

Daniel's been out on bail, but barely leaves his room. Nicholas stays out as much as he can. We've all taken to eating our meals alone, at different times. I've kept out of the house more than has been strictly necessary, and Tony's been spending even more time in the pub. He's been sleeping in the spare room, ostensibly because neither of us are sleeping well and we don't want to disturb each other, but that's not the real reason and we both know it. That side of our marriage was floundering anyway – drunks don't make great lovers – and it's well and truly over now.

Occasionally Tony and I make a pretence of sitting down together at the table if we are both in, but we struggle to find any words to say to each other and end up sitting in uncomfortable silence, bolting our food and retreating to our own private spaces as soon as possible. Our family life is broken. I thought we had years ahead of us all gathering around the table with boyfriends, girl-friends, friends, hangers-on – all would be welcome at the corner house, me dispensing my famous hospitality, Tony with a corkscrew in his hand. That dream is well and truly over.

Here comes Ellen now. I can see the rise and fall of her chest, hear the tremor as she confirms her name and takes the oath. I wonder if her nerves are because it's the most important, serious thing she's ever done in her life, or because it's somehow simultaneously a show, a performance.

High Cheekbones is back, more patrician than ever,

his confidence seemingly undented by the defence's suggestion of Karina's unreliability as a witness.

'Miss Mackinnon, I'm going to take you through the events of the night of the thirty-first of December 2006.'

He begins, covering every detail, starting with the moment Ellen arrived at the house, staggering like Bambi on her unfeasibly high heels, looking simultaneously older and younger than her years. I remember seeing Tony looming over her in the kitchen, wondering whether he was boring the poor girl to death, and Nicholas taking pity and rescuing her. Once we get past that, we are on to the real stuff, the part that matters.

'Did you see Mr Monkton and Miss Barton kissing?'

'Yes, I did.' She speaks clearly in her 'posh' voice, the one she puts on when she's trying to impress. She used to use it on me, but once she became more comfortable, she dropped it, going back to her natural Estuary drawl. 'At around ten o'clock I came out of the kitchen. It was getting stuffy in there. I saw Daniel and Karina in the porch section of the hallway. They were half-hidden in the coats. They were kissing.'

'And did Miss Barton appear to be a willing participant?'

'Yes.'

'And then what did you see?'

'He said something to her, I couldn't hear what, and they went up the stairs together.'

'Can you describe Miss Barton's demeanour as they went upstairs?'

Ellen hesitates. 'I don't know.'

'You don't know?'

'Well ... she looked as though she wasn't sure.'

'She looked nervous?' asks the barrister, concern etched on his noble features. 'As if she didn't want to go?'

'Your Honour!' Daniel's barrister is on her feet. 'My learned friend is leading the witness.'

'Agreed,' says the judge. 'Be careful, please, Mr Parkinson.'

'Yes, Your Honour. So, Miss Mackinnon, when did you next see Miss Barton?'

'It was about an hour later, around eleven. I was talking to someone in the corridor when Karina came stumbling down the stairs and ran past us. She looked upset, and a bit ... unsteady on her feet.'

'Did you go after her?'

'Not straight away. I was in the middle of a conversation, there was lots going on, I'd been drinking. I sort of registered that she looked upset, but I didn't think it was serious. I just thought she was drunk.'

'Did you see Daniel Monkton?'

'No.'

'And when was the next time you saw Miss Barton?'

'After about five minutes I thought I'd better go and see if she was OK, but I couldn't find her. I looked everywhere downstairs but she wasn't there, and I knew she hadn't gone back upstairs because I would have seen her. So I went out into the garden, and that's where I found her.'

'She was outside in the garden in the middle of winter?'

'Yes. It was freezing.'

'What was she wearing?'

'Just this little dress. She hadn't put her coat on. She was sitting on the ground under the mulberry tree at the bottom of the garden. I sat down next to her and put my arms around her. She was like ice. Her whole body was shaking. She had blood on her hands.'

'What sort of state was she in?'

'She was very upset, crying. She seemed drunk. I helped her back inside.'

'What, if anything, did she say to you at this point?'

'She said that Daniel had raped her and hurt her, cut her with a broken bottle.'

I look over at Daniel, who is motionless, looking straight ahead. I want to say to him that it's OK, this is all second-hand. Everything Ellen has said has been refracted through the prism of Karina. Ellen didn't see anything. She doesn't know anything. Her evidence means nothing, proves nothing.

'We have heard from Miss Barton that she had been involved in a relationship with Mr Monkton for the three months prior to New Year's Eve 2006. Were you aware of this relationship?'

'Yes, yes I was.'

I can't help it, I make a sound, a sort of involuntary cry. I clap my hand over my mouth but it's too late, everyone has heard. Dilys twists around in her seat to let me feel the full force of her triumphant stare. Daniel continues to look steadfastly straight ahead, but a muscle in the side of his face is twitching.

'Was Miss Barton aware that you knew about the relationship?'

'No, she wasn't.'

'So how did you know about it?'

'I knew she was seeing someone, I could just tell. She thought it was this big secret but it was totally obvious.'

'Your Honour!' Daniel's barrister is up again. 'I am loath to get up during my learned friend's questioning, but this is pure speculation from the witness without any factual basis. It is irrelevant.'

'I'm inclined to agree,' the judge says, regarding him sternly. 'Mr Parkinson, can you please get to the point?'

All eyes turn back to Ellen, trembling but resolute.

'Very well. How did you know that Miss Barton was in a relationship with Daniel Monkton, Miss Mackinnon?'

'It was about two weeks before the New Year's Eve party. I was round at Sasha's house after school. Sasha was staying back at school for a rehearsal for the Christmas concert, but she'd invited me over for dinner, so she gave me her key. I went back there on my own and let myself in.'

'Was that something you normally did?'

'No. I'd never done it before, but I knew Olivia and Tony – Mr and Mrs Monkton – wouldn't mind. I was . . .' She steals a glance up at me. 'They were like family to me, the Monktons.'

There's a lump in my throat and it swells a little more. Soon I won't be able to breathe at all.

'I made myself a cup of tea in the kitchen,' she goes on.

'I took it up to Sasha's room and sat on her bed, reading a magazine. I heard the front door opening and someone coming in. I was going to go down and say hello but I thought I'd wait and see who it was. Then I recognised Karina's voice. She was laughing, and there was a man there too. Daniel. They were coming up the stairs and there was something about the way they were speaking that made me stay silent. They went into Daniel's room – it was next to Sasha's and . . . the walls are not very thick. I could hear them.'

'What did you hear, Miss Mackinnon?'

'I heard them having sex.' She lowers her voice on the last word, still a child, incapable of saying it without embarrassment. 'And after a while there was a sort of banging noise, it sounded like a head hitting the wall, although I can't be sure, and I heard her say: "You're hurting me", but he didn't say anything, he just carried on.'

'What happened next?'

'I heard them both coming out of the room and then they left the house.'

'And what did you do?'

'I was a bit . . . shocked, I suppose. I texted Sasha to say I wasn't going to come for dinner after all, and went home.'

'So a full two weeks before the night in question, you heard Daniel Monkton and Miss Barton having sexual intercourse, possibly violent, in which she told him he was hurting her? Yet he denies entirely the existence of this relationship.'

'Yes.'

The judge calls for a break, and Ellen makes her way down from the witness box, her mouth set in a straight, tight line, every ounce of her concentrating on keeping her body still and upright, holding herself together.

Oh, Ellen, how could you? My almost-daughter. All those times she sat around my kitchen table, helping me cook, telling me about her day. I offered her a taste of culture, a window into a different life from the small one she led at home with her closed-minded parents; I showed her a better way. When I think that this is how she has repaid me, I burn with an unsettling fury.

Ellen

October 2005

Sasha cancelled the cinema, but for a brilliant reason. Nicholas and Daniel had complained that the party the weekend before had been totally lame, so Olivia and Tony said they could have another one, but with only their friends and Sasha's – no adults. Olivia and Tony were going to be there, but they'd promised to stay in their room unless things got out of hand. They were such cool parents.

Karina was invited too, this time. She tried to be all laid-back about it, but I could tell she was excited. She came over to mine beforehand and we got ready together. She was full of it: who was going to be there, what boys from our class had been invited, would Leo Smith come and if he did would he try and get off with Sasha or did she have a chance, what the two brothers would be like, if either of them would fancy her. She went on and on until I felt like screaming at her to shut up. I couldn't help thinking of Sasha, and how much cooler and funnier she was than Karina. Karina was so desperate.

When we got there, Daniel opened the door to us. He looked blank for a minute, and then recognised me.

'Oh, hi. Sasha's friend. Ellen, isn't it? Come in.' He stood back as we passed, Karina squeezing unnecessarily close to him.

'Hi, I'm Karina,' she said, holding out her hand.

It was so weird. I mean, who shakes hands apart from old people? Daniel took it, though, and bent low over it, kissing it lightly.

'Enchanted,' he said in a pretend posh voice.

Karina was simpering away, pink with delight. Didn't she know he was taking the piss?

'Sasha's in the kitchen,' he said, disappearing into the front room, the one with the piano and the piles of books. Karina looked longingly after him as if she might follow, but I tugged her towards the back of the house.

'Come on. Don't worry, you'll see him again later.'

'I'm not bothered,' she said, although I don't know why she even tried to pretend. She was like a dog on heat. I hoped she wasn't going to do anything embarrassing in front of Sasha.

In the kitchen, Sasha was sitting with her back to us at the kitchen table with a glass of red wine. All the other girls I'd seen so far were in jeans or tiny denim skirts and skimpy tops, but Sasha was wearing a full-length black dress, cut high at the front but sweeping very low at the back, so that the silken rope of her hair tumbled down her bare, tanned back. She should have looked comically overdressed, but she didn't. She looked magnificent, making the others look like silly little girls. Leo Smith sat opposite her, facing the door from the hall, but he didn't even look up when we came in. Sasha looked round when she heard the door, though, and jumped up to greet us. Her feet were bare, toenails painted a vivid scarlet. She hugged me first and then Karina.

'I'm so glad to see you both.' Her genuine delight was like a spoonful of warm honey. I'd never felt so important, so wanted, so good about myself. 'What do you want to drink?'

'Do they let you drink, then? Your par— I mean, god-parents?' Karina gaped as Sasha opened the fridge to reveal bottles of beer neatly lined up on their sides and a door full of white wine.

'Oh yes, they're frightfully liberal, aren't they, Sash?' said someone behind us. We turned to see Daniel leaning against the kitchen table, sparkling with amusement.

'Achingly so,' she said, smiling and pulling a bottle of wine from the fridge. 'No spirits, though. Although I'm sure some of the "older boys" may have brought some.'

'Did you get a lecture on older boys and how to avoid them?' said Daniel, laughing.

'I may have done,' she said. 'And on that note, we'll see you later. Come on, girls.' She grabbed three plastic glasses from the side and swept from the room, Karina and I following in her wake. Daniel looked after her with a smile on his face.

Upstairs, Tony was tiptoeing across the landing from the bathroom back to what I guessed was his and Olivia's bedroom.

'Sorry, sorry.' He held his hands up in a pantomime of apology. 'Just had to use the facilities. I promise it'll be the last time you see me. You're all looking very lovely, ladies,' he said, giving a little bow. 'Have a great night.' He slipped into the bedroom and closed the door.

Karina shot me a meaningful glance and I remembered how she had swooned over him the day they moved in. I shook my head, trying to warn her not to say anything. It would be too weird in front of Sasha. She must have got the message because she smiled and followed Sasha into her room.

We sat on the bed sipping our wine. Karina was forcing it down, clearly struggling to stop her face from betraying her inexperience at drinking.

'You seem to be getting on well,' I said to Sasha.

'Who?'

'You and Daniel. Last time you seemed a bit funny with each other.'

'Oh, that. Yeah, he's OK, I suppose.'

'What about the other one?' Karina asked.

'Nick? He's OK too. They're fine.'

We waited for her to say more.

'What?' she said, looking from me to Karina, bemused. 'Do you fancy them or something? Why do you want to talk about them all the time?'

'No!' we said in unison.

'I think it's . . . ' Karina halted, and I could feel her anxiety not to give away our summer of stalking. 'It's strange, that's all,' she said. 'You were living with your mum, and then all of a sudden you're in this new family with these two boys, and they're not your brothers, so . . .'

Sasha shrugged. 'It's fine. There's nothing to say.'

'But you must . . .' Did I dare say this? She never mentioned her mother. I screwed up my courage. 'You must miss your mum.'

Sasha pulled her knees up to her chest, her bare feet getting tangled in the folds of her dress. 'Yeah, I do,' she said quietly.

No one said anything for a while. Karina and I sipped our wine as if our lives depended upon it.

'Are you going to see her soon?' Karina ventured.

'Yes,' said Sasha, brightening up. 'She's coming over from LA next week to see me.'

'Oh, great. Maybe we could meet her?' I said, made bold by the wine.

'Maybe,' Sasha said. 'She's not here for long, though, and we'll probably want to spend the time together.'

'Right.'

Silence fell again, and I groped in my mind for an easier topic. We fell back on bitching about the teachers and the other kids at school. We were laughing about this boy in our class who no one had ever seen out of school and whether he even existed at all, when the door opened and Leo's face appeared. Karina's hands flew to her hair and even I pulled my top down where it had ruched up to show an inch of unappealing belly fat. Sasha was the only one totally unmoved.

'Can we help you?' she said, frost in every syllable.

'We're going to play truth, kiss or dare,' he said, grinning, apparently oblivious to her coolness. 'Want to join us?'

Karina was up and off the bed before anyone had even replied.

'Seriously?' Sasha said, eyebrows raised.

Karina sank back down, clearly thinking if she moved slowly enough, no one would notice how over-keen she had been.

'Oh, come on, it might be fun,' I said, throwing Karina a bone. She was supposed to be my best friend, after all.

'Yeah, might be,' she said gratefully.

'Oh God, OK,' said Sasha theatrically. She stood up and threw back the remains of her wine. 'Don't blame me if it all goes to shit, though.'

Leo practically jogged along the landing ahead of us, looking back every now and then to make sure we were still behind him. We followed him down the stairs and into the front room. A boy with long dark hair and acne was sitting on the piano stool playing the guitar, a couple of girls gazing on adoringly. I've noticed that a boy can be as unattractive as he likes but if he can play the guitar, it ups his fanciability by the power of about a thousand.

Most of the partygoers were now gathered in this room, sitting in a loose circle on sofas, chairs or the floor. I didn't recognise a lot of them, so I assumed they were Daniel and Nicholas's friends. There were a few of Leo's friends from school, and a few girls from our year who I knew by sight but had never spoken to. I didn't know who had invited them. An empty beer bottle lay on the floor in the centre of the room.

'OK everyone, let's start,' said Leo, who seemed to be in charge. I wondered if he had come up with the idea for the game purely as an opportunity to kiss Sasha.

Karina, Sasha and I squeezed on to one end of a huge, shabby sofa with a curlicued pattern of leaves and birds on it. My head was starting to swim from the wine and I guessed Karina's would be too. She was no more used to drinking than I was.

'We'll go round in a circle,' Leo went on. 'You have to choose truth, kiss or dare. Then we'll spin the bottle and whoever it lands on has to come up with the question, or the dare. Or tell you who to kiss.'

There were a few groans and mutters from around the room, and a lot of chat and laughter. I could feel the excitement pulsing out of Karina on my right, and a sort of weary indifference from Sasha to my left. I was somewhere in between.

'OK,' said Leo. 'I'll spin the bottle to decide where we start.' He gave it a great twist and it skidded, spinning round, getting slower and slower. My heart rose in my mouth as I thought it was going to be me, but it ground to a gentle halt pointing straight at Karina, who put her hand to her mouth, half-laughing, half plainly terrified.

'OK!' Leo said. 'Karina, is it? Come on, into the middle.'

Karina scrambled to her feet, her cheeks glowing red, and took her place in the centre of the circle, amid whoops and wolf whistles. Sasha had a tight smile on her face, but she looked anxious.

'Are you OK?' I whispered.

'Yeah, but ... I don't want her to make a fool of herself, you know?' she said under her breath. 'She's pretty pissed already.'

'What's it going to be?' said Leo in the manner of a TV talk show host.

'Um ... truth,' said Karina.

'OK, I'll spin again,' said Leo. 'Whoever it lands on gets to choose the question.'

He spun the bottle again. This time, it came to rest on one of Leo's mates from school, a thickset, dark-haired boy called Alex. Leo flung himself down in the space next to Alex, as if better to enjoy the show. Nicholas was on his other side and they exchanged a couple of remarks, laughing together as if they were old friends, although I didn't think they'd ever met before tonight.

They were interrupted by Alex's question. 'Are you a virgin?'

The pink that already stained Karina's cheeks darkened to red and spread down her neck and across her chest. This was the worst question she could have been asked. I knew she was, and everyone from our school probably had a good idea too and would know if she was lying. It was a fine line anyway. Say yes and you were naïve, unsophisticated, childish; say no and you were a slag. I willed her to get on with it. The longer she stood there, the worse it would be for her.

After what felt like hours, she spoke, muttering a low 'Yes' and slinking back to her seat next to me, shame burning from her like fire. I had little time to worry about her, though, because now it was my go. I took my place in the centre, my heart racing.

'So, what's it to be?' said Leo, standing up and joining me. The light from the lamp in the corner caught his eyes and they glittered in the dimness. I'd been skipping from one to the other in my mind during Karina's turn. My main fear about choosing dare was that I might have to take off some of my clothes, which would be beyond humiliating; and having witnessed Karina's question, I didn't fancy truth either. Kiss was probably the lesser of the three evils, so I took a shaky breath.

'I'll take kiss,' I said, aiming for nonchalance.

There was a chorus of 'oohs' and whistles.

'She's gone for kiss, ladies and gentlemen,' said Leo, getting into his role now. 'OK, I'll spin the bottle and whoever it lands on chooses who she kisses. Here we go.' He spun once more. This time the bottle caught on the carpet and didn't spin far, stopping on Daniel, who rubbed his hands together in glee.

'Hmmm, I think you can kiss ... my dear brother Nicky!'

Nicholas groaned and put his head in his hands, then quickly looked up at me and said, 'Sorry, no offence, nothing personal. It's ... well, thanks, Dan. And it's Nicholas, or Nick, if you must, not Nicky.' He jabbed his brother with his elbow and stood up.

'Aaah, Nicky's first kiss!' said Daniel, falling about laughing.

'Fuck off,' said Nicholas, shooting him an evil look.

'Don't forget the tongues, now!' trilled Leo. 'That's the rules!'

'What rules? You never said anything about rules!' protested Nicholas as he walked towards me.

'I'm saying it now,' said Leo, pushing me against Nicholas's chest.

Nicholas looked at me and raised his eyebrows. 'OK, here goes,' he said, bending towards me. His lips met mine, surprisingly soft and warm. My stomach flipped over as his tongue slipped into my mouth. It was only the second time I'd ever kissed a boy. At Tamara Gregg's party last summer, I'd been talking to a boy she knew from Venture Scouts. He'd unexpectedly loomed down at me mid-conversation, enclosing my entire mouth in his and lunging at it repeatedly and violently, his teeth grazing my skin. My lips were so sore the next day I felt like I'd been punched in the mouth. This was completely different, gentle and caressing, and my mouth opened in response, my body arching towards him. A loud wolf whistle brought me to my senses and I pulled back, blushing, and returned to my seat. Sasha's hand slipped into mine and I squeezed back. Thank God that was over.

Leo looked at Sasha triumphantly. She released my hand and sauntered casually into the middle, her dress flowing over her curves like water.

'The lovely Sasha,' said Leo. 'So, what'll it be?'

'Truth,' she said, looking him straight in the eye.

'OK,' he said, trying not to sound disappointed that she hadn't picked kiss, what with him being in charge of the spinning bottle. 'Truth it is.' He spun, and once again the bottle landed on his mate Alex. Everyone looked at Alex, but I kept looking at Leo, who raised his eyebrows at Alex, pointing at himself, wanting Alex to ask Sasha if she liked him, I suppose. But Alex had a one-track mind tonight (and possibly every night), and again he came out with his question with no hesitation.

'Do you masturbate?'

There was a second of shocked silence, then horrified laughter from the girls and whooping from the boys. I looked at Sasha, desperately sorry for her that she had to face such humiliation, but she simply smiled and said casually, 'Of course. All the time.'

As she sat back down, I looked around to see how this bombshell had gone down. The girls were still giggling and whispering to each other, but the boys . . . I thought what she had admitted to was embarrassing, but they were all looking at her with naked, unashamed desire.

The game went on, with various permutations of truth, kiss and dare being acted out. When it got to Daniel's turn, he chose kiss, and the bottle stopped at Nicholas.

'Kiss Sasha,' Nicholas said.

'Hang on a minute, they're related,' said Leo.

'No they're not, you idiot,' said Nicholas. 'Mum and Dad are her godparents.'

Leo looked in alarm from one to the other, trying to come up with another reason, but in the end, Daniel stood up, motioning Sasha to do the same. In the centre, he bent and kissed her lightly and briefly on the lips. They held eye contact for a moment, and then both sat back down.

'Hey!' said Nick. 'He said the rule was tongues. You can't do that.'

'I can do whatever the fuck I like,' said Daniel.

'Let's move on,' said Leo hastily. 'Who's next?'

As Nicholas glowered at Daniel, I caught a movement outside in the hall, out of the corner of my eye. For a confusing moment I thought it was Daniel, but he was still there across the circle, watching Sasha. When I looked back, there was no one there. Intrigued, I told Sasha and Karina I was going to the toilet, and went out into the hall. A man was making his way up the stairs, scurrying as if he'd been caught out. At the sound of my feet on the parquet floor, he stopped and looked back. Seeing me, he smiled and raised a finger to his lips.

'I wasn't here,' he said. 'You never saw me.'

It was Tony Monkton.

Ellen

September 2017

Back at the flat, I can't stop seeing Karina's face, guarded and hostile. I could still see in her the girl who used to be my best friend, but only just. I pray Dilys is right, that this is another case of Karina seeing Daniel where he is not, everywhere she goes, like I used to. I know it's not, though. Something tells me that this time, he is back.

And Olivia – does she genuinely not know where he is, or was she lying to me? What about Tony – has he seen Daniel? It could have been Tony upstairs at the corner house that day, but if so, why didn't he come down? I can't face going there again; can't cope with more hostility from Olivia. There is one person, though, who might know something: Nicholas. I have no idea how much contact he has had with Daniel since the trial. Did he visit Daniel in prison? Did anyone?

I go to Nicholas's page on LinkedIn. It's a Monday, shortly after 2 p.m. – he's probably at his desk at AVI

Solutions. There's no part of me that wants to pick up the phone and call him – in fact, it makes my skin itch to think about it – but I keep Sasha firmly in my mind: her face, her strength, her ability to make me laugh even in the deepest despair. I am doing this for her. I pick up the phone.

'AVI Solutions, can I help you?' She sounds bored, watching the clock hands as they creep unbearably slowly around to 5 p.m.

'Hello, can I speak to Nicholas Monkton, please?'

'Who's calling?'

Oh shit, I was so busy psyching myself up, I didn't think about this. I don't want him to refuse to speak to me.

'Sally ... er ... Wright.' I pluck a name from the air.

There's a few seconds silence, and then a man's voice says, 'Nicholas Monkton.' He is peremptory, as if I've interrupted him in the middle of something important.

For a moment, I think I've got the wrong person. He sounds so different. But his LinkedIn page is still open in front of me. It's definitely him.

'Hi, Nicholas.'

'Yes? How can I help you?' he says impatiently.

'OK, I'm sorry, it's not Sally Wright.'

As I say it, somebody asks him a question on the other end. It's a woman, and I imagine the bored receptionist poking her head round the door, telling him his next appointment is here.

'Hang on a sec,' he says to the woman, and turns back to the phone. 'What? Sorry, who is this?'

I am tempted to blurt out something about a wrong number and put the phone down, but I can't, I mustn't. I force myself to speak.

'It's Ellen Mackinnon.'

Silence echoes down the phone line.

'I need to talk to you about Daniel,' I go on, stumbling over my words now I've started. 'And Sasha. She's gone missing, and Karina said she thought she'd seen Daniel in London, although apparently she sees him everywhere when he's not there, and—'

'Hang on!'

I stop, out of words anyway.

'Can you give me a minute?' he says, and for a moment I think he means me, but he's talking to whoever's in his office. 'Sorry, Ellen, you've taken me a bit by surprise here. I can't really talk now, I'm at work.'

'I know, I'm sorry. Could we talk later?'

He doesn't speak, and I wait. He owes me nothing.

'OK, do you want to meet for a drink tonight?' he says. 'Presuming you're still in London?'

'Yes, that would be great. I live in Clapham. I've got to be at work at seven, though, in Wandsworth. What time do you finish?'

'I won't be able to get out till around five. I could pop over to you for an hour, if it's easier? It's on my way home, anyway. You don't want to come into town for an hour and have to go back again.'

I hesitate. 'OK.' It will make it easier for me, it's true.

I give him my address and put the phone down,

drawing a long, juddery breath. It's the first time I've spoken to him since New Year's Eve 2006, and it's plunged me back in time. I feel eighteen again, and not in a good way.

A few hours later, I watch from the kitchen window as he strides briskly along the pavement with the air of a man who knows exactly where he is going, both geographically and in life. There is no trace of the diffidence that dogged him in his youth. Although they were alike, Daniel was always the better-looking one, but Nicholas has grown into his looks, the heavy features, too much on a teenager, striking on a grown man. I wonder how Daniel has fared as he's grown older, what those years in prison have done to his dark good looks.

The door goes and I buzz him up, waiting for him to emerge out of the gloom. When he does, he's taller than I remember, broader. We halt, uncertain how we're going to greet each other, settling on an over-long handshake, topped off with a self-conscious kiss on the cheek. He follows me inside.

'Nice flat,' he says politely, looking around. 'Is it ... just you?'

'No ... I live with Sasha.'

'Really? I didn't know you two were still close.'

'Yes, that's why ... ' My face twists with the effort of not crying.

He looks alarmed. 'Sorry, I didn't mean to ... '

'It's OK, it's been a tough few days. I haven't slept much ... Can I get you a drink? Or a cup of tea?'

'I'd love a glass of wine if you've got one,' he says, looking relieved to be back on firmer ground. 'Any colour will do.'

I go into the kitchen and pour us both a glass of wine. When I come out he's still standing awkwardly in the hall, looking at a collage of photos of me and Sasha together, taken over the years.

'Oh!' I say, coming to an abrupt halt, wine slopping on to my hand.

'Sorry, I wasn't sure where to go,' he says.

'Come through here,' I say, leading him into the lounge. I'm reminded that he was always the more gauche of the two, and that I liked him the better for it.

He sits down straight-backed on the sofa, looking around him as if he's drinking in every detail. I sit on the armchair across from him.

'So . . . you said Sasha's gone missing?' he asks.

'Yes. Three days ago. She didn't come home from work on Friday and no one's seen her since. I went to see Karina today and—'

'Karina Barton?' he breaks in. 'My God, I haven't seen her for years, not since . . . you know. How is she?'

'Not great. I don't think she ever got over it. What happened.'

'No, I don't suppose she did,' he says grimly. 'Fucking Daniel.'

'That was what I wanted to talk to you about,' I say, grabbing my chance. 'Karina said she'd seen Daniel, in London, the week before last. I thought he was living in

155

Scotland, though? Didn't he go there, after he came out?' The questions tumble out in a rush, my words tripping over each other.

'Yes, he's been living in Scotland,' Nicholas says. 'As far as I know, he's still there. But I haven't been in touch with him for years, Ellen. I wouldn't have a clue where he is or what he's up to. For all I know he could be living next door.'

My face must have given away my horror, because he puts his hands up as if I'm waving a gun in his face.

'Hey, it was just a figure of speech. Sorry, I didn't mean to ... God, Ellen. I guess it's not only Karina who's not over it.' He presses the bridge of his nose. 'I'm so sorry, I had no idea.'

No idea about what? I want to say. No idea that your brother would still be scaring the shit out of me more than ten years on from violently raping my friend? No idea that the thought of him being back in the country makes me want to hide away and never come out? No idea that the repercussions of what happened in your house on New Year's Eve 2006 would still be reverberating through my life?

'That's OK,' I mutter instead, taking a big gulp of wine. 'When did you last see him?'

'Five years ago, when he got out. He lived at home for a bit – at Mum and Dad's, I mean. I tried to avoid him, to be honest. I had my own place by then, so I stayed away, but I did see him once or twice.'

'Your mum didn't tell me that.'

I think of Olivia, wielding the washing-up brush like a weapon.

'You've spoken to Mum?' He sounds suspicious, angry.

'Yes, I went to see her. Sorry, should I ... I thought she might know something, might have heard from Daniel. I ... I'm scared, Nicholas. That he might be back; that he's ... taken Sasha.'

'What makes you think that, though?' He sounds genuinely confused.

'Well, where is she, then? She's disappeared off the face of the earth at the exact time when your brother is apparently back in London, and nobody except me seems to give a damn! He wrote to us, Nicholas, after he got out of prison. Threatening letters. Accusing us of lying at the trial. If he hasn't got her, where is she?'

Nicholas looks at me strangely, as if he knows he has to tell me something unpleasant, something he can't believe I don't already know.

'But Ellen, don't you think ... I mean, isn't it typical of Sasha to do something like this? Take off without telling anyone? It wouldn't be the first time, would it?'

'I know,' I say, careful not to lose my temper this time. 'But I can't believe she would go without telling me. Not now.'

'But ... ' he spreads his hands helplessly, 'after ... everything that happened, she disappeared on us. She lived with your mum and dad, didn't she, for a while? And then she went off to university and Mum never saw her again. She can ... I don't know, cut people out.

She had this ability to switch off her feelings if they were no longer ... appropriate. Maybe it's because of her mum.'

'What do you mean? What about her mum?'

'Oh. Do you still ...? I thought you and her were close?'

'What do you mean? We were ... We are.'

He slides a finger inside the cuff of his shirt and fiddles with the button. 'Mum said it was up to her to tell people, so we never ... I thought you would know. I shouldn't have said anything.'

'Please, just tell me.' A sick feeling starts in my stomach and spreads upwards. I swallow it back down.

'OK ... What has Sasha told you about her mum?'

'That she was a model and they lived all over the world, and her mum wanted her to have some stability and get her A levels, so she came to live with you. She lives in America.'

'That's it? That's what she's told you?'

'Yes ... What do you mean? I figured they don't get on as they don't see much of each other, but Sasha obviously doesn't want to talk about it, so I've never asked.'

'Didn't you think it odd that you've never met her?'

'Not really. I've got lots of friends whose parents I've never met and they don't even live abroad.' Rachel, for example, I've never met hers. I try to stem the whisper in my head that says Rachel and I are nowhere near as close as Sasha and me.

'She doesn't live abroad, Ellen.'

158

'What?' I slide my hands under me, trying to stop myself biting the skin around my nails.

He leans forward, elbows on his knees, his face looming towards mine. 'She's a druggie. Homeless, probably, although no one's heard from her for years. She might even be dead for all we know.'

The room swims around me and I close my eyes for a second.

'Look, Ellen, I'm sorry to be laying all this on you. I can see it's unexpected. But you might as well know. Sasha's never lived in America. She didn't come to live with us because her mum wanted her to get her A levels. She came because her mum couldn't look after her any more. She . . . hurt Sasha.'

'What? What do you mean?'

'Mum knew that was the story Sasha told everyone, and she let her – it wouldn't have helped for Mum to have barged in and told everyone it was a lie. She thought if it helped Sasha, it wasn't hurting anyone. Mum didn't even tell us the full story at the time, although we knew what Sasha was telling people about Alice – that's Sasha's mum – wasn't true. Mum made us swear not to tell anyone. It's only recently that Mum told me the details. Alice was her best friend when they were younger, but she went off the rails. Mum had stayed in touch, and she saw a lot of them when Sasha was a baby, helped her out with babysitting and stuff. But then Alice went right off the radar, living in some dodgy squat in north London, and after that they moved up north somewhere, Hebden Bridge, I think, and Mum lost touch. The year Sasha came to live with us, Mum had got a call from Alice, saying social services had taken Sasha away from her. Sasha was fifteen, so she couldn't get her own place, and Alice didn't want her to go into foster care.'

'My entire world, which since Sasha's disappearance has been spinning wildly on its axis, flies off into outer space, leaving me utterly disorientated.

'What happened? Why was Sasha taken away from her?'

'Do you remember her face, when she came to live with us?'

'Yes.' The warmth of the sun on my forearms, the rough brick wall pressing into the back of my thighs, the pungent tang of blue nail varnish, the thud my heart gave as her golden hair swung round to reveal the scar on her cheek.

'Did you never ask her how she did it?'

'She said she did it on a piece of broken glass. Forgot her keys one day and had to break a window in her own house to get in.'

'That wasn't true. Alice did it. She was drunk, or on something, and she was flailing around and somehow ... accidentally pushed Sasha, who fell and hit her face on the corner of the fireplace.'

'Accidentally?'

'Quite. That was Sasha's story, and Alice's, but I don't think social services bought it. Even Alice realised it wasn't working out, so she asked Olivia if Sasha could stay with us for a while.'

'For a while?'

'Yes. Sasha was supposed to be going back, but Alice just ... disappeared. She called a bit, at first, to speak to Sasha and Mum. But the calls petered out, and one day Mum rang her at the house where she was staying and the bloke who answered the phone said she'd gone, no one knew where. She didn't have a mobile phone, so that was it. Mum tried social services, and the police, but no one was able to trace her. Mum never heard from her again.

'When was all this going on?' I try to remember the times Sasha spoke about her mum – what she told us and when.

'It was about six months after she came to live with us that she last heard from Alice.'

'But this flat ... Sasha owns it outright. She said her mum bought it for her.'

'I know Sasha's grandmother – Alice's mother – left Sasha some money in some kind of trust. I think she got it when she was eighteen. Maybe she used that. So you pay her rent, do you?'

'Yes.' If you can call it that. It's a paltry sum compared to what she could get renting it out on the open market. I've always thought she did it as a favour, because she knows how little I earn. But I wonder now if she has some other reason for wanting me around. If she needs me as much as I need her. More, maybe.

'Why didn't she tell me?' All those times we pressed her about her mum, Karina and I, wanting to meet this elegant model, who in my head resembled a mixture of Jerry Hall and Cindy Crawford. I can't believe now I didn't think it odd that I never saw a picture of her.

'She was embarrassed,' says Nicholas. 'She didn't want anyone to know, to judge her by her mum's actions. She wanted a fresh start, I suppose.'

There's a dull ache inside, a pain that's partly for me, for the lies I've been told. But it's for her too, for what she's had to endure, what she's had to hide.

'Maybe that's what she wants now – another fresh start?' he goes on.

'Not without telling me,' I say stubbornly, more to convince myself than anything else. 'You don't under-stand. You haven't seen her for years, and yet you waltz in here and tell me what she's like, what she's done. You don't know her. You don't know her at all.' Heat rises inside me, staining my skin red.

'Look, I'm sorry if I've been the bearer of unpleasant news,' says Nicholas, draining his wine and standing up. 'I'd better be going.'

I walk with him to the front door. There's no question of a handshake or a kiss this time, but as I'm closing the door behind him, he turns.

'Maybe you're right,' he says. 'Maybe I don't know her. But you know what, Ellen? Maybe you don't know her as well as you think you do either.'

And with that he is gone, leaving me alone again in the

flat I share with Sasha – my best friend, who has been there all my adult life. Yes, she has dipped in and out at times, but she has never before felt as she does now: a phantom, twisting and hiding as I reach for her, forever slipping out of my grasp.

Olivia

July 2007

'Miss Mackinnon, on the night of the thirty-first of December 2006, when you saw Miss Barton and Daniel Monkton kissing and touching each other, Miss Barton appeared to be a willing participant, didn't she?' Daniel's barrister smooths an imaginary out-of-place hair away from her forehead.

'Yes, I've already said that. But that doesn't mean—'

'Just answer the questions please, Miss Mackinnon.' She fixes Ellen with a gimlet stare, and I cheer inside.

'Yes,' Ellen says. She's getting quieter and quieter, and I'm glad.

'When you saw the two of them heading for Daniel Monkton's room just after ten p.m., was Mr Monkton pulling or forcing Miss Barton in any way?'

'No.'

'Did you hear her say she didn't want to go upstairs with him?'

'No.'

'You weren't in the room when the alleged rape took place, were you?'

'No, of course not—'

'And you didn't see Daniel Monkton inflicting any injuries on Miss Barton?'

'No.'

'When you saw Miss Barton running past you at the party at around eleven p.m., so upset, did you not see any blood on her, or notice any scratches or other injuries?'

'No, but—'

'Just answer the questions, please.' She smiled with her mouth only, her eyes watchful.

'No, I didn't notice anything like that.'

'So, you do not have any reason to believe, any evidence at all – *apart* from what she told you after the event – that Daniel raped Miss Barton, do you?'

'Well . . . ' She looks around, as if for help.

'Do you, Miss Mackinnon?'

'No,' she says to the floor.

'So is it possible that Miss Barton and Daniel had entirely consensual sex, and that the injuries that you saw on her thighs later were actually inflicted after she had left Daniel's room, either by another party, or by Miss Barton herself?'

'But why would she—'

'Is it possible, Miss Mackinnon?'

She looks down at her hands, one clasped around the other to hold them still.

'Yes, it's possible,' she says.

165

There are a few beats of silence. We all wait.

'I want to take you back to the day in mid-December, the day you say you heard Miss Barton and Daniel having sex in Daniel's bedroom.'

Ellen's face is composed, as if she feels more certain here. A wave of unexpected nausea rises in me. I think myself reasonably worldly. I know what teenagers get up to, but the thought of these conversations, these desires, bubbling under the surface of those candlelit evenings in the kitchen of my house makes me question everything. No, not everything; I mustn't question Daniel's innocence. I can't, or I will be lost.

'Did you at any point come out of the room you were in – Sasha's bedroom?'

'No.'

'Did you see Miss Barton and Daniel at any point?'

'No. After they'd . . . finished, they both left the house. I don't know where they went.'

'Mr Monkton's position has always been that he had never had any sort of sexual contact with Karina Barton before the night of the thirty-first of December 2006. Can you be absolutely sure that it was Daniel that Miss Barton was with?'

I can't be certain but I think a shadow of doubt crosses her face, mixed with something else. Fear?

'Yes,' she says firmly.

'What did you hear Daniel say?'

'I . . . I couldn't make it out, exactly. I—'

'So you couldn't hear him clearly enough to know what

he was saying, yet you are certain, beyond a shadow of a doubt, that it was Daniel Monkton that you heard having sex with Miss Barton?'

'They were in his bedroom!'

'Yes, and I'm sorry to repeat myself but I believe this to be an important point: you could neither see him, nor hear him clearly enough to make out what he was saying?'

Ellen glances around, as if looking for support, but none is forthcoming. The jury stare implacably, their faces unhelpfully blank. She looks back at the barrister, incredulous.

'I know it was him. I recognised his voice.'

'Answer the question, please. Could you see Daniel Monkton, or hear him clearly enough to know what he was saying?'

She twists her hands into her hair and then lowers them quickly, conscious of the advice she has no doubt received to appear calm.

'No,' she says. 'But—'

'Thank you,' the barrister cuts her off smoothly. 'You also said you heard Miss Barton say, "You're hurting me"?'

'Yes.'

'But if you couldn't hear well enough to make out what the man in the bedroom was saying, how can you be sure that you heard that correctly?'

'He was speaking quietly. She said it louder.'

'You didn't hear Miss Barton asking him to stop, did you? You didn't hear her say no?'

'No.'

'So is it possible that whoever was in there with Miss Barton was indeed doing something that was hurting her, but inadvertently? Perhaps he was lying on her hair, or squashing her? And when she told him that he was hurting her, he remedied the situation? Is that possible, Miss Mackinnon?'

'Yes, I suppose so, but—'

'Thank you, Miss Mackinnon. No further questions.'

I can tell as she descends the steps from the witness box that her legs are barely carrying her. I try to stem the ceaseless flow of questions running through my mind, the fears, the dark suspicions. I must concentrate on Daniel, on being here for him. Standing straight in the dock, he has his mask firmly in place, his skin perhaps a little greyer than it was earlier. He tries to look straight ahead, but at the last moment before Ellen steps down and out of his eyeline, he turns. The pain and distress that I have seen on occasion over the past few days have been extinguished. All that is left is pure, unadulterated fury, and for a second I wonder what the hell Ellen Mackinnon has done.

Ellen

September 2017

'Did you know about Sasha's mum?'

'What about her?' Leo sounds confused, as well he might be given that I've launched into my questioning with no preamble. He'd been reluctant when I called to ask him to meet me for a drink in my local pub, the Forresters, but was too polite to refuse.

'That she wasn't a model. She didn't live in America. She was an addict. Sasha was taken away from her by social services.'

'What? No, I had no idea. Who told you that?'

'Nicholas. I saw him last night. That's why I thought you might have known. You were good friends with him, weren't you? Back then?'

'Yes, I guess so. But he never said. Poor Sasha.'

'I know. She never said a word to me.'

My relief at having somebody sympathise with Sasha rather than accusing her of something is short-lived.

'Doesn't this make you think, though,' he says

cautiously, 'that you don't know her as well as you think? Can you be absolutely sure she hasn't taken herself off?'

I sip my drink, unable to let the words pass my lips, the words that admit the possibility that he is right.

'You've still got her on a pedestal, haven't you?' he says, but kindly. 'After all these years. Even now, when you know she's been lying to you.'

'She was only sixteen when she said that about her mum, though,' I say, desperate for an explanation that doesn't hurt. 'We'd just met. I can understand why she wouldn't want to tell me the truth.'

'Later, though? When you became so close. Why not then?'

'It's hard, when you've told a lie,' I say slowly. 'To go back on it. It's much easier to carry on with it. And the longer it goes on, the harder it gets.'

'How do you know she wasn't lying to you about other things, then? If you had no idea about this, can you honestly say you believe that was the only thing she lied about?'

'What is your problem? Why are you so keen for me to stop looking for her?' I'm aware that I'm being overly harsh on him, but I can't allow myself to believe she's been lying to me. I can't go there.

'I'm not!' The couple at the next table look at us, and he lowers his voice. 'That's not what I'm saying. I just . . . I don't want you to get hurt, I suppose.'

'Thanks.' There are hot tears pressing behind my eyes. I don't want him to see them fall. 'I shouldn't have asked you to come,' I say, standing up, my drink unfinished. 'Silly idea. Sorry.'

'It's fine. Stay and finish your drink at least.'

'No, I'd better go. I've got to get to work anyway.'

I can feel his puzzled stare on my back as I thread my way between the tables. I've nearly made it to the door when someone says my name and there's a hand on my arm.

'Oh! Hi, Rachel.' I suppose I shouldn't be surprised to see her here – the Forresters is our local, we're in here all the time. She's texted me a couple of times over the last few days, asking if I've got any news, but we've not spoken since Saturday.

'What are you doing here?' Her eyes roam over the tables, looking to see who I've been with.

'Oh, I was meeting an old friend for a drink. No one you know.'

Her gaze halts on the table I've recently vacated and her eyes widen. 'Were you with Leo?'

'Yes.' A hollow feeling creeps into my stomach. 'How do you know him?'

'He's an old friend of Sasha's, isn't he? He was at a party we were at, about a month ago. I met him there.'

'Oh. You never said.'

'I don't think I've even seen you since then, have I? Anyway, I hardly spoke to him. It wouldn't have been worth mentioning.' I get the sense she's backtracking, trying not to give away her emotions, whatever they are.

'Did he and Sasha . . . spend much time together?'

'No, I don't think so. I'm not even sure she knew he was going to be there.' She looks quickly over at him again.

'Have the police spoken to you?' I ask. I gave them her details on Saturday.

'Yes, they called. Not sure I was much help, though. Do you want a drink or . . . ?'

'No, thanks, I've got to be at work soon.' Not for an hour or so, in fact, but I hadn't anticipated that my meeting with Leo would be so brief.

'Oh, right.' Am I imagining it or does she seem relieved? 'Let me know if you hear anything about Sasha, won't you? Anything at all?'

'Yes, of course.'

At a loose end, I decide to walk to work instead of getting the bus. It's still light and there are plenty of people around. I shouldn't feel vulnerable, but I start to get the feeling someone is watching me. I don't have any specific reason to think it, but once the idea is in my head, it's hard to shift. There's a shortcut across a small park, and at the gate, I stand aside to let out a mother clutching a grubby, wailing toddler with one hand and struggling to push a buggy containing a baby, also screaming, with the other. She smiles her thanks through gritted teeth. The last families are leaving the brightly coloured play park, and as they do, a group of teenagers, smoking and drinking cans of cheap beer, climb over the perimeter fence, the girls climbing on to the roundabout and screaming as the boys spin them around.

I cut across the middle of a large area of scrubby grass beyond the play park. On hot days, groups of friends gather here for picnics and illegal barbecues, but today there's no one around apart from a homeless man asleep under a tree, surrounded by tatty carrier bags. Every now and then, I snatch a look behind me, but there's no one there. The last part of the shortcut is through a small wooded area. It's so quiet in here, the traffic just a distant hum. A twig snaps in the undergrowth and I can't help it, my feet speed up and then I'm running, my armpits prickling with sweat, heart pounding, bag banging against my hip. I take another look behind me as I turn the corner on to the path that will lead me back to the street, and as I do so I run smack into someone. I give a half-scream, and he takes me by the shoulders.

'Hey, Ellen, are you OK?'

It's Matthew from work.

'Has something happened?' He looks behind me. I still can't speak, my chest heaving. 'Ellen, what is it?'

I force myself to take a long, slow breath. 'I'm OK,' I say. 'I spooked myself walking through the woods.'

'Are you sure?'

'Yes.' I plaster a smile to my face.

'All right. Well ... I'll walk you back to the studio,' he says. 'Come on.'

I don't argue, and Matthew distracts me with his usual enquiries about Sasha, insisting on taking me right to the door and waiting until I've been buzzed into the building. It's not until I'm ensconced in the studio, headphones on and ready to play my first piece, that I realise I've had Simply Classical on all day today and Matthew wasn't presenting. He lives way across town, so what on earth was he doing here?

Ellen

December 2005

'Take a book, that's my advice,' said Mum. 'I had a boy-friend years ago who thought it'd impress me to take me to the opera. Oh my God, it was the longest night of my life.' She flipped up the lid of the bin and chucked the teabags in. 'I had literally no idea what was happening, and it seemed to go on and on . . . ' She trailed off as she handed me my tea and saw my stony face.

'Sorry, love. I'm sure it'll be good.'

'Olivia's one of the most well respected sopranos in the country, Mum. It's not some am-dram production in a village hall. This is at the Barbican.'

'I know, I know. Like I said, I'm sure it'll be very good.'

I refused the proffered cup of tea and swept from the room, sensing Mum's worried gaze on my back. She was doing my head in. She didn't understand what life was like at the Monktons'. Her and Dad had no interest in music, or politics, or books. Their conversation revolved around people they knew, what was on the telly, what room in the house to do up next. It was all so bloody boring. The other night at Sasha's, they'd had this journalist over for dinner and they'd all got embroiled in a long debate about the Iraq war. I couldn't get a handle on exactly what was what, or who I agreed with, but it was electrifying to be in the middle of all this passion. To be around people who cared about stuff, and who made their opinions known. Sasha had rolled her eyes at me during one particularly heated exchange, and Daniel and Nicholas were having their own private argument at their corner of the table, but I'd ignored Sasha and immersed myself in the words and ideas that flew back and forth across the kitchen.

Up in my room, I flipped through the hangers in my wardrobe. What did people wear to classical concerts? Olivia had her own style, of course: bold colours, lots of floaty layers, dramatic jewellery. Sasha, too, had an innate ability to dress in a way that was completely unlike anyone else, and yet was somehow perfect for the occasion. I couldn't attempt to emulate either of them – I'd look ridiculous. It would be humiliatingly obvious, too, that I was trying to copy them. In the end, I settled on a dress with a bold (for me) print and knee-length boots, hoping I looked the right amount of dressed-up without appearing try-hard.

'You look very smart,' said Mum as I came down the stairs. I cringed inwardly at her attempt to wheedle her way back into my good books, her shaming need not to lose me to an experience she would never understand.

God, I hoped she wasn't going to try and get herself invited to the Monktons' some time. The thought of her trying to engage Olivia in a conversation about how they've moved the coffee and tea aisle at Sainsbury's was more than I could bear.

'Thanks.' I studied my make-up critically in the hall mirror.

'You look fine,' Mum said. 'It's only a concert. You're not going to Buckingham Palace.'

'Oh, for God's sake, I'm just checking I haven't got lipstick on my teeth. If that's all right with you.' I grabbed my coat and bag from the newel post. 'I'll see you later. I'm going to stay at Sasha's tonight.'

'Again?' said Mum as I opened the front door, letting an icy blast in.

'Oh, for God's sake, Mum. Olivia wouldn't give me all this crap. Sometimes I wish she was my mum.' I slammed the door behind me, but not before I'd seen the look of utter devastation on her face.

I hurried down the road, guilt coursing through my veins like a noxious chemical, until I reached the Monktons', where Daniel opened the door.

'You're all dressed up,' he observed.

'Thanks,' I said, although it hadn't been a compliment. 'Sasha in her room?'

'Yep.' He came behind me up the stairs, and I thought for a moment he was going to follow me into Sasha's room, but at the last minute he swerved and went into his own room, closing the door firmly behind him.

Sasha was lying on her bed in her dressing gown, staring blankly out of the window.

'You're not dressed,' I said stupidly.

'No shit, Sherlock.' She swung her legs round and sat up on the edge of the bed. 'I don't know if I'm going.'

'What? Why not?' I'd never been out anywhere with the Monktons before, and the thought of going without Sasha made me feel panicky, with an undercurrent of something that might have been a nauseous sort of excitement.

'Oh, I don't know. It's going to be so boring, and we'll all have to fawn over Olivia afterwards and tell her how amazing she is. I don't know if I can be arsed.'

'Oh. Right.' I rubbed the fabric of the cuff of my dress between my finger and thumb.

'Do you actually want to go?' she said incredulously.

'It's just . . . I've never been to a classical concert before.'

'So? Nor have I.'

I shrugged, ashamed of the anticipation that had been building in the weeks since Olivia had invited me, the excitement I'd felt as I got ready earlier, the shivery feeling I got in my stomach when I imagined seeing her on stage.

'Oh, all right.' She slipped off her dressing gown and sauntered over to the wardrobe in her matching black underwear, pulling a dress seemingly at random from the overstuffed rail and slithering into it. It was black and clinging, high necked and low hemmed but simultaneously revealing. She gathered up her hair and

178

pulled it into a messy bun, secured with a couple of hairbands.

'Right, I'm ready.' I was probably imagining it, but I thought I detected a sly note that told me she knew exactly how much I'd been looking forward to the evening. 'Come on, then.'

I followed her downstairs, shaky with relief. The Monktons were gathered in the kitchen, Tony looking smarter than I'd ever seen him in a dark blue suit, pale blue shirt and silk tie. Even Daniel was wearing a shirt and jacket over very dark jeans. Only Nicholas was in his everyday wear of frayed jeans and a long sleeved T-shirt. I started with a foolish stab of jealousy when I saw Leo sitting beside Nicholas, rivalling Tony in the best-dressed stakes in a grey suit. I knew he and Nicholas had become friends as I'd been seeing him more and more at the Monktons' recently, but I hadn't known he was coming tonight. I had thought I was the only non-family member to be invited.

I noticed how all four pairs of eyes were drawn to Sasha as she slipped into a chair at the kitchen table, the light from the pull-down lamp pooling in front of her, spilling on to her hair. I stood awkwardly behind her in the shadows. There were a few seconds of silence, as if the four of them had been discussing something they didn't want to talk about in front of me, or perhaps Sasha, and then Tony pushed back his chair.

'Right,' he said. 'Shall we be off?'

Sasha and I trailed behind the others on the way to the

station. On the train, Tony and the boys sat in silence at a four-seat table, Sasha and I in a two behind them. I tried to engage Sasha in conversation but she kept shutting me down, so in the end I gave up and we stared out of the window as London flashed past in the darkness.

Once we were on the tube, the atmosphere lightened. It was busy and I found myself squashed up against Tony, who, on discovering I'd never been to a classical concert, told me about the different pieces we were going to hear. It was ostensibly a Christmas concert, so there would be a few carols and songs I might recognise, but Olivia was also singing various arias from operas, so he explained the plots of those, and the stories of the particular songs she was doing. Daniel, squeezed in between us and the door, chipped in when he thought Tony was getting things wrong. Nicholas, Leo and Sasha were chatting on the other side of the carriage. Sasha had shaken off her earlier mood and was laughing up at Leo, occasionally touching his arm.

As we walked into the foyer of the Barbican, a wave of noise and warmth rose up to greet us. There were twinkly lights and a Christmas tree. Small groups stood chatting, laughing, waving at acquaintances across the room. There was a feeling of comfortable anticipation in the air. These were people going to see a famous singer doing well-known songs. They knew they were going to have a nice time. Sasha, Leo and Nicholas were still laughing together in their little cluster. Daniel and Tony were looking at the programme, and didn't notice a glamorous woman of about Tony's age in a silk trouser suit making her way towards us, jet black hair tumbling over her shoulders.

'Tony, darling!'

He looked up in surprise. 'Oh! Hi, Elizabeth.' They did the two-cheek kiss thing I was finally becoming accustomed to, having never seen it first-hand before meeting the Monktons.

'How *are* you, darling?' the woman said, with a sympathetic head tilt.

'Fine!' said Tony, with a glance at Daniel, who had slipped off to join Nicholas and the others. He seemed to have forgotten I was there.

'I *heard*,' she said. 'Such bad luck.'

'Oh, it's fine,' he said with a forced smile. 'Plenty of other work around for a willing bassoonist.'

'Oh, of course, darling. But the LSO's the biggie, isn't it? For someone like you? I mean—'

'Actually, I'd been hoping for the chance to try something different, so it came at a good time.'

She laid a hand on his arm and was about to say something when there was an announcement on the tannoy: 'Ladies and gentlemen, please take your seats in the auditorium. Tonight's performance will begin in five minutes.'

'Ah, better go and find our seats,' said Tony with obvious relief. 'Lovely to see you. Right, come on troops,' he called to the others. 'Where's Ellen? Ah, there you are. Come on, let's go in.' He put one arm out to usher the others in the right direction and the other protectively behind me, hovering an inch or so behind my back, as the crowd surged towards the auditorium doors. As we headed up the steps to our seats, I realised I hadn't given any thought to who I would be sitting next to and that it was too late to engineer anything. Nicholas filed in first, followed by Leo and then Sasha. Daniel was next, and Tony turned to me.

'I'd prefer to sit on the aisle, if that's OK – stretch my legs,' he said, so I slid in next to Daniel.

Leo was telling a story about something that had happened at a party he'd been to, but Daniel wasn't listening, instead watching the empty stage intently, his hands twisting around and around each other.

'Are you ... Do you get nervous for her?' I asked.

He gave an embarrassed laugh. 'It's stupid, I know. I suppose I know what it feels like.'

'Have you done a lot of concerts, then?' I asked, realising how little I knew about his musical talent, other than hearing him playing at the Monktons', usually at Olivia's insistence.

'Yeah, quite a few. At college, obviously, and I've done some others as well.'

'What, for money?' I was impressed.

'Well, yeah. Not that there's a lot of money in it. Even at her level.' He indicated the stage.

'Really? But Olivia's famous!'

'She's classical music famous, not *famous* famous. You don't see her on the TV, do you?'

182

'No, but you've got that big house, and the piano, and ...'

'A big mortgage is what we've got.' He speaks quietly, not wanting Tony to hear. 'That and a massive credit card bill.'

I wasn't sure what to say to that, so I scanned the audience, which was mostly a sea of grey hair and balding pates. Then something caught my eye about ten or fifteen rows in front of us, not far from the front row. A young woman sat alone with empty seats either side of her. Something about the way the brown hair was twisted into a clip looked familiar, and as she looked over to her left, I saw I was right. It was Karina. What on earth was she doing here, and by herself? I hadn't told her I'd been invited by the Monktons, for the very reason that I didn't want her muscling her way in, as I was sure she would have done.

I was about to lean across Daniel and tell Sasha, but the orchestra started tuning up, and an expectant hush settled across the audience. A moment later, a disembodied voice asked us to please welcome Olivia Monkton to the stage, and there she was, gliding across in a long, black, silk dress I'd never seen before, cut low to expose her white shoulders, her hair swept up in an elaborate up-do secured with a red rose, thunderous applause echoing around the auditorium. She smiled warmly, her eyes sweeping the audience until the clapping finally died away.

'Good evening, everyone. It's so wonderful to see you

all here tonight. Christmas is one of my favourite times of year, so I couldn't have been more delighted when I was asked to do this concert. As you will have seen from the programme, I will be singing some Christmas classics later, but I'd like to start with one of my own particular favourites: Dido's Lament from Purcell's *Dido and Aeneas.*'

She took a slight step back from the microphone and looked down at the orchestra. After a few seconds of silence, a chord chimed from the pit, although I wasn't sure from what instrument. I expected Olivia to have to take in a huge breath, so I wasn't fully prepared when she casually opened her mouth, as if to ask me if I wanted a cup of tea, and this noise came out. It was simply the most beautiful sound I'd ever heard. I didn't know the story of the opera beyond what Tony had told me on the tube, but it didn't matter; I could hear the pain and despair in every note that flowed from Olivia's lips. I was aware that my mouth was hanging open, like a dumb-founded cartoon character. Tears gathered in the corners of my eyes and I let them fall. I wasn't hearing it only with my ears; it swelled inside me, sending a sprinkle of tingling goosebumps that started at my neck and spread out across every inch of my skin. Something intruded into my trance and I looked in annoyance to see who could possibly think it appropriate to talk during this transcendent experience. It was Nicholas, leaning in to whisper something to Sasha, who smirked and whispered something back. An elderly lady sitting behind them shushed them sharply, and they made faux-guilty faces at each other, Sasha with her hand across her mouth as if to keep from laughing.

I realised I was wrong to assume everyone would have the same reaction as me, and sat back in my seat, not wanting her to see my wet cheeks. It was then that I noticed Daniel, sitting statue-like beside me. He didn't appear to have even registered Nicholas and Sasha messing about. His eyes were fixed on his mother, the suffering in her voice reflected in his face, and I realised he was as moved as I was – more so. I watched him for a moment, thinking there was no chance of him observing me doing so, but he turned and saw my tears. I smiled, ready to make a joke of it, but he shook his head and took my hand, giving it a brief squeeze before releasing it. For that one extraordinary second, I experienced something: not love, or lust, or anything like that, but it was as if I was inside his head, or he in mine, and I knew that what we were feeling was the same. I suppose it was the first time I realised what music could do, in the right hands. I didn't think I would ever be the same again.

Ellen

September 2017

I'm unable to resist peering at the corner house as I pass it on my way to Mum and Dad's for dinner. Funny to think how all I ever wanted to do was spend every second I could there, day and night. At the time, I thought the way they lived was everything – so exciting, so vibrant – my own parents seeming unutterably pedestrian in comparison. I can see now, though, that nothing like what happened on New Year's Eve 2006 could ever have happened at my parents' house. Olivia and Tony thought they were doing the right thing, I suppose, but was it their permissiveness that allowed events to unfold as they did? Or is that unfair to them?

I'm level with their house when Olivia comes out, a clutch of hessian shopping bags in her hand. She gets into the car and drives away. I slow, checking the clock on the dash. Mum and Dad won't mind if I'm a bit late. I pull up and sit there until Olivia's car has disappeared around the bend in the road. I'll never get a better chance to speak to Tony alone.

As I wait for him to answer the door, I wonder whether Nicholas has told his parents about our meeting. Seeing him again has left me with a faint feeling of unease, although I can't put my finger on why. I shake my head, my brain twisted in a cobweb made of silken strands that look ethereal, harmless, but are actually weaving around and around me, so gently I can't tell I am being tied up.

The first thing I notice is that, like Olivia, he's lost weight. His skin has a yellowish tinge and his cheeks are all shadows with a dusting of grey stubble. His eyes are cloudy and spidered with red, his once-raffish good looks faded into ravaged disarray. He can't be more than sixty, but he looks much older, that summer day when Karina swooned over him a faded, distant dream. For a few seconds he looks at me expectantly, waiting for me to start selling him double-glazing or some such, but then realisation dawns.

'Ellen!' His face lights up, a glimmer of the old Tony visible: Tony the host, bottle of wine in hand. He pulls me into a hug, which takes me by surprise, my body stiff and unyielding in his embrace, my nose wrinkled at the sour, unwashed smell that emanates from him. 'Come in, come in. Liv told me you were here the other day. I . . . I wasn't feeling too well, or I would have come down.'

So he was here that day. Was that what made Olivia so edgy? Why wouldn't she have wanted me to see him, though?

'That's OK,' I say, following him down the hall. 'Is Olivia here?'

'No, she's out, but she shouldn't be too long. Do wait, she'd love to see you.'

I'm not so sure about that.

'Drink?' he says, heading for the fridge.

'Not for me, thanks, I'm driving.'

'Oh yes, of course, I meant tea or coffee,' he says with a laugh, which fools no one, getting the milk out of the fridge door. I notice an angry, purple bruise on the back of his hand.

'Tea would be great, thanks. Do you know how long she'll be, Olivia?'

'Oh, not long, not long,' he says, filling the kettle. 'But what about Sasha? Is she back?'

'Olivia told you, then?'

'Of course she told me.' He looks at me in surprise. 'We've never given up on her, Ellen. I know Sasha may have given you a different impression, but there's not a day goes by that we don't think of her. We couldn't ... well, we couldn't keep trying for ever. She made it very plain she didn't want anything to do with us. She knows where we are if she wants us. Have you heard from her?'

'No.' My voice wavers and he leans against the Aga, his face sympathetic.

'When did she go missing again?'

'Friday.' Five endless days ago.

'Hmmm.' I can tell he wants to say something, something he thinks might upset me. I save him the trouble.

'I know what you're going to say. This is who she is; it's what she does. She runs, she disappears, she doesn't care who she hurts. But I thought that was what she did to other people. Not to me.' I know I sound deranged, blurting these things out, but the longer she is gone, the less I care about the social niceties.

'Yes, you always were very close, I know that. We were so happy when she found you. So good for her to have a friend. Especially after . . . ' He is clearly unsure what I am supposed to know.

'It's all right, I know about her mum. Nicholas told me.'

'You've seen Nicky?' The childhood nickname slips out. I'd forgotten that was what they called him. He used to hate it, said Nicky was a girl's name.

'Yes. He assumed I knew about Sasha's mum.'

'She never told you? But Liv said you've been sharing a flat for years.'

'Yes, we have,' I say shortly. I am trying to keep that particular pain at bay; the pain of what she kept from me, when I thought we told each other everything.

He puts my tea down in front of me and I notice a slight tremor in his hand.

'Tony, you don't think Sasha's mum could have anything to do with this, do you? Did she ever get in touch at all?'

He sits down opposite me. 'No.' His face drops. 'I could never quite forgive her for that. I know she had her problems, and maybe she could never have had Sasha to live with her again, but to drop out of her life

189

entirely like that ... Anyway, if she wanted to get back in touch with Sasha, she would have come through us, I'm sure, and we haven't heard a word from her for over ten years.'

'Do you have an address for her? Even an old one?'

'Oh goodness, I don't know if that would be a good idea, darling. Not at all.'

'Please, Tony.' I steel myself and lay my hand over his on the table between us. 'I don't want to drag up anything unpleasant, but I'm so worried about Sasha.' We're close, our faces a couple of feet apart. There are patches of dry skin on his face and a couple of long hairs curl from his nostrils.

'All right, I'll have a look in the book and see what's the last address we've got for her. Hang on.'

He goes to the dresser and takes down a battered black book, with a few remnants of gold lettering that used to say *Addresses* on the front. He flips through to 'N', running his finger down the page until something makes him stop and frown.

'What is it?' I say eagerly.

'It's just ... I didn't realise Olivia had updated it. I thought the last address we had for her was up north somewhere, but she's crossed that one out and written in a new one in London.'

'Sasha's mum is in London?'

'Apparently. Here.' He passes the book over to me and I tap the address into the notes on my phone.

'Right, well, it was good to see you, Ellen.' His eyes

swivel to the fridge, just for a second. He's trying to get rid of me so he can have a drink. I gather all my courage.

'What about Daniel?'

'What about him?' He's guarded, but the shutters haven't come clanging down the way they did when I asked Olivia about him.

'Karina said—'

'Karina Barton? You spoke to her?' he says in horror.

'Yes!' I slap my hands down on the table. 'Of course I have! Sasha has disappeared! I'm doing everything I can to find her because no one else seems to care!'

'Sorry,' he says quietly. 'Go on.'

'She said she'd seen Daniel. In London. Mum said she thought she saw him too. Coming in here.'

'And what?' The bonhomie from a moment ago has completely disappeared. 'You've immediately jumped to the conclusion that he's done something to Sasha?'

'So you have seen him?'

'He's my son! Yes, I've seen him. What do you think? To be brutal, Ellen, I'm dying.' The tremor in his hand, the sickly yellow skin. Something in me had already known. 'I'm not prepared to go to my grave estranged from my son when he has done nothing wrong.'

'Nothing wrong?' I know they've been through hell, Olivia and Tony, but I can't let this pass.

'Yes, Ellen. Do you really still believe Karina Barton was telling the truth?'

'Yes. Yes, I do. And so was I.'

'Oh, Ellen—'

He is interrupted by the sound of a key in the door, and seconds later Olivia bustles into the kitchen.

'I forgot the bloody list— Oh!' She stops dead. 'What are you doing here?' Her tone is unfriendly, without a hint of the warmth she showed me last time I was here.

'I saw Nicholas last night. He told me about Sasha's mum.'

'Didn't you know?' Her expression softens. 'Had she never told you?'

'No.' I can't say any more or I'll betray how devastated I am that Sasha never confided in me.

'Is there still no word from her?' she asks.

I shake my head, not trusting my treacherous voice.

'But surely you can't think Alice has got anything to do with it? No one's heard from her for years.'

You have. You've noted down her new address in your black book. 'I thought maybe she might be in touch with Sasha or . . . '

'Alice North has got absolutely zero interest in her daughter, or in anyone else, for that matter,' she says, picking up her list and checking in the fridge, presumably for anything she's forgotten. 'I wouldn't waste any time trying to find her. Even if you do, you'll get no sense out of her. Honestly, Ellen, you're barking up the wrong tree there.'

'What about Daniel?' I say, suddenly fearless. 'Is he the wrong tree too?'

She slams the fridge door shut. 'I told you last time,

192

I don't know where he is or what he's doing. I'm sorry about Sasha, I really am, but I think you'd better go.'

'Tony's told me you've seen him.'

'Oh, for God's sake.'

Tony shrugs apologetically at her, gets up and takes a small glass from the dresser. He pours himself a whisky from a bottle on the side, Olivia watching despairingly.

'He had no right to tell you anything of the sort!' She takes my arm to guide me out into the hall. 'Look, Ellen, you need to take anything Tony says with a pinch of salt, I'm afraid.' She's calmer now, confidential. 'As you can probably tell, he drinks too much. Always did, anyway, but since everything that happened, it's been much worse. He's barely functioning, to be honest. You don't want to set any store by what he says. Yes, we've seen Daniel, but only recently. Tony's ... not very well.' She breathes in deeply through her nose. 'He begged me to reconsider our decision not to see Daniel, and I couldn't very well refuse. But he's got nothing to do with wherever Sasha is, I can promise you that.'

Tony emerges from the kitchen, the glass of amber liquid in his hand.

'I had to see him, you can see that, can't you, Ellen?' He takes a gulp of his drink and his face softens. 'It's all so long ago now.'

Pity blooms within me as I look at them, these ghosts, shadows of their former selves. I say goodbye, and while Olivia stays where she is, arms firmly crossed, Tony moves forward to squeeze my arm, kissing my

193

cheek as he does so. I try not to wince at the smell of his breath.

As I walk down the road towards my parents' house, a journey I made so many times all those years ago, I can still feel his hand on my arm, the place where he kissed my cheek burning like a brand.

Ellen

March 2006

I suppose it was the money going missing that was the first sign that something was wrong. It was a couple of months ago, not long after Christmas. I was round at the Monktons', sitting at the kitchen table putting the Christmas decorations away, while Olivia made a boeuf bourguignon for what I was learning to call 'supper'. Sasha had been there earlier, but had gone out shopping a couple of hours before, and Olivia had urged me to stay until she got back. I hadn't taken much persuasion. Ever since the concert at the Barbican, I'd wanted to spend as much time as possible with Olivia, treasuring it like a precious jewel. Not only was I in awe of her talent, she was also everything I'd ever wanted in a mother: laid-back and permissive, but warm and loving. She treated me like an adult but at the same time she made me feel safe, protected. I'd never had that sort of relationship with an adult. Sasha had noticed and occasionally made fun of me about it, as did Nicholas if he was around, but

Daniel never did. We'd never talked about it, but ever since the moment we had shared when Olivia opened her mouth and let the pure sound of it pour out, wrapping itself around us, there had been a kind of silent understanding between us.

At home, our Christmas tree was lifted down from the loft and unfolded each year, to be topped by a gaudy fairy, the rest of it festooned with tinsel, glittery baubles and multicoloured flashing lights. The Monktons had a real tree peppered with tiny white lights, its piney scent making me nostalgic for a storybook Christmas I'd never had: one filled with homemade gingerbread houses and moonlit walks through crisp snow to midnight mass, rather than dry turkey and falling asleep in front of the TV. Olivia's decorations were a mix of handmade ornaments made of wood and gingham and twisted cane, and malformed cardboard Father Christmases and reindeer made by the boys when they were little.

'I can't bear to throw them out,' she had said to me that day as I wrapped a tatty felt bell in a piece of ancient tissue paper with the lines of Christmases past folded into it. I placed it reverently in the dark green Clarks shoebox with a label on the side that said size 12 and a half.

'Bless you for helping me,' she went on. 'No one else is interested. Do you want a cuppa?'

'Yes please,' I said, glowing with pleasure as she reached up for the Earl Grey tin.

'Oh damn,' she said, peering into the fridge. 'Those

wretched boys have drunk all the milk. Would you be a love and pop to the corner shop? I don't want to leave this.' She gestured to the bubbling Le Creuset casserole on the stovetop.

'Yes, of course.'

'We need some tinned tomatoes too, if they've got any, and can you get a paper as well?' Olivia said, rummaging in her bag for her purse. 'Oh.' Her expression changed to annoyance as she opened it. She walked into the hall and bawled up the stairs. 'Daniel! Nicky! Have you been in my purse?' They both came out of their rooms and stood belligerently at the top of the stairs.

'What?' said Daniel.

'Have you been in my purse?' she repeated. 'I had three twenty pound notes in there earlier.'

'Nope,' said Daniel.

'Me neither,' Nicholas said.

'Don't worry, I'll get it,' I called from the kitchen table, eager to be of use.

Olivia sighed as she came back in. 'Those bloody boys,' she said. 'All right, darling, if you wouldn't mind. Just get the milk, don't worry about the rest of it.'

I came back with not only the milk but the tomatoes, the paper (the *Guardian*, naturally) and some of the fancy chocolate biscuits I knew she liked. When Sasha finally reappeared, laden down with shopping bags, I expected Olivia to ask her about the money, but she didn't mention it.

This week it was a different story, though. I didn't see

Sasha over the weekend because we'd had my auntie and uncle staying, and Mum wouldn't let me go out. When I called for her on the way to school on Monday morning, she came out almost before I'd lowered my hand from the bell. She looked pale and her eyes were red.

'Are you OK?'

'Let's go.' She grabbed my arm and pulled me down the street.

'What's up?' I looked back at the house in confusion.

'I just want to get away from there,' she said through gritted teeth. Once we were a hundred yards or so from the house she spoke again. 'Fucking Olivia.'

'What's happened?' I said, horrified.

'She's had more money go missing.'

'What do you mean, more?' I said, although as I spoke I smelled beef stewing in red wine, felt the crackle of tissue paper under my fingers, saw Sasha waltzing in laden down with shopping bags.

'There's been a couple of times recently where money's gone from her purse,' she said, sliding me a sideways look. 'You were there the first time, remember? Not long after Christmas.'

'Oh yeah,' I said, pretending to remember, in one of my futile attempts to keep from her how important the Monktons, and particularly Olivia, had become to me, in case she thought it was weird.

'There were a couple more times after that. She always asked Nicholas and Daniel if they'd taken it. But never me. Until now.'

I waited in silence, unable to rid my mind of the image of her swinging into the kitchen with those bags.

'She had a couple of hundred quid in her bag – it was expenses from a job she'd done, to reimburse her for food and stuff while she'd been away. The other times it wasn't as much, and she just thought it was her being scatty. But this time, she knew the money had been there, and she knew it had gone missing.'

'And she's accused you?'

'Not accused, exactly. She sat me down yesterday morning, "terribly concerned".' She did ironic quote marks in the air. 'Was there anything I wanted to talk to her about? Did I need money for some reason? God knows what she thinks I'm doing with it.'

'So she definitely thinks it's you that's taking it? That's so unfair. What about Daniel? He always seems to have money.'

'What, her golden boy?' She hoisted her bag defiantly up on her shoulder. 'He swears blind it wasn't him, and she believes him. Nick's the same.'

'Tony?' I said, clutching at straws. 'Maybe he's … I don't know, a secret gambler or something?'

'Nope, she's pretty much made up her mind that it's me. The cuckoo in the nest.'

'I'm sure that's not how she thinks of you, Sash.'

'That's what I am, though, isn't it?' She was tight with tension. 'I don't fit. She's done her best, but to her I'm an outsider. I always will be, and that's where she likes me. She doesn't want me to get too close.'

'You're not alone, Sash, you do know that, don't you?' I said. 'It must be so hard for you, Olivia saying those things, but you've got me. I'm on your side.' I so wanted to ask about her mum, if Sasha had spoken to her about all this, if Olivia and Tony had talked to her. It was such a forbidden subject I was frightened to introduce it, but I took a deep breath and launched in.

'What about your mum? Can't you talk to her about it?'

Sasha closed up like a fan. 'I don't want to worry her with it.'

'But she'd want to know, surely?' I tried to think how my mum would feel, if I were living far away with another family and had been accused of something I hadn't done. She'd be up in arms, I realised, storming in, all guns blazing. Mum was pretty non-confrontational in everyday life, but there had been a few times when she'd come to my rescue. At primary school there was a girl called Joanne Speer, who had made my life hell for a term, and when my mum found out, she was incandescent with rage.

'The little bitch,' she said to my dad when she thought I was in bed. It's the only time I've ever heard her swear. I don't know what she said when she went into school the next day, but I do know Joanne never bothered me again.

'No, she won't be able to do anything and she'll only worry about me,' Sasha said. I started to protest but she cut me off. 'Trust me, Ellen. It's better if she doesn't know.'

'So what did Olivia say? How did you leave it?'

'She was nice about it, I suppose. I mean, even though she thinks I've taken it, and I suppose I can't blame her, all she said was if I need money I only have to ask, or if there's anything bothering me, I should talk to her about it.'

'So who is doing it? Who's taking the money?'

'One of the boys' friends, maybe? Or Karina? She's there all the bloody time at the moment. Or Leo – he and Nicholas are joined at the hip. I don't know – there's people in and out of the house all the time. You know what it's like.'

She was right. It was one of the things I especially loved about their house: its open-door policy, how Olivia and Tony encouraged all of them to have friends over, to feel that the house was their home too, not just Olivia and Tony's. Selfishly I hoped this money business wouldn't change that.

'She'll simply have to be more careful from now on,' Sasha said. 'If she doesn't leave money lying around, nobody will be able to take it, will they?'

'You don't think . . . one of the boys is doing it, hoping that you'll get the blame?'

'No! Why would they?'

We walked on in silence for a few minutes, and then Sasha spoke with the bright energy of someone deliberately trying to move the conversation on.

'So, we're definitely going to go away, yeah?'

'Yes, absolutely.' I'd finally managed to persuade my mum to let me and Sasha go travelling around France and Spain by train in the summer holidays. I was saving up my wages from my Saturday job at the Body Shop. I wasn't sure where Sasha was getting the money from, but she always seemed to have plenty.

'Have you had a word with Karina?' Sasha asked. When we'd first started discussing it at school one day, Karina had been there and had been keen to come too. Later, in her bedroom, Sasha had admitted that she didn't really want Karina to come, she wanted it to be just the two of us, and I had felt a surge of guilty relief. Sasha had asked me to break the news to Karina, but thankfully it hadn't come to that.

'Oh, it's OK, her mum won't let her.'

'Thank God,' said Sasha, giggling, and I laughed along traitorously. Ever since I'd spotted Karina on her own at the concert, I'd been feeling increasingly uncomfortable about her interest in the Monktons. I hadn't mentioned seeing her there to any of them, even Sasha, out of some sort of residual loyalty to my former best friend, but I had asked her about it. She was defiant, saying why shouldn't she have gone, she wanted to hear Olivia sing as much as I did – this last with a nod to the teasing I had taken at the hands of Nicholas and Leo last time we were all at the Monktons', about my devotion to Olivia. I'd left it – after all, she was right. There was no reason why she shouldn't have been there, but something about seeing her sitting there alone had left a peculiar, lingering taste in my mouth, and a vague, unformed question in the back of my mind.

Ellen

September 2017

'I wish you'd told me about the letters at the time,' Mum says, helping me to too many potatoes.

'There didn't seem much point, and I didn't want to worry you.'

'You should have taken them to the police,' Dad says.

'They couldn't have done anything. He wasn't threatening us – well, only vaguely in that first one. The others were just accusing us of lying.'

'I know you didn't lie, sweetheart,' says Mum. 'Or Karina. I went round to see Dilys the next day, to see if there was anything I could do.' This is news to me. 'I saw her, the poor girl. She looked terrible.' I remember. Curled in a ball on the frozen ground, her skirt hitched up, catatonic with shock. 'But Sasha . . . I wouldn't put it past her.'

A piece of chicken lodges in my throat. I take a sip of water, trying not to react. The days when Mum and I would argue about the Monktons are long gone, buried in a past where I was so blinkered I couldn't see the value in my loving, stable parents.

'Sasha didn't lie, Mum,' I say evenly. 'Let's not talk about it.'

'You still haven't heard anything?' asks Dad.

'No, nothing. The police don't seem that interested. And also . . . ' I am torn between wanting to tell them that Daniel is definitely back, so someone else understands the seriousness of this, and the desire to protect them. If Daniel has got Sasha, I am in danger too.

'What?' she asks, concern clouding her features.

'Nothing. Just ... Olivia and Tony, they weren't that helpful.'

'You've seen them?' There's something of the old animosity still there. Neither of us mention the night of Olivia's concert and the hurtful remark I flung at her as I left, but I know we are both thinking of it. Part of me is surprised it still hurts her, but I suppose I shouldn't be, given how much the whole thing still haunts me. Live in the present, that's the advice, isn't it? Look forward, not back. However much you try to do that, though, you can never escape your past, the way the things that have happened to you shape you.

'Yes, I went to see them at the weekend, and then again tonight. I thought they might be able to help, might know something that would help to find her.'

'Why would they know anything?' says Dad. 'To be honest, I wouldn't trust anything Tony says these days, anyway. I saw him once in the street at 10 a.m.,

204

staggering about, reeking of drink.' There's a back note of satisfaction that makes me wonder if he, too, suffered from my teenage infatuation with the Monkton parents.

'Yes, that's what Olivia said. Also, he's really not very well. He said ... He told me he was dying.'

'Oh. Poor man.' Mum can't help but be compassionate. Vengefulness isn't in her nature.

'I found out something else, too ... about Sasha's mum.'

'Oh yes?' Mum is suspiciously neutral.

'Did you know?' I ask, aghast.

'I don't *know* anything. It's just ... I wouldn't be surprised if what she told you wasn't entirely true. It certainly sounded made up.'

'Why didn't you say anything at the time?'

'Are you kidding?' Mum laughs. 'You would have bitten my head off at the mere suggestion. Plus I figured it must be something pretty unpleasant for her to want to conceal it. Who was I to say she had to tell the truth?'

'Well, you were right. Her mum wasn't a jet-setting model. She was a drug addict. Sasha was taken away by social services. That's why she came to live with the Monktons.'

'Ah, I see.' Mum says this as if it explains a lot.

'What do you see?'

She looks at Dad.

'She seemed like a troubled soul, that's all Mum means.'

My instinct is to argue, to defend her, but of course they are right. They were always right, about it all. I was too involved with Sasha, too invested in the Monktons.

I lost my heart and my head to them, and nothing has been the same since.

'I'm sorry,' I say, poking a piece of broccoli around my plate with my fork.

'What on earth for, sweetheart?' says Mum.

'You know – how I was back then. Always going on about the Monktons . . . '

'Water under the bridge,' says Dad firmly.

'All teenagers argue with their parents,' says Mum. 'There's no need to apologise.' She starts clearing the plates. 'But thank you,' she adds as she places them on the serving hatch and walks round to the kitchen.

My phone buzzes in my bag. It's a text from Rachel: Are you doing anything tonight? Can we meet for a quick drink in the Forresters?

It's only 8.30 p.m. Mum and Dad are probably hoping I'll stay the night, but I text back: OK, I can be there at 9. All OK?

Yes fine, she texts back instantly. See you there.

I make my excuses to Mum and Dad, who are disappointed, but let me go without a fuss, and hop back in the car. When I arrive shortly before 9 p.m., Rachel's already there, immaculate as ever in dark jeans and a crisp, white shirt, a large glass of wine half-drunk on the table in front of her.

'Have you heard anything?' She cuts straight to the chase as soon as I sit down with my drink.

'No.' My heart sinks. She doesn't have any new information, she's ambulance-chasing, wanting in on the action as usual. 'Have you?' I know she hasn't. Why would she?

'No, but ... there's something I need to talk to you about.' She's being cagey, but you never know with her if she's dramatising for effect, to make herself seem important.

'What's that?'

'I've been going back and forth about whether I should say anything, but I've decided if there's even the tiniest chance it could have something to do with where Sasha is, I should tell you.'

'What?' The sounds of the pub around us fade away and all I can see are her eyes, dark and anxious.

'When I saw you in here with Leo yesterday, I said I knew he was an old friend of Sasha's. But I didn't tell you I also knew he was an old boyfriend of yours. Sasha told me.'

'When we were teenagers, yes. So what?'

'That's why I didn't tell you last night. I wasn't sure if you'd be upset or ... '

'Tell me what?'

'That night, a month ago, when I met Leo at that party ... Jackson wasn't there, and ... '

I know what's coming, but I wait for her to say it, giving myself a few more precious seconds of unknowing. Part of me wants to get up and run, and never stop, so I don't have to hear her say it.

'Sasha slept with him. It only happened the once, I'm sure.'

Something inside me crashes and crumbles, like a

tower block being demolished by dynamite. It's stupid, shaming, how hurt I am. Leo and I went out for six months when we were eighteen. I don't have any rights over him. So why do I feel as though they have both betrayed me in the most horrible way possible?

'She made me swear not to tell you. She said you'd be really upset. It was only one time. She never meant it to happen. She felt terrible.' She's babbling now, the words she's had to keep in pouring out like a waterfall.

So Jackson was right about her. Beneath the anger and despair, there's a tiny part of me that feels vindicated for my teenage self, the girl who flinched every time Leo glanced in Sasha's direction. Not so paranoid now. What I felt, what I feared – it was real. I concentrate on breathing in and out. I need to be present for this. I need to hear it, to understand it.

'How? What happened?'

She looks away, out of the window into the darkness. 'Will it help, Ellen? Really?'

'Please.' I put my hand out and grasp her arm. 'I want to know.'

She swallows. 'OK.' It has taken courage for her to come here and tell me this, I realise.

'Thank you,' I say, withdrawing my hand jerkily.

'I don't know much. They were drunk. I saw them talking for hours in the corner at this party. I don't know all the details, and I'm sure you don't want them anyway.'

Don't I? Part of me does; part of me wants to see how the curve of her body fitted into his, to hear the sounds she made, to know if he did the things to her that he did to me.

'I saw them kissing. I didn't know then that he was an ex of yours, but I knew she was cheating on Jackson, obviously. The next day she called me. She said she felt guilty, about Jackson, but you too. She said she needed to get it off her chest, needed someone to confide in, but . . . '

'What?'

'She likes it, doesn't she, inviting you into a secret? Making it something just the two of you know.' She speaks quietly, and I realise how brave she is being to admit that she liked it, as I did. That we both thrived on feeling like Sasha's confidante, her one and only. That we craved her attention, her love; blossomed under it.

'I wasn't going to say anything, but when I saw you with him last night, I thought . . . maybe he's got something to do with it? Maybe he knows something. I'm sorry. I hope I did the right thing.'

'It's OK.' I'm not angry with Rachel. I'm not sure that I'm angry at all. I am shattered, yes, but I'm also resigned. Of course this has happened. It feels, if not right, then expected. I've been waiting for it to happen since the day when she sat on her desk, swinging her legs, and he couldn't take his eyes off her. There's a nub of anger growing, though, and it's directed at Sasha. However foolish it might be on my part, she would have known exactly how I would feel about her sleeping with Leo – that's why she didn't tell me. Yet she went ahead

209

and did it anyway. The anger burns a little brighter, but I don't know what to do with it. I'm so unused to being angry with her.

As I watch Rachel making her way through the tables to get us more drinks, another thought eases its way in. I've been so busy focusing on Sasha's betrayal (and it does feel like a betrayal, no matter how I try to rationalise it), I've failed to fully take in that Leo lied to me too. Was it because he knew I'd be hurt? Or did he have another reason for wanting to keep his relationship with Sasha from me?

Ellen

May 2006

'Someone's been in my room.'

'What do you mean? Who?' I slid my tongue around the edge of the cone to stop the ice cream dripping on to my fingers. The weather had been unseasonably warm this half-term, so Karina, Sasha and I had decided to make the most of the last couple of days of the holiday by coming to the park with a rug, snacks and magazines.

A group of boys I recognised from school, including Leo Smith, had set up their own camp not far from us, where they were blatantly trying to impress Sasha with their football skills, self-consciously swearing and taking the piss out of each other. Sasha was totally oblivious, as ever.

'I don't know,' she said, pushing herself up on to her elbows and gazing into the distance. 'But things have been moved. Nothing important: the book I'm reading, my make-up bag, my pencil case. But they're not where I left them.'

'Maybe it's Olivia cleaning up, dusting,' said Karina, without taking her eyes off the boys. She'd been lying on her front facing them, chin on hands, since they arrived.

'No, she doesn't clean our rooms. She says we're old enough to do it ourselves or live with the consequences.'

'That's weird,' I said.

'I know.' Her face crumpled and I realised she'd been worried we wouldn't believe her.

'Have you told Olivia?'

Sasha sighed. 'She still thinks I took that money. She'll think I'm making it up.'

'Why would you do that, though? I mean, why would she think that?' I said.

'Oh, she thinks I want the attention. She'll want to sit me down and have a serious talk, try to get to the bottom of my "issues". Psychoanalyse me. Well, she can forget that.'

'Are you sure? She seems so ... '

'What? Wonderful? For God's sake, Ellen, just because you think she's the perfect mother, doesn't mean it's true.'

'I know,' I said, reddening. I'd been trying to keep my mum-crush on Olivia under wraps, but I'd obviously failed. 'What about ... Could you ... ' I paused, unsure whether to go on. 'I mean, have you thought about asking your mum to talk to Olivia?'

'I've told you, I don't want to bother her with stuff like this,' she snapped. 'She's got enough on her plate.' She lay back down and closed her eyes.

Karina and I exchanged glances. Every now and then,

one of us would gently probe Sasha about her mother, but neither of us had ever got anywhere. I picked up the suncream and rubbed some more into my legs. I hated myself for it, but I began to wonder if Olivia was right that Sasha was making the whole thing up. It sometimes felt as if she moved around the world in a little bubble, nothing touching her; that other people's opinions of her streamed off like rainwater. But could that be true? Was anyone truly impervious to how others saw them? Did she have some reason for wanting to paint herself as the victim of a stalking campaign?

'Sorry,' she said after a minute, her eyes still closed.

I waited for her to offer an explanation for her shortness, but none was forthcoming, so I picked up a magazine and started to read, or pretend to. If she was going to be like that, I wasn't going to indulge her by asking all the questions she wanted me to ask. If she wanted to talk to me, let her. If not, fine. Karina resumed her surveillance of the football game, and the three of us lay there in silence for twenty minutes or so. I was just dropping off, lulled by the sun on my face and the sounds of other people having fun, when something whacked into my leg. I sat up too quickly, head spinning. Someone was standing above us, his head blocking out the sun, making his face appear dark, so that for a moment I couldn't tell who it was.

'Sorry,' he said to me, picking up the ball, and I realised it was Leo.

I hastily pulled part of the rug over the top of my legs. I was attempting an early-season tan in a navy one-piece that had seen better days. Karina was in a strappy sun-dress and Sasha was sporting a white halter-neck bikini and an all-over butterscotch tan.

She opened her eyes lazily and stretched like a cat. 'Oh, hi, Leo.'

He smiled at her, seemingly oblivious to the acres of tanned, smooth flesh on display, and then at me, jiggling the ball from hand to hand as he spoke.

'We're going to have a game of volleyball. Do you guys want to play?'

'No thanks.' I was hopeless at ball games and had no desire to embarrass myself.

'I will!' Karina jumped up eagerly, adjusting the shoulder straps on her dress. I realised she wasn't wearing a bra at the same time Leo did. He caught me looking and gave me a wicked grin.

'Lovely jubbly,' he said, and I couldn't help smiling back at him, a little thrill running through me at the idea of having a private joke with Leo Smith.

'Sasha? How about you?'

She shrugged her shoulders. 'OK, why not?'

She stood up and started walking over to the boys without putting so much as a T-shirt on over her bikini. Some of them could barely close their mouths. It was like something out of a Bond film. Karina followed awkwardly a few paces behind. I looked back up at Leo, expecting him to be gawking at her too, but instead he was looking down at me.

'She's laying it on a bit thick today, isn't she?'

I blushed. 'What d'you mean?'

He flung himself down next to me on the rug. 'You know, strutting around in that tiny little bikini, laying it all out there . . . I know you and her are close, and I'm not being funny or anything, but . . . '

I watched as the boys set up a makeshift net consisting of a piece of rope strung between two trees. A couple of other girls had also joined them, and I saw them looking at Sasha in her bikini with a mixture of distaste and naked jealousy.

'I thought . . . ' I kept watching the volleyball game, a barely perceptible tremor in my voice at my disloyalty. 'I kind of got the impression you liked her. Fancied her, I mean.'

'Yeah, I did when she first started at school,' he said breezily, unfazed. 'But now I think she's a bit obvious. A bit fake. I prefer someone more down to earth.'

'Like Karina?' I said. Actually she'd seemed less interested in him recently, but I was sure she'd still be delighted if he liked her.

He nudged me gently with his elbow. 'No, dummy,' he said. 'Like you.' With that, he got up and walked over to the others without looking back.

I stared motionless and breathless after him, electrified and terrified in equal measure.

Ellen

September 2017

I sit bolt upright, heart racing. Something has jolted me from sleep, but the flat is silent except for the usual strains of the traffic thundering up and down the road outside, and the sound of distant sirens that forms the backdrop to London living. I can feel every breath I draw, juddery from the pounding of my heart. I look at the clock. It's 3 a.m., and I think of seeing Rachel in the pub earlier, and her 'three a.m. friends'. Could I call her now and tell her I'm frightened? If Sasha was here, I'd go padding into her room. She'd shift and wake briefly, shuffling over to make room in the bed, letting me huddle in close to her, knowing without me having to say anything that I needed comfort, company. Someone to make me feel less alone.

I lie back down, but my sheets are clammy with sweat, so I move over to the other side, trying to breathe slowly and deeply, clearing my mind to let sleep come. I'm on the edge where my thoughts start drifting out of my control into the unpredictability of dreams, when I hear a noise and my eyes snap open. I know what it is. It's the creak that the floorboard near the front door gives when somebody steps on it. Someone is in the flat. I lie rigid, petrified, feeling every ridge in the mattress beneath my back.

It never gets completely dark in my room because of the streetlights, and I slide a look left to where my phone sits on the bedside table. I want to reach out for it but my brain spirals ahead of my body and sees my arm reaching over and a hand shooting up from beneath the bed to grab it, hard. However much I tell myself that the danger is out there in the hallway, not here in my room, under my bed, I cannot stretch out my hand. Those childhood monsters that lurked under my bed cast long shadows, reinforced by every schlocky horror movie I've ever seen. This isn't a movie, though, or an unfounded fear. This is real. My whole body is made of jelly. I couldn't get out of bed even if I wanted to, the power drained from my limbs, replaced by unadulterated terror. Whoever it is, they are moving very quietly, but I hear them opening the door to Sasha's room, which also gives a slight creak. Is it her? Could it be? Part of me wants to run in there and shake her by the shoulders, scream at her to tell me where she's been, but even if I was capable of movement, I wouldn't. What if it isn't her?

My stomach lurches and for one terrifying moment I think I'm going to be sick, but I clench my fists and swallow, forcing myself to hold it together. There are noises, rustling sounds through the wall, drawers being opened slowly, papers being moved around. Whoever is in there is trying not to be heard but it's impossible to be entirely silent unless you remain motionless. I have no choice but to be utterly still, frozen beneath the bedclothes, every muscle strained to breaking point. I don't know how long the rustling and stealthy moving of objects around goes on for. It feels like an eternity. I will it to end, to stop, but at the same time the fear of where the intruder will go next consumes me and part of me wishes they would stay in Sasha's room for ever.

Agonisingly, the movement in the next room stops and there is a moment of stillness. A thrill of pure fear shoots through me and I hold my breath, beads of sweat breaking out on my forehead and trickling down towards my ears. Sasha's door creaks again and then the footsteps are coming my way, I'm certain of it. I can feel a presence on the other side of my door. I close my eyes, thinking I can't bear to see the moment my door handle goes down, then open them again, unable after all to bear not knowing. A raft of images flash through my mind, ranging from Daniel Monkton, a silvery knife flashing in his hand, to Sasha, penitent and sobbing, begging my forgiveness. I sit up, looking around at the last minute for a weapon, anything I could use to defend myself, but I don't even have a glass of water. I promise myself that if I come out of this alive I will sleep with a kitchen knife by the bed for the rest of my life.

I swear I hear a breath, sense a movement, and I brace

myself, but then a police siren springs into life outside the flat, the blue light flickering on my bedroom walls. It makes me jump and I slap my hand over my mouth to prevent any sound escaping. For the first time I hear footsteps – the siren has frightened the intruder as much as me because they are retreating, thank God. There's another creak and I recognise it, with a thud of relief, as the floorboard by the front door. I hear the faint click of the Yale as it is pushed down, and a soft thud as the door closes. Then silence; beautiful, utter silence.

Even though I am as sure as I can be that the intruder has gone, I lie there frozen for another twenty minutes, my ears pricked for any sound. There is nothing, and eventually I am forced out of bed by a pressing need for the toilet. I reach out a still-trembling hand and switch on my bedside lamp. Nothing reaches out to grab me, and the room seems instantly less frightening in the light. I pad as quietly as possible to the door and open it a crack, sliding my hand around and fumbling for the light switch in the hall. I snap it on and slowly push open the door. The hallway looks as it usually does: Sasha laughs at me from the central photo of a clip frame containing a collage of pictures of me and her. We are at a festival that was held in the local park a couple of years ago. She's wearing a pink vest top and a cowboy hat to shade her face from the fierce sun. Her arm is around my shoulder and she's throwing her head back, laughing. I look hot and uncomfortable in a long-sleeved T-shirt, smiling grimly straight at the camera.

I walk down the hall to the door. There is no sign of a forced entry. It's closed, but when I push down the Yale lock, the door swings open. I'm sure I double-locked it. How did they get in?

I slip noiselessly back along the hall and into the bathroom to pee. The relief is tempered by the noise of urine hitting water, which echoes around the flat. I stop and stuff a handful of toilet paper down there, dulling the sound. When I've finished, I re-emerge into the brightly lit hall. I can't go back to bed without finding out what has happened here. I'll never get back to sleep, anyway. I check the kitchen and the lounge, which are exactly as I left them. That only leaves Sasha's room. The door is ajar and I stand outside under the harsh overhead light, my breath coming faster and faster, ragged in the silence. Slowly, I reach out my hand and push. The room is in semi-darkness, lit by the streetlamps outside and the light from the hall, but I can see straight away that someone has been in here.

Sasha's room was a mess anyway, but it's worse now. The drawers under the bed have been pulled out and what was in them strewn on the floor; likewise the bedside cabinet. Clothes have been taken from the wardrobe and chest of drawers, and piled on the bed. The mirror, which stands on an old chest, has been laid on the floor and the contents of the chest (bank statements, old wedding invitations, exercise books I recognise from school) lie discarded all around. Nothing is untouched. I stand in horror at the door, my skin prickling, my mind struggling to comprehend what I am looking at. I can't tell yet if anything is missing, but clearly somebody has been in here looking for something. But who was it, how did they get in and what the hell were they looking for?

Olivia

July 2007

Sasha's perfect face is as smooth and polished as ever. Her molten gold hair is neatly pulled back from her face and rolled away where the jury can't be distracted by it. She's wearing a conservative dress and jacket, but even if she was in a voluminous kaftan, there would be nothing she could do about the glow that emanates from her like a scent. Yes, she's beautiful, but it's more than that. There's something about her that draws people to her – an empathy, perhaps, unexpected in one so beautiful. I know Ellen felt it – basked in it, bloomed in its warmth. It gives Sasha power, and power is always dangerous. That's why I had to do what I did.

She begins her account of the evening. She and Ellen came down to the kitchen around 9.15 p.m. While Ellen was being bored to death by Tony and subsequently rescued by Nicholas, Sasha was talking to Leo and some others from school in the kitchen. She didn't see Daniel and Karina kissing in the hallway, or going up the stairs.

Shortly after they went upstairs, at around 10.15 p.m., she herself went back up to her bedroom.

'Your bedroom is directly adjacent to Daniel Monkton's, I believe?' The barrister adopts a marginally different tone with Sasha than he has with the other witnesses. It's so subtle I doubt anyone but me has even noticed. Even he, with all his years of experience, all the different types he must come up against in this room and others like it, cannot help but be drawn under her spell.

'Yes.'

'So when you got into your bedroom, what, if anything, could you hear?'

'I could hear Daniel and Karina through the wall.'

'Who else was there in the room with you?'

'No one. I just wanted to lie down for a minute. I'd been drinking and I was exhausted.'

When the others talk about their teenage drinking, it sounds kind of sordid, but from her lips it has a sort of glamour. Even I am nearly sucked in – probably would be if it weren't for what I know about her.

'And can you tell us what you heard through the wall?'

'At first, just low voices, and then silences in between. I guessed they were kissing.'

'Did you hear anything else?'

'I could hear the sounds of . . . well, you know.' She looks down, biting her lip. For God's sake. She's playing the jury like a trombone – the sweet, innocent little girl, being forced to talk about these unpleasant things, things she has no experience of. As if.

'I'm afraid, Miss North, that the jury needs to know exactly what you did hear. There is no need to be embarrassed.'

'It's just ... ' She clasps her hands in front of her, as if to keep them still, throwing another look at the jury.

'May I remind you that you are under oath, Miss North,' the barrister says gravely, 'and that what you say has consequences. It is imperative that you tell us exactly what you observed, truthfully and without obfuscation.'

'I heard them having sex, but it was sort of ... quick. I mean, it was over quickly, and I couldn't hear anything except the bed creaking, and Daniel. I couldn't hear Karina at all. It was as if she wasn't there. Then he came out of the room and crossed to the bathroom.'

'How do you know it was him, rather than Miss Barton?'

'I heard him say something to her as he came out, about seeing her downstairs in a while.'

'And what did you do then?'

'I stayed in my room a little while longer. I didn't hear anything from Daniel's room. Then I went back downstairs into the kitchen and chatted to some friends from school.'

'And when was the next time you saw Miss Barton?'

'It was around ten past eleven, I think. I heard some sort of commotion in the hall, and then Ellen brought Karina into the kitchen.'

'And what sort of state was Miss Barton in?'

'She was dreadfully upset. She was saying that Daniel had raped her.'

'And was there any doubt in your mind about whether she was telling the truth?'

'None at all,' she says, still addressing the jury. 'She was in a terrible state.'

'Thank you, Miss North. Now, I'd like to take you back, if I may, to the afternoon of the fifteenth of December 2006. You stayed back at school, I believe, for a rehearsal for a Christmas concert?'

'Yes, I did.'

'And did you stay for the entirety of the rehearsal?'

'No. I wasn't feeling well, so I left early. Around four o'clock.'

My heart starts to beat a little faster. What's going on? Dilys has her arms folded across her in smug satisfaction, a slight smile on her lips.

'And where did you go, when you left the school?'

'Home. I went home. Only ... ' She trails off. The innocent little girl is back.

'Yes?' The barrister leans forward, as if to reassure her as you would a small child, and you can feel the jury mentally doing the same.

'As I approached the house, I could see Daniel and Karina standing outside. I was surprised, as I didn't think they knew each other that well. They looked as if they were arguing. Karina went to leave, but he grabbed her by the arm, quite roughly, and pulled her back. He came right up close to her and said something, I couldn't hear what. Her shoulders dropped and she followed him inside.'

Daniel's face is a stony mask, chiselled in granite, but there is something in the set of his jaw that tells me he is perilously close to exploding. Dear God, he mustn't. An outburst from him at this stage would be his death knell. His barrister is also watching him anxiously, unclipping and replacing the lid of her pen over and over.

'Did you go into the house?' Karina's barrister asks.

'No.' She hesitates, and then goes on. 'I didn't like to. There was something . . . not quite right about the way they were with each other. I felt as though I'd be intruding.'

'So what did you do?'

'There's a café on the corner of the next street. I went and sat there for an hour, and then I went home. When I got back, there was nobody in. Ellen was supposed to be coming for dinner but she texted me to say she couldn't make it.'

'Did Miss Mackinnon subsequently tell you what she had heard from your bedroom?'

'Yes, she told me the next day.'

My God. I was so stupid, so self-satisfied, so complacent. I'd painted myself as the benevolent matriarch of this alternative, relaxed, welcoming household, when in fact I was sitting on a nest of vipers, deceit and poison lurking in every corner. I keep thinking of Ellen's face, sitting across the table from me, my adoring subject. She never breathed a word of this, yet I'd prided myself on being her confidante, the mother figure she was missing in that bland, conventional home of hers. As for Sasha . . . I can't get to grips with this at all. I can't believe she would lie about something so serious, but how does this fit with what I know about her?

'What, if anything, did you tell Miss Mackinnon, or anyone else for that matter, about what you had seen?' he asks.

'I didn't tell anyone.' Sasha lowers her eyes again, the picture of demure girlhood. 'I was confused by it. I didn't know what to make of it. And also, I didn't want to spread gossip. So I didn't mention it.'

'Thank you, Miss North. No further questions.'

He sits down, and Daniel's barrister stands. She reminds me of a lioness, sleek and beautiful in her quiet watchfulness, barely concealed ferocity within.

'On New Year's Eve, as you lay in your bedroom, listening through the wall—'

'I wasn't listening.' Sasha's head snaps up. 'I could hear.'

'My apologies.' The barrister's tone is deliberately bland, but still manages to convey the sense that she's doing an elaborate, sarcastic bow in Sasha's direction. 'As you lay in your bedroom, *unable to avoid hearing what was going on in the next room*, did you suspect that Miss Barton was not a willing participant in whatever was going on behind the wall?'

'Yes, I did.'

'But you did not go and knock on the door to see if she was all right? She's your friend, isn't she?'

'I didn't want to interrupt, in case it wasn't . . .'

'In case, in fact, the sexual intercourse was entirely consensual?'

'Yes,' she says in small voice, and I am darkly happy at seeing her deflated.

'But surely, if there was even a small chance that Miss Barton was being raped, the minor embarrassment of walking in on them would have been a small price to pay?'

'I ... I wasn't sure. I'd been drinking.'

'You weren't sure. You'd been drinking.' She doesn't actually do this, of course, but she gives the impression of turning to the jury and giving a comedy eye roll and shrug.

Sasha's not looking at the jury any more, and I rejoice inwardly.

'So, other than what Miss Barton herself said, do you have any evidence that the sex that Miss Barton had with Daniel Monkton was not consensual?'

'No,' she says.

'No further questions.' She sits down, with the air of one who has provided meat for a whole pride's worth of cubs.

Sasha throws an uncertain look at the prosecution barrister, who gestures for her to step down from the witness box. The jury are all watching her as she makes her way down the steps, as everyone watches her everywhere she goes. She is mesmerising, every curve and angle and sway of her. I am watching her too, against my will, and as I do so, I wish with all my heart that I'd listened to my instincts and never agreed to take her in.

Karina
July 2006

Oh my God, I can't believe he's interested in me. He's so gorgeous. He wants to keep it a secret for now, something that's just for us. I totally understand why. People can get so jealous.

Ellen would go CRAZY if she knew. Since she got friendly with Sasha, she thinks it's all about her. She's so worried about me. Even worse, she feels sorry for me. *Poor Karina, we must make sure she's included.* If only she knew!

There have been times when I've almost told her, when she's going on about Sasha this and Sasha that, Sasha's got such amazing clothes, she's had such a cool life, her mum lives in America, Leo is totally obsessed with her, blah blah blah. I've had to hold myself back, desperate to see the look on her face if I told her.

We used to have all these conversations about how far we've gone with boys, and who's done it in our class and stuff. We haven't talked about it in a while. For her, I think it's because she's embarrassed that she hasn't gone past first base. Mind you, as far as she's concerned, I'm the same, apart from that time Andrew Papadopoulos felt my tits at Tamara Gregg's party, and that doesn't really count because he was squeezing them like stress balls. I've gone so much further than that now. I bet she doesn't know some of the things I've done even exist.

He looks after me, though; cares about me. I know it's a cliché, but he really does think I'm something special. A lot of girls my age are so silly, so childish. I'm more mature, and he can see that. Sasha and Ellen are a couple of little girls, sometimes, trying on clothes together, laughing over something totally stupid. We have proper conversations about life and stuff. He's committed to me, doesn't want me to have anyone else, only him. He says I'm enough for him, and he is enough for me. We don't need anyone else. I think about him all the time, and he says he does too.

It's so romantic, I could die.

Ellen

September 2017

Surely they will have to believe me now. I tap in the numbers from the card PC Bryant gave me, figuring it will only be switched on if she's on duty. If I can't get her, I'll call 999, but I would rather speak to her than to somebody who doesn't know the circumstances, to whom I would have to start from the beginning.

'Bryant,' she says, sounding as if her mind is on something else. There's a buzz of chatter and the faint sound of music in the background.

'Oh, hello,' I say, suddenly unsure I've done the right thing in calling her. 'It's Ellen Mackinnon. I reported my friend Sasha missing last week.'

'Yes, Ellen, of course. Hang on one second.' She issues instructions to someone, then I hear a door slam and the background noise fades away.

'That's better,' she says. 'How can I help you? Is there any news of Sasha?'

'No, it's not that. I'm ... sorry to call at this time.'

'It's fine, I'm working tonight.'

'Someone was in my flat just now. They broke in.'

'Were you awake? Did you hear them?'

'Yes. I hid in my room. I couldn't move.'

'Oh, Ellen. That must have been very frightening.'

I swallow, determined not to crumble. 'Yes. Yes, it was. I think I know who did it, though. Remember I told you about the boy who raped my friend? He—'

'Ellen, hang on. I'll come over to you now and we can discuss it properly. Are you absolutely certain the intruder has left the property?'

'Yes, yes I am.' I've checked under the beds, even in the wardrobes, snatching the doors open, my heart in my mouth, my pulse only subsiding when I'd checked every possible hiding place.

Half an hour later, the buzzer goes, and for the second time I hear her shoes clip-clopping up the stairs. We sit at the kitchen table, and despite my head being thick and hot with lack of sleep, I manage to give her a coherent account of what happened.

'And there was no sign at all of a forced entry?' says Bryant.

'No. Is there any way someone could get in without a key, without breaking the door or the lock?'

'It's possible. Did you double-lock it, or was it just the Yale lock?'

'I usually double-lock it, but I don't know. I can't remember.'

'Do you think anything's missing?' she asks.

232

'Not as far as I can tell, no. Neither of us has anything particularly valuable, anyway. And if it was a robbery, wouldn't they have taken the telly or something?'

'Possibly,' she says. 'We'll double-check in a minute, though, just in case. Now, you said on the phone that you thought you knew who had done this?'

'Yes.' I keep my hands in my lap, twisted together to keep them still.

'You think it was Daniel Monkton, the one who raped your other friend?' says Bryant.

'Yes.' My fingers thread around and around each other, my legs crossed at the ankle, the outside of one foot pressing into the other. 'Have you spoken to him yet?'

'No. We have spoken to Mr and Mrs Monkton, and they've given us a mobile number for him, but as yet we haven't been able to contact him. They say they don't know where he's staying.'

Of course they know.

'They were able to give us an address for Sasha's mother, but we haven't managed to speak to her yet, although of course we'll keep trying.' That's on my list, too, although I don't tell Bryant that.

'The other thing we have to consider,' Bryant goes on, 'especially given that there are no obvious signs of a break-in, is that it was Sasha herself who was in the flat.'

I knew she would suggest this, and even I can see it's the most likely explanation, but despite everything, I can't believe she would deliberately frighten me like that.

'Can you think of any reason why she might have

wanted to come back to the flat without you knowing?'
Bryant goes on.

I think of her strange mood that Friday, a couple of
weeks ago, when she got back from work; her unex-
plained absences; the truth about her mother that she's
been hiding from me for twelve years; the night she spent
with my ex-boyfriend a month ago; the fact that I'm not
sure I know her at all.

'No,' I say. If I say any of that, they won't look for her,
and I want them to. I need answers.

'The first thing I would suggest, if you're worried, is
to get the locks changed. The fact that there's no sign
of a break-in suggests that if there was someone in here,
they had a key.'

If there was someone in here. Does she not believe me?
Does she think I was dreaming, or making it up? Maybe
she thinks I messed up Sasha's room myself, or perhaps
she can't tell the difference between the Sasha-mess
and what it's like now. I want to protest, take her by the
shoulders and shake her, make her see what is going on
here. There's no point, though; it'll make me look even
crazier than she already believes me to be, so I leave it,
assuring her I'll let her know if anything else happens
that makes me concerned. I won't, though. I can see now
that I'm on my own, unless something worse happens, of
course, and by that time it will be too late.

She's right about one thing, though: I do need to change
the locks. When she's gone, I search for locksmiths on
my phone, but pull a face when I see the prices. So far,

Sasha's absence hasn't affected me financially, but next month, will I be facing paying all the bills alone? I can't afford a locksmith. There are forums online suggesting I could replace the locks myself, but I don't even understand the instructions, let alone have the ability to carry them out. I go on the website for a DIY store instead. I can afford some bolts, a heavy-duty chain. That will have to do. Even those I can't fit myself, though. I don't own a drill and even if I did, I wouldn't have a clue how to operate it. I curse myself for my stupid, stereotypical femaleness, while simultaneously running a list of people through my head who might be able to help. My dad is famously hopeless at DIY – my parents have a handyman they get in to do work in their house. I can't ask him to do it, though – he'll tell my parents and I don't want to worry them.

The one person I can think of who has a drill and the necessary know-how is Jackson. Sasha used to laugh about it, his old-fashioned manliness. She was taking the piss but I could tell she liked it really. I text him, explaining briefly what has happened and asking if he can help. It's five in the morning, so I'm not expecting him to reply now, but I know there's no way I'll be able to sleep. I grab my duvet and decamp to the lounge, putting the telly on. A sunburnt retired couple are trying to decide whether to move to Wales or Portugal. I must have fallen asleep eventually, because I'm woken just after 7 a.m. by my phone ringing. It's Jackson.

'Shit, Ellen, I've just seen your text. Are you OK?'

'I'm fine, but I need to add some security to the door – bolts and a chain. I was wondering if you might . . . with your drill . . . '

'Don't you need a locksmith? How did they break in?'

'They didn't. Either they had a key or . . . maybe I didn't double-lock the door – someone could have broken in somehow.'

'They had a key? Don't you think . . . ?' He is wary of upsetting me.

'Don't I think it was Sasha? That's what the police said.' I can't bring myself to mount a vociferous defence of her, not this time. 'Would you be able to come over? I'll go and get the stuff this morning. I'm working tonight, but you could come round when you've finished work, just let yourself in.'

'I don't have a key,' he says, embarrassed. 'Sasha didn't want me to have one. I'm not working today, anyway. I can come over this morning, if you like?'

There's a DIY store about ten minutes' walk from the flat, and I'm there shortly after it opens at 9 a.m. On the way home, bolts and chain clanking in the carrier bag, I screw up my courage and call Leo.

'Hello.' He sounds pleased to hear from me. 'What's up?'

I'm not in the mood for pleasantries, particularly after the night I've had. 'Why didn't you tell me you'd slept with Sasha?'

There's a stunned silence.

'Don't bother denying it – Rachel told me.'

'Ellen,' he says under his breath, 'I can't talk now. I'm at work.'

'I don't care where you are.'

'Bloody hell. Hang on a sec.' It sounds as though he's walking, and then there's a clang and the background office sounds die away. 'OK, I'm on the fire escape. I'm sorry. I didn't tell you because I thought you might be upset, and it sounds like I was right. But you and I went out a million years ago. I don't think I've done anything wrong here. If I'd done something back when you and I were together, maybe you'd have a right to be pissed off. But not now. Not ten years later.'

'That's not why I'm upset!' This is a lie, of course.

'Really?' he says. 'What is it with you and her, anyway? What have you actually got in common, other than the trial? You seem to think she's been this amazing, supportive friend to you, but if you ask me, it's the other way around.'

'What's that got to do with anything? You still should have told me. It might have something to do with Sasha's disappearance.'

'I didn't because I know it doesn't have anything to do with it. Unless ... unless you're accusing me of having something to do with it. Jesus, is that what this is? You think I've done something to her?'

'No, that's not what I'm saying ... but any information helps. The police might want to talk to you if they know you slept with her recently. You need to tell them.'

'What, or you will? Bollocks to that, Ellen. I slept with her once, a month ago. It's got no relevance at all to whatever's happened to her now. I've got to get back to work. Goodbye.'

He cuts me off, and I walk the rest of the way home with stupid, hot tears stinging my eyes. Jackson arrives not long after I get back, toolbox in hand, and gets to work straight away.

'Did they take anything?' he asks.

'I don't think so.'

'So if it wasn't Sasha, who do you think ...?'

I wait for the drill to stop, weighing up my options. Ten seconds is enough to decide I don't owe Leo or Sasha anything as far as this goes.

'I don't know. But I have found something out. I saw Rachel last night, and she told me that about a month ago, Sasha slept with someone else.'

'I knew it. I fucking knew it.' He stares at me, drill in hand like a gun. 'Who was it?'

'Leo Smith. He's an old friend of ours from school. My ex-boyfriend, in fact.'

'She mentioned him. She bumped into him recently, didn't she?'

'Yes. I've only just found out about that too. She didn't say anything to me.'

'I bet she didn't, the stupid cow.' Despite echoing my own secret feelings, the ugliness of his words makes me recoil.

'Sorry, Ellen. But honestly. Hang on, I think I met him. He was there in the pub one night. Jesus. And your ex as well. What is she like?'

'I know. What's going on, Jackson?'

He doesn't answer but starts drilling again with renewed vigour. I lean against the wall and watch him. He said he doesn't have a key, and that may well be true. But as he skilfully fits two bolts and a chain with a minimum of fuss and mess, I reflect on how, if I had to pick one person out of everyone I know to break into a house without leaving a trace, I would pick him.

Ellen

August 2006

It was obvious from the moment I arrived that something wasn't right. When Leo texted me to say Nicholas
and Daniel were having a party, my heart had leapt
even more than it did normally when he contacted me.
Nothing had happened between us since that day in the
park, but every time I'd seen him, at school or at Sasha's
house, there was something between us, like an electrical
current that nobody else could feel. He texted occasionally, jokey little messages, not mentioning what he'd said
on the rug that day, but enough to fuel the connection
between us.

This time, though, it was the thought of being back at
the corner house that made my pulse skip. It had been
disconcerting without Sasha around. Once my anger at
her running off to France without me had subsided to a
low-grade, nagging gripe, I'd realised how difficult it was
going to be to spend much time at the Monktons' without
her. I often stayed on if I was already there when Sasha

went out, chatting to Olivia in the kitchen. A few times I'd even shared a bottle of wine with Tony when Olivia wasn't there, although he drank so quickly I didn't get more than a glass and a half. But turning up when there was no chance Sasha would be there felt like a different matter altogether. This party would give me a completely legitimate excuse to spend hours there. I could probably even stay the night in Sasha's room if I wanted.

I dressed with extra care and hurried along the road slightly before the appointed time of 8 p.m., an addict desperate for a fix.

'Ellen! You're looking lovely, as ever.' Tony kissed me on both cheeks, his face whiskery against mine, his familiar smell of whiskey and the dry, citrusy aftershave he wore assaulting my senses.

I followed him into the kitchen, where Olivia was getting glasses out and banging them down on the table. 'Hi, Ellen,' she said, barely looking up.

'Hi.' I stood awkwardly in the doorway. It was the first time I'd spoken to her since she'd called to tell me Sasha had phoned from France. I'd been expecting a hug, or at least a bit of interest.

'The boys are in the piano room,' she said, opening the fridge and putting in some bottles of beer from the kitchen worktop.

'Oh, right. I'll just go and . . . ' I drifted across the hallway, sharply conscious of Sasha's absence. Was it that which was causing the frosty atmosphere? In the front room I found Nicholas, alone, idly picking out notes on the piano. He stopped abruptly when he saw me, slamming the lid shut.

'Oh, sorry,' I said, starting to back out of the room. Where was I going to go now?

'It's fine, you don't have to run away,' he said.

I stopped, but was grateful to be liberated by a ring on the doorbell.

'I'll get it,' I said, gratefully rushing to the door.

Leo was wearing a pale blue shirt, his skin lightly tanned, the natural golden highlights in his hair glistening in the last rays of evening sunshine. I'd never been so glad to see anyone in my life, and without thinking, I stepped forward and gave him a hug. We held each other a fraction of a second too long, and then I stepped back breathlessly.

'Come in. Nicholas is in the piano room. Do you want a drink? How are you, anyway?'

'I'm fine.' He smiled. 'I'd love a beer, please.'

I bustled off to the kitchen with more urgency than the task required. Tony was pouring wine for a girl I'd seen at Monkton parties before. He grabbed my arm as I passed on my way back from the fridge with Leo's beer.

'Here, let me top you up, darling.'

'I'm all right, thanks, Tony.'

'No, no, come on, drink that last bit up and I'll pour you another. Never let it be said that anyone goes thirsty at the Monktons'.'

Reluctantly, I drained my glass and held it out for him to fill.

'That's better. Good girl. On you go.' He patted me on the back, rather as if I was a horse, and I escaped back to the piano room. Leo and Nicholas were sitting on the sofa, and I self-consciously passed Leo his beer.

'Where's mine then?' said Nicholas.

'Oh! Sorry. I can get you one.' I braced myself for another encounter with Tony.

'Oh, for God's sake, Ellen. I was only joking. Sit down.'

I perched on the armchair opposite.

'Have you heard from Sasha?' I asked.

'Nope, not a word. She hasn't even called Mum since that first time. She's texted her a couple of times, to say she's OK, but that's it, I think. Have you?'

'She texts quite a bit,' I said. She'd texted me twice in three weeks, perfunctory messages to which I'd replied with multiple questions that remained unanswered. 'I haven't spoken to her, though.'

'What happened? Why did she go off like that?' asked Leo. This was the question I had dearly wanted to ask myself, but I was ashamed to reveal how little she had confided in me.

Nicholas took a sip of his beer. 'She told Mum she'd run into some couple she knew from before. It was a spur of the moment thing.'

'That's weird, though, isn't it?' persisted Leo. 'Going off without telling anyone?'

'Not really. Maybe to you. Mum and Dad are cool with stuff like that. They want us to be independent. Why are you so interested, anyway? Do you fancy her too?'

243

'Piss off,' Leo said good-naturedly. 'What d'you mean, "too"? Who else fancies her?'

'Just about everyone. Hadn't you noticed?'

'Fair point. Anyway, I don't. Obviously she's an attractive girl, but I'm not interested.'

I took a too-large gulp of my drink and choked. Leo came over and patted me on the back, Nicholas observing dispassionately from the sofa.

'Hmm, so that's the way the land lies, is it?' he said. 'I think I'll leave you to it.' He left the room as my coughing fit died away.

'Are you OK?' Leo said.

I nodded, not looking at him. He balanced uncomfortably on the arm of the chair beside me.

'Look, what Nicholas said . . . ' he began.

'It's OK,' I said hurriedly. 'He's just being an idiot.'

'Yes, but, the thing is . . . he's right. I do like you.'

Blood rushed to my cheeks. I stared into my drink.

'Ellen?' he said.

I looked up and he leaned down towards me and kissed me softly. I was glad I was sitting down as otherwise my legs would have given way. He drew back and smiled at the wineglass that was shaking in my hand.

'Do you want to put that down?' he said.

I did so, but as he bent to kiss me again, I heard a sharp inhalation of breath and we both started. Leo jumped to his feet and I turned to see Karina silhouetted in the doorway, looking at us with an unreadable expression on her face. All the conversations I'd ever had with her about Leo spooled in fast-forward through my head.

'Sorry,' she said, still staring.

'It's fine, come in,' Leo said, oblivious to the undercurrent of confusion, or jealousy, or whatever it was.

'I'm going to get a drink,' Karina said, and left.

'Right, where were we?' said Leo. 'Shall we sit on the sofa? I'm kind of uncomfortable up here.'

'Sorry.' I stood up, almost kicking my wineglass over. 'I'm just going to go and see if Karina's OK.'

'Oh. Right.'

'Sorry, it's not ... It's just that ... I'll see you in a minute.' I picked up the glass and hurried from the room, face burning.

I found Karina in the kitchen, pouring herself a glass of wine from a bottle on the table.

'You two looked very cosy,' she said. 'Sorry to interrupt.'

'It just happened, just now ... I've never kissed him before, I swear.'

She laughed. 'I'm not upset, Ellen! Is that what you think?'

'Well ... '

'I was surprised, that's all, and I could see I was intruding, so I thought I'd leave you to it. God, I've got no interest in Leo Smith, I promise you. You're welcome to him.'

'Are you sure? I know you used to like him. I wouldn't want to—'

'Ruin our wonderful friendship?' she cut in. 'Hardly.'

'Karina . . . ' I wanted to say something, to acknowledge what we'd been to each other, to tell her I knew things had changed between us but that didn't mean we couldn't still be friends, but as I struggled to find the words, Daniel came in, going straight to the fridge and taking out a beer.

'All right, you two?' he said as he searched for the bottle opener in the kitchen drawer.

'Yes, fine,' I said. We'd never again come close to sharing a moment like the one we had in the audience at Olivia's concert, had never discussed it, in fact, not even later that night when we all went backstage to congratulate her. Sometimes I wondered if I'd imagined it.

'Here you go.' Karina took the bottle opener from the worktop behind her and handed it to him with a smile.

'Thanks, Karina,' he said. 'What would I do without you?' It was spoken lightly, but I thought there was something else behind his words, a flirtation, perhaps, or a question at least.

'Shall we go and sit down?' she said.

He made his way back to the piano room, Karina following with the bottle of wine in her hand.

Leo was back on the sofa under the window, and I self-consciously sat down next to him, relieved to feel the pressure of his leg against mine. Nicholas was on the other sofa, and Karina joined him there, Daniel taking the armchair.

'Will you play something, Daniel?' Karina asked.

'Oh, no. Maybe later. Nick might?'

'Oh, I didn't know you played too,' I said. I'd seen him strumming a guitar a couple of times while someone else sang, but I hadn't thought him as musical as the others.

'Oh, I don't, not really. Not like Daniel,' he said.

'Of course you do!' said Daniel. 'We both had to learn, didn't we? Mummy's little musicians.' It was meant to be a joke, I thought, but it came out more bitterly than he had intended, and there was a brief silence in which nobody looked at him.

'Let's play a drinking game,' said Nicholas, clearly trying to save the situation. He proceeded to explain the rules of a complicated game based around the characters in a TV show I'd never seen. As a consequence, I had to drink on practically every go, and even though I was a good deal more used to drinking than I had been at that first party nearly a year before, my head was soon spinning. After an hour or so, I got up to go to the toilet. On my way back, I went to get a glass of water. Tony and Olivia were alone in the kitchen, whispering furiously at each other. I paused outside the door. If they'd looked round they'd have seen me, but they were engrossed in their argument.

'It's not my fault,' Tony said. 'You can't blame me for this one.'

'You don't help, though, do you, always pouring the drinks, and creating this ... party atmosphere, just so you feel better about drinking all the time?' hissed Olivia. 'What did you think was going to happen?'

'She's an attractive girl,' said Tony. 'I can't—'

I must have swayed slightly, because Olivia noticed me standing there.

'Ellen, darling! Are you all right?'

'Fine, fine. Need some water.'

'Of course you do.' Olivia eyed Tony ominously as he left the room. She ran the cold tap. 'Had a bit too much to drink?'

'No, no, just a bit thirsty,' I said, enunciating carefully. She handed me a large glass of water. 'Thanks, Olivia.' I drank half of it down, then started to make my way back to the piano room.

'Wait, Ellen.' Olivia sounded uncharacteristically nervous. 'Have you heard from Sasha?'

I was too drunk and weary to pretend in the way I had earlier. 'No, hardly at all. The odd text to say she's having a great time.'

'Did she give you any idea why she took off like that?'

'Nope, not a clue.'

She reached out a hand and stroked my hair, the way my mum used to before we started arguing all the time. 'I know how much you were looking forward to going away with her,' she said. 'I'm so sorry.'

'It's not your fault.' I was horrified to feel tears springing to my eyes. 'Better get back,' I muttered, beating a hasty retreat.

Lots more people had come into the piano room while I had been away, and a boy I didn't recognise was now sitting next to Leo, who had earned the dubious reward of downing an entire bottle of beer in one go. I stood in the doorway, watching him for a minute, unseen. Nicholas was laughing as everyone chanted, 'Down it, down it'. Karina had moved across the room and was sitting on the arm of the chair, her hand resting lightly across the back, just inches from Daniel's head. Suddenly, everything seemed unbearably sordid. I noticed the dark, grease-stained areas on the backs of the sofas where countless heads had rested, the threadbare patches on the carpet, the thin film of dust that coated every surface. Despite the no smoking in the house rule, somebody had stubbed a cigarette out in the fireplace and the air was thick with warm, alcohol-scented breath and something even more noxious that I couldn't identify.

Something inside me snapped. Without thinking, I put my water glass on the hall table, opened the front door, stepped out and closed it quietly behind me. I walked home as the shadows lengthened towards my traditional, completely un-bohemian, boring parents and the glorious, clean quiet of my own bedroom.

Ellen

September 2017

After Jackson leaves, I lock up with slight trepidation. The bolts will keep me safe when I'm in the flat, but I can't draw them when I go out. Alice lives in a part of west London I've never been to before, sandwiched – as these parts often are – between pockets of huge wealth. As I walk the ten minutes from the tube, well-kept Edwardian villas gradually give way to smaller houses, and then to tower blocks, kebab houses and pawnshops. I wonder if Tony has confessed to Olivia yet that he has given me the address. I know the police will be speaking to Alice, but I need to see her myself, this woman who I had longed to meet, who I had thought was going to be the most exciting, glamorous woman I'd ever seen. I find the house on a road of small, scruffy terraces that, despite their size, appear to have been broken up into several flats or bedsits each.

I ring the bell for the ground-floor flat and wait. When the door opens, it is a shock to be looking into eyes identical to Sasha's. This woman's face is sunken, with wrinkles spidering out around her mouth and eyes, her blonde hair thin like straw, but she must have been very beautiful once. She probably could have been a model.

She looks at me in suspicious silence.

'Hello. I'm a friend of Sasha's.'

She starts to close the door, but I put out my hand to stop it.

'Please. I'm worried about her.'

'Why?' She narrows her eyes. 'She can look after herself, can't she?' Her voice speaks of years of late nights and cigarettes and too many drinks, or worse, but underneath, her original cut-glass accent stubbornly refuses to disappear.

'She's disappeared,' I say quickly, trying to hold her attention, stop her from closing me down.

'So?' she says, but she's not pushing on the door any more.

'I thought you might be able to help. If you've got any idea where she might be . . . '

'Me? You're joking, aren't you? You do know she waltzed out when she was sixteen and never looked back?'

I think of the ugly scar on Sasha's face and the way her body would instinctively curl up when we asked about her mother. I want to shout and rage at Alice for letting her down so badly, for daring to describe being removed by social services as 'waltzing out'. I don't, though. I smile through gritted teeth.

'Yes, I know, but I wondered if she'd been in touch at all?'

A group of teenage boys turns the corner at the end of

her road, and as they get closer I can hear them swearing and jostling each other. One of them spots me and says something unintelligible to the others.

'Can I come in?' I say. 'Just for a minute?'

She looks at the boys. 'All right.'

We step into a small hallway and through a door into the flat, which, I realise, is not really a flat at all, it's a bedsit, with a mattress on the floor in one corner. There's a small faux leather sofa with two large rips in it against the wall, and a flimsy coffee table in front of it. It's clean and tidy, though, with very few personal possessions. There's a suitcase open on the floor next to the mattress. Alice flips the lid closed and gestures for me to sit down on the sofa. She remains standing, leaning against the sink in the kitchenette opposite.

'Not what you were expecting, eh?' she says shrewdly, as I look around in surprise. 'Thought it would be filthy, with needles everywhere and fag butts on every surface? That's how Olivia painted it, I dare say.'

'No . . .'

'Save it. I know what they think of me. Look, I don't know why you're here. I haven't seen Sasha for years. I can't help you. All I can say is, if she's disappeared, she's probably got good reason. Like I said, she knows what she's doing.'

'There are things you don't know, though.' As I say it, I realise she probably does know at least some of it. The case was widely reported in the press at the time; she must have seen it.

'Probably.' She shrugs. 'Anyway, like I said—' She is interrupted by her phone ringing in her pocket. She pulls it out and looks at the screen. Fear crosses her face and she waits a couple of seconds before answering.

'Hi.' Her bright tone is at total odds with the pallor of her face as she listens to whoever is on the other end.

'Yeah . . . but I thought you were . . . OK, fine, see you in a bit.' She hangs up. 'You've got to go.'

'Why?' I remain seated.

'You don't want to know, darling. Just get out.' I stand up and she bundles me out of the room. 'I hope you find her,' she says. I step out on to the street and she immediately slams the door behind me.

I am nearly back at the tube station when my phone rings. It's PC Bryant. I stare at it for a few seconds, wondering if this is the call that changes my life, the bridge between Before and After. I can't not answer it, though.

'Hello?' I step into a doorway, my finger in my other ear to keep out the traffic noise.

'Hi, Ellen. I just wanted to keep you posted, and ask you a couple of questions. We've been looking at CCTV footage of the day Sasha disappeared. We've picked her up leaving work at twelve-thirty and going into the bar that forms the ground floor of her place of work.'

Café Crème. I've met her there before. They go there to celebrate promotions, her and her colleagues, and to drown the sorrows of those who have been made redundant.

'She was there about half an hour, and then she got on the tube and went to Fulham Broadway.'

I look across the road at the tube station. Fulham Broadway, says the sign. She was here.

'We assume that she went to see her mother, so we'll definitely be trying to contact her again.' Now that I've met her, I can't imagine Alice taking a visit from the police too kindly. 'Sasha then got back on the tube and went to Victoria station. We haven't been able to ascertain yet where she went after that, but we are continuing to check CCTV footage.'

I should tell Bryant that I've just been there, that Alice claims to know nothing. But maybe they will get something out of her that I couldn't.

Bryant hangs up, reassuring me that they are still doing everything they can. I step out of the doorway and cross the road. Outside the station, I stop. Sasha was here. She must have gone to see Alice, who won't tell the police anything. I have to try again.

I retrace my steps. The street is quiet now, and I rehearse what I'm going to say in my head. *The police said* ... No, better not mention them. *Somebody saw Sasha* ... I'm so busy planning my opening gambit that I'm already reaching up to ring the bell before I notice that the front door is ajar. I ring anyway. No answer. I knock.

'Alice? It's Ellen, again, Sasha's friend,' I quaver in the silence.

I push the door open and take a cautious step into the hallway.

'Hello?'

Still nothing, save the beating of my own heart. Slowly, I push the door open into the flat. I stop, my hand to my mouth. The place is in utter disarray. The kitchenette cupboards are open and there is broken glass and china on the floor; the coffee table is missing a leg and is upended on the floor; someone has punched a hole in the wall. I stare around, aghast. There's a noise from the street outside, a man's voice, and I stand very still, praying he's not coming in here. It fades, he is passing down the street, but that's enough to make me scurry out and run back to the safety of the tube station, my lungs burning, sweat running down my back.

As I sit on the tube, my breathing slowly returning to normal, all I can see is Alice's eyes, so like Sasha's. I'm exhausted, but I've got one more call to pay.

Café Crème, despite the continental name, looks like the bar of a cheap hotel, the sort of place low-grade business travellers stay on their way to a meeting in Peterborough. It's a stupid long shot, but Sasha was in here the day she disappeared and maybe I'll learn something.

I stand at the bar with my phone in my hand, feeling utterly foolish. The sole bartender is a young man in a white shirt and black waistcoat, and he comes straight over in the absence of any other customers.

'What can I get you?'

'Small glass of white wine, please.' As he bends to open the fridge, I force myself to say in a rush, 'There was something else too, actually.'

'Sure.' He takes a glass down and begins to pour.

'This is going to sound odd, but do you recognise this woman?' I hold my phone out with a recent picture of Sasha, full face and smiling. He puts my wine down on the bar.

'That's four pound fifty, please. Let's see.' He takes the phone. 'Oh yes, I know her. She works upstairs, doesn't she? There's a group of them, come in after work a lot. Is ... everything OK?'

'She's gone missing. I'm trying to find her.'

'Oh, right.' He doesn't sound that interested. 'I don't know anything about that.'

'No, of course not. It's just ... was she in here last Friday, can you remember?'

'No idea, sorry. She might have been.'

'She might have been meeting someone ... Would you mind having a look at some other photos?'

He sighs. 'All right, it'll have to be quick, though; people will be coming in for lunch soon and I'm on my own.'

'Of course. Here.' I show him Leo and Jackson's Facebook pages, and Nicholas's LinkedIn picture. I couldn't find anything recent of Daniel, but he and Nicholas are alike enough that I thought it might spark a memory.

'No, sorry, I don't recognise any of them,' he says. A group of men in suits comes jostling through the door into the pub, shuffling off the morning's work like snakes shedding their skin. The barman looks past me expectantly, ready to serve them.

'Sorry, just quickly ... ' I say in desperation. 'Did you ever see her with an older woman? Very skinny, blonde hair.'

'No, sorry. Oh, hang on, she was with a woman one day, but it wasn't last Friday, it was longer ago than that. A couple of weeks ago – the Friday before, maybe?' That's the night Sasha came home in such a strange mood, shut herself away in her room. 'They looked like they were having a very intense conversation. I remember wondering what they were talking about.'

'This other woman – was she late fifties, a bit ... rough-looking?' I can't be bothered to prevaricate.

'Oh no, not that old. About the same age as you and her.' He gestures to my phone. 'Quite a big girl, pale skin, mousey brown hair, thick-rimmed glasses.'

My heart skips a beat. It could be one of many people, of course, but I know without a shadow of a doubt that he is describing Karina Barton.

Ellen

September 2006

Sasha only got back the day before school started. It had been two weeks since I walked out of the party at the Monktons'. I hadn't been back to the house or seen any of them since. Leo had texted about an hour after I'd left, asking me where I was. I told him I'd felt really drunk and gone home. Which was the truth, although maybe not the whole truth. He came round in the morning to see if I was OK. Mum was delighted by his interest. I think she had feared I would fall for one of the Monkton boys, and then she really would have lost me to them. He'd agreed with me that there had been a weird atmosphere that night, although he'd stayed on anyway, sleeping over in Daniel's room. He'd started on the floor, but about four in the morning he'd woken to find Daniel still not there, so he'd climbed into his bed and spent the rest of the night there. He'd found Daniel curled in a ball on the sofa in the morning, and had left without speaking to anyone.

Sasha texted me two days before we were due back at

school to say she'd be home around lunchtime the next day and did I want to come over. My instinct, of course, was to text back immediately, effusively, saying yes of course. And I did want to, that was the stupid thing. She'd skipped off to France without telling me, and barely been in touch all summer. I ought to be furious with her, and part of me was, but a larger part of me, the part that had missed her badly, wanted to fall back into our friendship and have everything be exactly as it was before. Plus I had lots to tell her, not least that I was now officially going out with Leo. For reasons I couldn't fully articulate, even to myself, I didn't want to see her at the Monktons', so I forced myself to wait a couple of hours, then sent her a message suggesting we meet at a coffee place on the local high street.

I was deliberately late, but still there before her. I sat in the window with a cup of tea and watched her running through the drizzle in denim cut-offs and a white T-shirt, her skin the colour of toffee, turning heads as ever. She came through the door and shook her hair as if she were a dog, garnering more admiring looks from male customers and staff. She walked over and hugged me, disarming me straight away by apologising.

'Sorry I've been so shit at keeping in touch. There was hardly any signal in the place where I was staying, and I had no money, so I ended up picking apples and pears on this farm. Oh my God, it was fucking exhausting. When I bumped into Will and Eloise in London, I thought it seemed like such a fun idea, taking off, but I got the wrong end of the stick, thought they had a villa. I didn't realise they were going out there to work. So if I wanted to stay in the place they were staying, I had to work there too. Nightmare.'

I wanted to ask why she hadn't come back if it was so bloody awful, but I wasn't sure I wanted to know. Instead, I steeled myself to tell her about Leo. I knew she'd never fancied him, but he'd made it very clear he liked her when she first moved here, and I suspected she'd enjoyed his adulation even if she didn't want to reciprocate. I poured myself another unwanted cup of tea and added too much milk, turning it grey and watery.

'Something happened while you were away.'

'What?' She seemed to pale under her tan.

'Me and Leo, we're going out with each other.' I sipped my lukewarm cup of dishwater.

'Oh, that!' She sat back in her chair. 'Yeah, I know, Nicholas told me this morning.'

'Oh. So ... are you OK with it?'

'Why wouldn't I be?' She looked at me as if I'd lost my mind.

'Because Leo used to like you, I thought it might be a bit weird for you.'

'God, no. I was never interested in him, was I? It was all him. More likely to be weird for you, if anyone.' She looked at me slyly. 'What if he still likes me?'

This, of course, was my greatest fear. I'd tried to talk to Karina about it the other day when we went shopping, but she'd been distant and uncommunicative. I had thought that with Sasha away we might have regained some of our previous closeness, but if anything she'd felt further away from me than ever.

Sasha must have seen the horror on my face and her smile dropped. 'Oh, Ellen, I was only joking. Sorry. It was a stupid thing to say. How did it happen? Tell me all about it.'

I relented, the pleasure of telling the story of me and Leo to an appreciative audience too tempting to pass up. She asked all the right questions, wanting to know exactly what he'd said, how he'd kissed me, how far we'd gone. I was glad to have someone to talk to on this last point, as we hadn't yet gone as far as Leo would have liked. He wasn't putting any pressure on me, but I felt it nonetheless.

Once we'd exhausted everything that had happened while she'd been away, I asked her how things were at home. I knew relations between her and Olivia hadn't been the same since the conversation about the missing money back in March.

'Did you ever tell her you thought someone had been in your room?' I asked.

'No. Like I said, there's no point. Actually ... ' She fiddled with her teaspoon, twisting it over and over.

'What?'

She looked scared – and something else. Ashamed?

'I think someone's been in there again. While I was away.'

'Oh, Nicholas and Daniel had a party. I think they let

someone sleep in there. I'm sure Olivia will have changed the sheets. Your things probably got moved around a bit.'

'It's not stuff being moved. Some things have … gone missing.'

'What things?' I asked.

'A pair of my knickers,' she said quietly, glancing over at the elderly women at the next table.

'What? Are you sure? Maybe they've got mixed in with someone else's washing?'

'No, they haven't. I've never worn them since I've been living there. They've never been in the wash. They're part of a matching set and the bra's quite uncomfortable, so I don't wear either of them.'

'Shit, Sasha.'

'I know.'

I was going to say more but she changed the subject, and I knew from experience that once she had done so, there was no diverting her. We sat there for another hour, ordering more tea and chatting, pretending everything was the same, but it wasn't. Before she left for France, Sasha and I had been best friends, but there was a barrier between us now. I had no idea if anything she had told me about her trip was true; despite his protestations that he had no interest in her, I was frightened about what would happen between Leo and me now Sasha was back; and somebody had stolen Sasha's underwear and was keeping it for God knows what purpose.

Everything had changed, and I couldn't suppress the feeling that things were only going to get worse.

Karina

October 2006

He turned up outside school yesterday. I came out of the gates and he was there, staring at me from across the street. I hurried over, said I thought it was meant to be a secret, what if somebody sees? He said it didn't matter any more.

Sometimes when we're doing it, he gets a funny, faraway look, and I can tell he's not there with me, not really. I want to ask him afterwards what he was thinking about, but he doesn't usually want to talk. I wonder if other blokes are the same, or if some of them want to cuddle up and whisper together like I do. I haven't got anyone to ask.

I'm used to sharing everything with Ellen – all the milestones. We went shopping for our first bras together, with our mums. They took us for hot chocolate and toasted teacakes afterwards, and I remember looking at the bags hanging from the backs of our chairs and wondering if anyone in the café guessed what was in them. Plain white triangles of soft fabric, with a complicated hook and eye system at the back that I thought I'd never get to grips with.

We almost started our periods together – her one month and me the next. We'd been waiting for ages. Our mums had bought us the same book: *Have You Started Yet?* We'd pored over it together, both hopeful and horrified at the prospect.

We even had our first kiss the same night, at Tamara Gregg's party. She was first. I saw her with this boy, all acne and greasy hair coaxed into peaks. They were chatting for ages and I didn't want to interrupt, so I went to the kitchen to get a drink. When I got back, he had her pushed up against the wall, her whole face practically inside his mouth. I watched as he slid one hand up her side towards her boob, but she pushed it down again. He did it again and again, waiting a couple of minutes between tries, but every time her hand would force his down again. That was the only reason I got off with Andrew. I didn't want to be left behind. But when his hands snaked up, I closed my eyes and let them. I remember how she squealed when I told her that night as she lay on a blow-up mattress on my bedroom floor. I wish I could talk to her about this. She feels so far away at the moment.

The other weird thing is he keeps asking me about Sasha. What she's like at school, who her friends are, if there are any boys she's interested in. I keep telling him

I don't know her that well, that Ellen's better friends with her than I am, but he keeps on asking anyway.

I need to try harder to find a way to keep him interested in me. I don't want this to end.

Ellen

September 2017

My phone rings just after 6 p.m. I'm on my way out for a late shift at the station and am tempted to ignore it, but of course I don't, can't.

'Ellen? It's Nick. Nicholas Monkton.' He sounds hesitant, apologetic. 'Sorry to bother you.'

'That's OK.'

There's a silence, which he seems to be waiting for me to break, as if it were me that had called him. What I should say is that I'm terribly sorry, I'm on my way out and could we speak later. I'm not sure if my inability to do so is due to the fact that he is a Monkton, and therefore sacred in my absurd world view, or simply my natural feebleness, an aversion to confrontation.

'So?' Of course I ask him.

'You were right,' he says. 'Daniel's back. Mum told me.'

'I know. I went to see your dad.'

'I can't believe they've been seeing him.' His voice

266

rises and I hear him take a breath. 'After everything he's put them through.'

'Did they tell you what he's doing here? Is he back here to live?'

'I don't think so. He's come back because of Dad being ill ... you know ... '

'Yes, he told me. I'm so sorry.'

We are quiet for a moment. I stand in the hall, looking at the pictures of Sasha on the wall.

'Are you going to see Daniel?' I ask tentatively.

'No!' The violence of his reply seems to surprise him as much as me. 'No,' he repeats more quietly. 'I've got nothing whatsoever to say to him. Have you heard anything about Sasha?'

'No,' I say uncertainly.

'What is it? Have you heard from her?'

'No, nothing like that.'

'But there is something?'

'I went to see her mother today.'

'Wow, really? What was she like?' There's fascination in the question and I can tell that Alice North is a mythical creature to him, like a mermaid or the evil stepmother in *Snow White*.

'What you would imagine, I suppose. She wouldn't tell me anything. After I left, I got a call from the police saying they'd picked Sasha up on CCTV near Alice's flat on the day she disappeared. I went back, but Alice had gone, cleared out. The flat was all messed up; looked like someone had smashed the place up in a rage.'

'Shit. You should be careful, Ellen.'

He's right. What do I think I'm doing?

'So Karina was right about Daniel. She did see him,' Nicholas says. 'Have you spoken to her again?'

'No, not yet.' I consider telling him what the barman in Café Crème said, but something stops me. 'I'm going to her birthday party tomorrow.'

'Are you? I didn't think you two had been in touch for years.'

'We haven't. Dilys invited me when I was there on Monday.'

'God, what's that going to be like?' I thought I detected a jeering note.

'I don't know,' I said coldly. 'Why do you say it like that?'

'Like what? I didn't mean anything by it. I genuinely wonder what it will be like. I've thought about her a lot, over the years. Poor girl.'

'Yeah, me too,' I say. 'Sorry, I didn't mean to jump down your throat, I'm just a bit ... '

'Yeah, I know,' he says. 'Me too. It's all so messed up. What have the police said about Sasha? Will they still not do anything?'

'They are looking for her, but they don't seem to be looking that hard. They still think she's taken herself off somewhere.'

'God, I can't believe this is all starting up again. I thought it was over. I thought it was done, that I'd never have to face him again.'

I am horrified to realise he is crying. If he was here, I'd

probably put a stiff arm across his shoulders, but I don't know what to say to offer any comfort.

'I'm sorry,' I say uselessly. 'I've never really thought about how hard this must have been for you.'

'Hard? My whole family was torn apart by it. Everything was fine until that year. I wish to God she'd never come to live with us.'

'It wasn't Sasha's fault!' I say, my breath coming faster. 'How can you blame her?'

'If she'd never come to live with us, we wouldn't have had to move house, we would never have met Karina.'

'I know he's your brother, but Daniel is ... ' I'm unsure of the right word. Evil? I'm not sure I know what that means. It sounds like something from a trashy made-for-TV movie. 'What I mean is, this was always going to happen. If it hadn't been Karina, it would have been someone else. For some reason, it made him feel good to take what he wanted, to have power over her. It wasn't some spur of the moment thing, Nicholas, some ... mistake. It had been going on for months.'

'I know that. God, of course I know that. But it was something about her, Karina; she made it too easy ... '

'How dare you! First you're trying to blame Sasha, and now it's Karina's fault? That she got raped? You think she was asking for it? What do you think this is, the nineteen fifties?'

'Sorry, Ellen.' He sniffs, breathes out in a whoosh of air. 'I didn't mean it. I know it was Daniel's fault, all of it. He's a fucking bastard.'

'I'm sorry, I've got to go, I'm due at work soon,' I say.

'OK. Listen, Ellen, if you hear anything about Sasha, will you let me know?'

'Yes, of course.'

It feels for a moment as if he's about to say something else, but the moment passes and we say an uncomfortable goodbye. I put my phone in my bag, and unexpectedly sink down on to the floor, my knees pulled up to my chest. In the quiet of the hallway, all I can hear is the hammering of my heart.

Karina
November 2006

We don't normally see each other at the corner house, but he'd already told me we'd have the place to ourselves. Olivia's away at a concert in Vienna and everyone else was going to be out. I love being there with him; it feels so ... forbidden. Obviously I'm at the house sometimes, hanging out with Sasha and Ellen – when they deign to invite me. That has a thrill all of its own, especially if he's there. Knowing that I've been in parts of the house Ellen's never seen; brushing past him casually in the kitchen; catching a glimpse of an expression on his face that only I know is just for me.

He pushed me back hard on to the kitchen table, before we'd kissed or even had a proper conversation. The sharp edge of it dug into my back. I tried to look into his eyes but they were fixed on the dresser with its collection of mismatched teacups and family photographs.

I told him he was hurting me, but it was as if he couldn't hear me. My head was banging against the table

271

with every thrust, hitting the exact same place over and over. It hurt a little more every time, and I began to focus solely on that spot, telling myself that this wouldn't go on for ever, that he would finish soon and my head wouldn't hurt any more. I tried to put myself forward mentally to a time when this wouldn't be happening, when it would have stopped. And then it did, him wiping himself casually on a piece of kitchen roll, me pulling my knickers back into place, tugging down my skirt, putting a tentative finger to the back of my head.

While he was doing it, it sort of felt like he was raping me, but afterwards I realised that was silly of me. He's my boyfriend. We've had sex loads of times before. How could it have been rape? And he was totally normal afterwards, talking to me about what he'd been up to, a film he'd seen, Sasha.

I suppose that's how he likes it sometimes. I'll try and enjoy it a bit more if it happens again.

Olivia

July 2007

I am struggling to find it in Daniel today, his little boy's face. I thought I would always be able to see it but the layers of experience and age are piling on faster than I ever realised they could. Today is the day when I am going to have to hear it from his own lips. I suspect there will be harder days to come; days when I will have to fight to keep on believing in him. But today is about him, and I have to be strong. I can feel his need for me streaming out of him, as it has done ever since he was born, equal parts burden and privilege.

Daniel's barrister takes him through the events of the evening again. She looks so young – not much older than him, although she must be. This constant telling and re-telling is like a hideous, Ancient Mariner-style punishment, making us all relive the night over and over again, each time with tiny, subtle differences. Maybe if we hear it enough times, the truth will start to emerge of its own accord, blinking in the sunlight.

As I hear again about the first time Daniel spoke to Karina, I risk a sideways glance at Dilys, crammed into her usual seat at the end of the row, a sheen of sweat on her round face. I wonder absently how old she was when she had Karina. Is Dilys younger than she looks or was Karina a last-chance baby, a miracle?

His account of the evening up until he and Karina went into his bedroom is the same as everybody else's. It is once they are in the bedroom that his story differs.

'As we have heard from several witnesses, after spending some minutes kissing you in the hallway downstairs, Miss Barton went willingly with you to the bedroom shortly after ten p.m.'

'Yes, she did.'

Even the prosecution doesn't dispute this, although I'm not sure what it means, or why it matters. How many times has it been drummed into us – no means no at whatever stage a woman chooses to say it; and if a man continues after she has said it, it's rape. Gone are the days, surely, when a woman could be blamed for being raped because she was wearing a short skirt? Because she took her clothes off and got into bed with a man? Because she was asking for it? Perhaps I'm being totally naïve to believe that. On the one hand, I am outraged at the idea that they might try and blame Karina for putting herself into an unsafe situation; on the other I want them to throw everything at her, use everything in their arsenal to prove that my son is not a rapist. I don't let myself consider what that makes me.

'And what happened when you got into the bedroom?'

'She closed the door behind her and leaned against it. I sat down on the bed. I . . . I asked if she was OK, if she wanted to do it. And she said yes.' I have a horrible feeling that there is something missing from his story, a space between his words that he is not filling.

'And by "do it", are you sure Miss Barton understood that you meant sexual intercourse? Are you absolutely certain that she consented at this point?'

'Yes,' he says firmly, and my shoulders drop because now I believe him. 'She came and sat down next to me. We talked for a bit, and then we . . . we lay down and we had sex.'

'Was there any point at which Miss Barton said no, or stop, or anything at all to suggest that she was not consenting?'

'No.' He reddens but doesn't look my way. I imagine he is pretending I'm not here, although I know he is glad that I am. They've obviously told him to keep his head up, look at the barrister or the jury, maintain eye contact, but he's struggling. I yearn to reach out and hold him, take him in my arms and tell him it's going to be OK.

'Miss Barton has testified that she had been drinking alcohol. Did you have any indication that she was so intoxicated as to be unable to consent to sexual intercourse?'

'No, I did not. She was fully in control of her actions.'

'After you had finished having sex, what happened?'

'I got up to go to the bathroom. She needed to go too,

so I said I'd see her downstairs when she was ready. I waited for her in the piano room but she didn't come down. Mum asked me to play the piano, and I couldn't very well say no, I didn't want to tell her what had happened . . . ' His eyes stray to me again and I try to smile. *It's OK, I'm here.* 'So I started playing, and then people wanted me to play songs for them to sing, and I couldn't get away. I assumed Karina had got chatting to someone in another room. Then Ellen came in to the piano room and whispered something to Mum.'

I couldn't really hear Ellen over the singing, just that something had happened and I needed to come. I thought someone had broken a glass or spilled red wine on the carpet.

'A few minutes later, Mum came in again and said I needed to come out and talk to her. We went upstairs to her room and she told me . . . what Karina had said.'

I'll never forget how I felt as I climbed the stairs with my son to tell him he had been accused of rape: the pure shock that flooded me, a shakiness that pervaded my whole body; the way my breath caught in my throat, making me feel as if I was choking; the treacherous way I wondered if it might be true.

'We have heard about the injuries found on Miss Barton's thighs – injuries consistent with being cut with broken glass. Did you at any point inflict such injuries on her?'

'No.'

'Were those injuries present the last time you saw

her, when you left her in your bedroom to go to the bathroom?'

'No.' He pulls at his collar, trying to loosen it, and I will him to stop. To keep his hands folded in front of him as he's been told.

'Do you have any idea how those injuries came to be inflicted?'

'No. I . . . I can only assume that she did it herself.'

A large man on the jury scribbles something in his notebook. What on earth can it be? *Did it herself???*

It's an enormous relief when the judge proclaims a lunch break and brings the session to a close. I wish I had a better idea of how it was going. I can't tell anything from the jurors' faces. Is anyone feeling sympathetic towards him? There's a feeling of suspension in the air, as if we are all waiting for something.

Maybe we are waiting to see which of the two Karinas is the true one. One is a naïve, helpless victim, a mere girl; a girl who was taken advantage of in the most horrible way by a sexual predator; the other is a troubled young woman, who for reasons unknown has developed a vendetta against Daniel, which has also had the effect of attracting longed-for attention to herself.

It seems entirely possible to me that the jury could believe either of these things. I try to focus on the second Karina, the attention-seeking little madam that I have seen her be. I try not to think about how easy it would be for me to believe in the first.

Ellen

September 2017

Karina's house looks at me blankly, the street quiet, with no sign of a party. I think back to those evenings at the Monktons': the illicit sourness of the wine Tony would pour for us; the rise and fall of posh voices all around, debating politics and literature; classical music being bashed out on the piano; singing, but like nothing I'd ever heard before; the burning at the back of my throat as I inhaled on my first joint. I take a firmer hold on the bubble bath set I have wrapped for Karina (a Christmas gift from my aunt last year) and the bottle of wine I've brought, walk up the path and ring the bell.

Dilys answers the door wearing a yellow flowered dress that strains under the arms where it is pulled tight across her chest. She breaks into a smile when she sees me, taking the proffered bottle of wine with one hand and pulling me into an awkward half-hug with the other. I try not to breathe in her musty scent as the soft, papery skin of her arm presses into my neck. I wish to God I had trusted my gut feeling and stayed away.

'It's so good to see you, Ellen.'

I follow her in. There are still no discernible sounds of a party. She leads me into the front room, and I stand, stricken, in the doorway. It is worse, so much worse, than I feared. Two women smile at me from a green velour sofa that has seen better days. They could be any age from forty to sixty, but they look so similar to Dilys they must be her sisters. On a wing chair in the corner, an elderly man with a startlingly white moustache looks to be on the verge of nodding off. On two wooden dining chairs set out by the bay window are a couple around my parents' age, who I vaguely recognise. That's it. There is no sign of Karina.

'This is Auntie Meryl and Auntie Jane.' One of the sisters gives a little wave and the other one giggles.

'And Uncle Stanley.' The moustached man's head jerks up at this.

'Very nice to meet you,' he mumbles.

'And you remember Pat and Ian, from next door.'

Of course. The neighbours from Karina's old house. We used to go round there selling 'perfume' that we had made by crushing rose petals into little bottles of water. Pat would buy them for 5p and Ian would give us a mint humbug from a stash he kept in his desk drawer. We were fascinated by them because they had no children. Karina said it was because they had never had sex, and I had pretended to know what she meant.

279

'Where's Karina?' I ask, trying to sound normal.

'Oh, she's upstairs getting changed. She'll be down in a minute. Sit down,' says Dilys.

'Could I use the toilet?' I can't stay in this room a moment longer; I'll suffocate. Dilys points me along the hall to a downstairs toilet, and I close the door behind me, leaning against it, my need to breathe deeply to calm myself fighting with the peach air freshener that fails to mask the underlying odour of damp and urine. What could I say to get me out of here now? Nothing is worth this, not even finding out what Karina and Sasha were doing in Café Crème two weeks ago. Feigning illness seems to be the best course of action, so I emerge from the toilet trying to look unhappy and sick, which, given how I feel, is not hard. I am hovering outside the door to the front room, hand on my stomach, prepared lies on my tongue, when I hear footsteps on the stairs and see Karina, in smart black trousers and a peacock blue silk shirt, her make-up immaculate. Her face is transformed when she sees me; she lights up.

'Ellen! I'm so glad you came.'

Slowly, I lower my hand and try to arrange my face into a suitably festive expression.

'Happy birthday.' I hand over the bubble bath. It looks very small in its gaudy wrap.

'Thank you. I'll open it later, with the others.' Her words conjure a table piled high with beribboned gifts, instead of the few small, square boxes I had seen on a side table in the front room, wrapped in paper so cheap

280

that the corners of the contents were beginning to poke out. 'Come through.'

Back in the room of doom, Dilys has opened a bottle of sparkling wine and is pouring it into rarely used champagne glasses, sticky with kitchen grease to which a film of dust has adhered. I sit on a hard chair by the door, taking a glass and sipping at it, trying not to retch at the bits floating on the surface. Dilys hands round a bowl of plain crisps. They are a bit softer than they should be and I chew at one, forcing it down with another reluctant sip of my drink.

'So, how have you been?' asks Pat. She smiles warmly, and I have a sudden, crystal-sharp memory of her kindness to me as a child. 'It seems only yesterday that you were knocking on my door every minute to ask for your ball back!'

'I'm very well, thanks,' I say, wondering briefly what would happen if I did what no one ever does and answered that question truthfully. 'And you?'

'Oh, all right apart from my usual trouble.'

I smile sympathetically and try to look as if I know what her usual trouble is, although how she thinks I would is beyond me.

'What about your mum? She all right?'

'Yes, she's fine.'

Karina is standing by the fireplace, the wine in her hand untouched.

'Mum,' she says now. 'I wanted to show Ellen that dress I bought.'

'Oh yes, love, you two go upstairs. I know what you girls are like: you'll be up there for hours giggling and trying on clothes. It's just like the old days, isn't it?'

I smile weakly and follow Karina out of the room and up the stairs. I half expect her bedroom to be exactly as it was in their old house in 2006, but the walls in here are painted duck-egg blue and the bed clothes are a tasteful pale grey linen. There are no pictures on the walls, no photos or personal touches. It looks like an unused spare room. Karina slumps down on the bed, her back to the wall. I sit beside her, on the very edge, as if poised for flight.

'Oh God, I'm sorry, Ellen.'

'What for?'

'This terrible party. I'm not so far gone that I can't see how awful it is. But when Mum invited you, I thought . . . you being here would make it better. Stupid of me.'

'It's fine. I was happy to come.' The words sound forced even to me.

'That's kind of you, but it's bloody awful, Ellen.' There's an echo of the old Karina there, and I start to laugh, and so does she, and there are tears in our eyes, and I'm not sure if they are of laughter or not, but it feels like old times, like Dilys said. I wish I didn't have to break the spell by confronting her about Sasha, but I know I have to.

'How are you, really?' I ask first, seizing this moment when it feels like we might be able to talk about real things.

'Let's see: I've got no job, I live with my mum, and you've seen my birthday party. How do you think I am?' She could sound sharp, barbed, but she doesn't. She just sounds sad. 'And now I've got the police sniffing around, dredging up the past. Why did you tell them I'd seen Daniel?'

'Why do you think? I'm worried about Sasha. I'm sorry if it brought back unpleasant memories but—'

'Unpleasant? That's putting it mildly.' Bitterness creeps in. 'This has got nothing to do with me. Why are you dragging me into it?'

'Nothing to do with you?' I say, a pop of anger bursting inside me. 'So it wasn't you having a cosy chat with Sasha in Café Crème two weeks ago?'

She flushes, and if I had any doubts about whether it was her, they are gone.

'That was nothing to do with this,' she whispers.

'What was it to do with, then? You have to tell me, Karina.'

'I'd seen Daniel. I wanted to talk to someone about it, that's all. Someone who'd understand.'

'Sasha *knew* Daniel was back? Why didn't she say anything to me?'

'I don't know,' Karina says. 'Maybe you didn't know her as well as you think you did.' There are shades of the old Karina, the one who wanted to win the competition of who knows most about Sasha and the Monktons. Is she still in thrall to them?

'Why choose her? Why didn't you come to me?' Maybe

283

I'm competing too, but for Karina's affections. We were so close once, before Sasha arrived in our lives.

'You don't understand, Ellen. There was a lot going on back then that people didn't see.'

'Like what?'

'Oh, I don't know. Lots of things.'

'What d'you mean, Karina?' I cannot let this pass. All these lies, this secrecy, and now Karina's hinting that there is more to discover. What was really going on at the corner house in 2006? 'If there's something you know—'

'Girls! Come and have some cake!' Dilys's shrill call interrupts me.

Karina jumps up, looking relieved.

'Coming, Mum!' She bounces up and makes for the door.

'Wait, Karina, please.' The urgency in my voice makes her stop, but when she looks at me, her face is carefully blank.

'What do you mean, there was lots going on that people didn't see?'

'It's nothing, Ellen, honestly. I just meant when you're a teenager, you have all these thoughts and feelings, and you don't know whether anyone else will understand, or laugh at you, or whatever, so you keep them inside. That's all.'

It's useless to push her, so I follow her back downstairs, and sip the warm wine and eat cake that's dry like dust on my tongue. I suggest a couple of times that we go back upstairs but Karina acts as if she hasn't heard me, chatting brightly to her aunt as if she hasn't a care in the world. At 9 p.m. I can bear it no longer and make my excuses. Karina says goodbye to me in the lounge in front of everyone, leaving Dilys to see me to the door.

As I drive home, cake crumbs still claggy between my teeth, the truth clangs into me, over and over, like repeated hammer blows to the head. Sasha knew Daniel was back. She saw Karina a week before she disappeared and didn't tell me. She slept with Leo a month ago. It looks extremely likely that she saw her mother the day she disappeared. She has been lying to me at every turn. Do I really know her at all?

Safely in the flat, I slide the bolts into place with a satisfying clunk of metal on metal. I chuck my handbag on the floor by the hall table and go straight into the kitchen to put the kettle on.

I've just opened the milk and am poised to pour it into my tea when I hear it: the creak of the hall floorboard. I whirl around, dropping the bottle on its side on the worktop, narrowly missing knocking my tea over. Milk spreads from it, a widening pool that drips down on to the floor and splashes my shoes, pale splodges on dark suede. I grip the teaspoon in my hand, the edges of it digging into my palm, but the pain of it is not enough to stop the shaking, the way my insides have turned to liquid, the fire in my head.

Daniel Monkton is standing in my kitchen.

Karina
December 2006

This afternoon, he wanted me to do something so horrible it finally prompted me to say no. He said it would be a Christmas present for him. I've never said no to him before, and now I know why. He turned me around and for a terrifying second I thought he was going to do it anyway, my whole body braced for it, but then he pulled my top up and I felt a searing pain. I opened my mouth to scream but he was ready for it, clapping his hand over my mouth.

'Don't even think about it,' he said.

It wasn't until I smelled sickly-sweet burning flesh that I realised he had put a cigarette out on my back. I stared at a smudged pencil mark on the wall that looked like a bird in flight. Something bitter on his hand made me want to gag, but I held it in.

'Don't think about telling anyone,' he said. 'Don't forget I've taped you on my video camera. I can show everyone what a slut you are with the press of a button. Even your mum.'

I staggered from the room and went straight to the bathroom, locking the door. Gingerly, I lifted up my top and saw an angry red mark, a perfect circle on my back. I didn't want to meet my own eye in the mirror, so I closed the toilet lid and sat down. I had a half bottle of vodka in my bag, which was still hanging over my shoulder. I took it out and had a swig. Then another. It was all I could think of to dull the pain. I knew he would be waiting for me in the bedroom. There was no one else in the house. No one to hear me scream.

I picked up my bag and slid the bathroom door bolt open as smoothly as I could. I tiptoed along the landing, holding my breath. Down the stairs, avoiding the fourth one, which creaks. At the door, I shoved my feet into my shoes, not stopping to do them up, and grabbed my coat from the peg. I slipped out into the freezing air, easing the door shut behind me.

I know he'll find a way to make me pay for this. I just wish I knew what it was going to be.

Ellen

December 2006

On New Year's Eve, I tottered down the road to the Monktons' in a pair of heels that had seemed reasonably comfortable in the shop. From a couple of hundred yards away, I saw Karina come out of her house and cross the road. She paused on the pavement outside, head down, as if engaged in internal debate. After a few seconds, she shook her hair back and marched up the path, and by the time I got there she had disappeared into the house. I wondered if she'd been thinking about what I had heard through Sasha's bedroom wall a couple of weeks before. I hadn't said anything to Karina, supposing that if she wanted to tell me what was going on, she would.

A man I'd never seen before answered the door to me. He was around Tony and Olivia's age and he cheerfully looked me up and down.

'Good evening, young lady!'

Oh God, I'd forgotten this was one of those Monkton parties where they all invited their friends, including the parents. It had seemed so exotic to me at first, adults drinking and socialising like teenagers, something I had never seen my parents do; but recently I'd started to find it a bit weird, although I couldn't put my finger on why. They were all musicians, artists, actors – larger than life, extravagant. Until one recent night I'd thought they were all successful too, on the verge of making it big. But as the evening wore on, and they talked more about what they were actually doing work-wise, I had started to realise that was not the case.

I extricated myself from the conversation with the man at the door. Karina was in the front room talking too fast to a girl from our year and laughing unnaturally loudly. I ignored her and made my way upstairs. As I reached out to open Sasha's door, it almost hit me in the face as it was flung open from the inside by Daniel, who walked swiftly past me without saying hello, or even registering I was there. I walked in, smiling, ready to tell Sasha about the creep who had opened the door, when I was brought up short. She was sitting on the bed, white-faced, looking down, holding her hand to her mouth, as if to keep something from flying out.

'Are you OK?' I said, standing uncertainly in the doorway.

Her neck snapped up and she lowered her hand, forcing her mouth into a bright smile that didn't touch her eyes.

'Hi! Yes, I'm fine. Just Daniel being an idiot. Wow, you look great. Where did you get that dress?'

I allowed her to lead me into an inconsequential

conversation about clothes and shopping, understanding that she was silently asking me not to press her any further. I wished afterwards that I had done, but it was too late by then. A few minutes later the door burst open again and Karina came in and flung herself down on the bed.

'Hello, girls,' she said, gleaming with a strange light. 'What's up with Daniel?'

'Oh, I don't know, he's in a mood about something,' said Sasha. 'How are you?'

'Great!' she said, lying back on the bed. After a few seconds she sat up again. 'Woah, that's making the room spin.'

'Are you pissed already?' I asked. 'It's only early.'

'I'm fine, had a couple of drinks in my room before I came over, that's all.' She folded her hands in her lap and smiled brightly. She reminded me of how I was when I got home after an evening around the Monktons' table, pretending to Mum and Dad that I was completely sober, enunciating every word while simultaneously trying not to be too garrulous. 'Have you got anything to drink up here?'

'No. There's plenty in the kitchen, though,' said Sasha, pointedly.

Karina didn't seem to notice her snarkiness, and stood up unsteadily. She opened the door as Nicholas was walking past towards the stairs.

'Where d'you think you're going?' we heard her say.

'To the kitchen, to get drinks for me and Daniel,' he said.

'Ooh, I'll come with you.'

Sasha and I looked at each other as their voices faded.

'What's up with her?' I said.

'God knows,' said Sasha. 'She's been acting so weird lately. Weirder than usual, I mean.'

I laughed disloyally. Things between me and Sasha were finally returning to normal after her flit to France, and it felt so good to be back on her team that I didn't care if I was being mean to Karina. She didn't know what we were saying anyway, so it wasn't hurting her.

'What does she look like, as well?' I said, warming to the theme.

'I know! Did she put that make-up on with a trowel?' Sasha mimed slapping handfuls of something on to her face and we both collapsed in giggles.

As the hours wore on, everyone got drunker and drunker. I'd never known adults to drink as much as the Monktons and their friends. I spent a trying fifteen minutes trapped in a corner of the kitchen while Tony stood too close and talked at me loudly about how wonderful it was that Olivia's career was going so well, and how happy he was for her, how pleased to be able to support her by being there for the family when his own work commitments allowed. I'm not sure who he was trying to convince, but I got the opposite impression to the one he'd been trying to give. Because she was so careful to disguise it, I hadn't realised until recently how much higher profile than him Olivia was, nor how disappointed Tony was with his own career. I had another reason, apart from boredom, for wanting to get away from Tony. Out of the corner of my eye I could see Sasha and Leo engrossed in conversation in the far corner of the kitchen. I'd been trying to signal my need for assistance to them, but either they hadn't noticed or they were deliberately ignoring me. The longer they talked, the more my anxiety rose. Both of them had sworn to me that they weren't interested in the other, but looking at them, so beautiful, so perfect, laughing in the lamplight, they looked right together. Leo wasn't meant for someone nondescript like me. He ought to have been with someone extraordinary. Someone like Sasha.

It was Nicholas that rescued me in the end. He'd been watching for a few minutes as I nodded and smiled and cast desperate glances at Leo and Sasha, and then at anyone and everyone, hoping someone would sense my distress signals and come over. It was useless, though – they were all talking about themselves, or waiting for whoever they were talking to to finish speaking so that they could start talking about themselves again. Only Olivia, the one genuine star among them, was immune to this endless self-promotion, self-validation; the idea that if you said you were successful, then you were, or would be. I felt a light touch on my arm and turned thankfully to see Nicholas standing there, proffering a glass of wine.

'You look like you might need this,' he said. 'Dad, you're boring Ellen to death.'

This was another thing that had taken some getting used to – the Monkton children's casual rudeness to their parents. If I'd said something like that to my dad, he would have gone mad.

'At least she listens to me, unlike my own children,' Tony said, putting his arm around my shoulders. I must have stiffened because he dropped it straight away.

Nicholas looked at him with distaste. 'You're not giving her any choice, Dad. Come on, Ellen, let's leave him to bore someone else senseless.'

I smiled at Tony, but let Nicholas lead me away and sit me down at the table with him.

'Thanks,' I said. 'It was getting a bit much.'

'Was he giving you the full sob story? How if only he hadn't had to take a back seat to Mum, he'd have been first bassoon by now? How selfless he is, stepping up to the plate and raising the family so she could shine?'

'He didn't say exactly that ...'

'No, but I bet that was the general idea, wasn't it? Never mind the real story, where Mum struggled to build her career while simultaneously doing pretty much everything at home.'

We sat in silence for a few seconds, me unsure how to respond and him seemingly lost in thought. Nicholas was the one to break it. 'Have you seen Karina? She looks hammered.'

I thought, with a lurch, how drunk she had already been a couple of hours ago. There was a sharpness about her recently that hadn't always been there, a jagged edge of unpredictability that made me fearful of her, or for her.

'She was in the hall when I came down here,' I said.

'Talking to Daniel, I think.' The sounds I had heard through the wall a couple of weeks ago echoed uncomfortably through my mind. 'I probably ought to go and check on her.' It was stifling in the kitchen anyway. I could do with getting out.

'OK. I'm sure she's all right,' Nicholas said lightly. 'She seems to know what she's doing.'

'Yeah, I'm sure she's fine, but . . . '

He waved a hand, as if to dismiss me. I left the room and stood for a moment in the corridor, leaning against the wall. The world spun hazily around me and I breathed deeply. What I really wanted to do was go home and lie down in my own quiet bed, but it was New Year's Eve, I told myself. I couldn't leave before midnight. It was dark in the corridor and I was wearing a black dress that blended into the shadows, so they didn't see me. I nearly didn't see them, half-hidden by the coats that bulged from the pegs by the front door. At first I couldn't work out what I was looking at because all I could see was someone's back, burrowing into the coats; I thought it might be someone rummaging for something in their coat pocket. But then I recognised the shirt from earlier, and I slowly realised that what I was looking at was Daniel pressed up against someone, kissing them. I looked down at the floor and saw a familiar pair of black shoes, just as he stepped back and whispered something. Karina emerged from the coats, smiling, her hair mussed and her sparkly dress pulled down at one shoulder. She glanced at the coat pegs, and her lips moved but she was speaking too low for me to hear what she was saying. Daniel leaned forward and whispered in her ear again and as he did, her smile faded. As his face moved back into her eyeline, she smiled again, but it was fake, as if painted on for his benefit. He slipped his hand round her waist and led her up the stairs.

I had my back to the kitchen door, so although I looked round when I heard it click shut, I was too late to see who it was that had closed it, and whether they had seen what I had seen.

Olivia
July 2007

He stands up, the prosecution barrister, and there's a pause before he speaks. As he looks over the papers in his hand, which I'm sure don't pertain to the case, he somehow manages to give the impression that he is shocked and horrified at what Daniel has done. Allegedly done. Without even speaking, he has the jury in the palm of his elegantly manicured hand. They are waiting with bated breath to see how he will begin. He pinches the bridge of his nose.

'Mr Monkton, I'd like to take you once more through the events of the evening of the thirty-first of December 2006.'

Daniel nods, but he looks frightened. I clench my fists a little tighter, wishing I had a hand to hold, someone who wouldn't care if I squeezed so hard it hurt. I think of Tony's face at our silent breakfast table this morning, the way he leafed through the paper without seeing it. I have pretended to understand his absence from court; I have let him off, but I wonder if I will ever be able to forgive him for not being at my side for the most terrible experience of my life.

'This New Year's Eve party at your parents' home – at what time did proceedings begin?'

'The . . .' He stops to clear his throat. 'The first guests arrived around seven p.m., I suppose.'

'And did you start drinking alcohol at around that time?'

'Yes, I think so.'

'You think so?'

'No, I did.' He runs out of breath and has to stop to gulp in air. 'Around that time.'

'And what were you drinking?'

'There was some champagne; I had a bit of that. And then beer, mostly.'

'Champagne and beer.' The barrister looks down for a few seconds, as though lost in thought, then appears to remember himself and turns to Daniel again.

'And what time did Miss Barton arrive at the party?'

'I don't know. I didn't answer the door to her.'

The barrister consults his papers. 'In her evidence, she says she arrived at around eight p.m. You don't have any reason to disbelieve that, do you?'

'No.'

'And at what time did you first encounter her at the party?'

'Not for a while. I was in my room with my brother and some friends. I think we came down around eight-thirty to get some more beer from the kitchen. That was the first time I saw her.'

'Did you speak to her?'

'Yes, just hello, that sort of thing. I think she said Happy New Year, maybe.'

He's saying too much. He sounds as if he's trying to please the barrister, give him the answers he wants. Why is he doing that?

'You then went back to your bedroom, with the beer?'

'Yes.'

'At ten o'clock, only an hour or so later, you kissed Miss Barton passionately in the hallway, and went upstairs with her.'

'Yes, that's right.'

'So what happened in the interim period? How did you get from drinking in your room with friends, to taking Miss Barton to your bedroom?'

Daniel looks uncertainly at the jury and back to the barrister. 'I wouldn't say I took her. She wanted to go.'

The barrister stops a fraction short of raising his eyes to the heavens. 'I do apologise. How did you get from drinking with friends to kissing Miss Barton in the hall-way and *going together with her* to your room?'

'We all came down to get some more drinks, me and my friends.'

'At what time?' He sounds ... bored. I know it's a tactic, it must be, but it's working. He's managing to subtly discredit everything Daniel says without appear-ing to be doing so. I am horrified at how theatrical it is. I want to stand up and shout at him: THIS IS NOT A GAME! This is my son. His life. My life.

'Around nine-thirty, I guess. It's hard to remember. We'd been drinking.'

'Indeed,' he says smoothly. 'And how intoxicated would you say you were?'

'It's hard to say.'

'Well, were you, for example, in full control of your actions?'

'Yes,' he says, his brow furrowed in the way it used to be when he bent over the kitchen table doing his homework.

'And so you came down at nine-thirty, and that was when you began talking to Miss Barton?'

'Yes. I was going from the kitchen to the piano room, and I saw her in the hall, rummaging through the coats. She seemed upset.'

'You thought she was leaving?'

'Yes. She was crying.'

'And did she tell you what was wrong?'

'She said it was nothing, that she'd had too much to drink.'

'How well did you know Miss Barton at this point?'

'I'd seen her around the house a lot. She was a friend of Sasha's, my parents' goddaughter who lives with us. I'd chatted to her before, seen her at parties. But I didn't know her very well. I'd probably never had a conversation longer than about five minutes with her.'

'So you'd never kissed her before?'

'No! Nothing like that.'

'You and Miss Barton had never had sexual inter-course, or any kind of sexual contact?'

'No! I hardly knew her.'

The barrister makes a little moue with his mouth, as if to express doubt.

'So you began to talk, and what … one thing led to another?' He says this with slight distaste, as if this is something that would never happen in his own life: *one thing leading to another*.

'Yes, I suppose so,' he says, with a brief, agonised glance up at me. My heart clutches in my chest at this evidence of his boyish embarrassment at having to talk about these things in front of me. Last night he offered me a way out, said he would understand if I couldn't face it, but I could hear what he was saying underneath his words: *please be there; please don't abandon me*.

'Miss Barton was intoxicated, wasn't she?'

He looks down at his hands, which are folded together in front of him.

'A bit, I suppose. It was a New Year's Eve party.'

'Mr Monkton, when you and Miss Barton were engaged in sexual intercourse, she asked you to stop, didn't she?'

'No.'

'She said no. She told you that you were hurting her?'

'No.'

'When I asked you a moment ago if Miss Barton seemed intoxicated, you said …' He makes a great show of consulting his notes, although he clearly knows perfectly well what comes next in this drama he is starring in. 'You said: "A bit, I suppose. It was a New Year's Eve party." Miss Barton was incapable of consenting to sexual intercourse. Did she consent, Mr Monkton?'

'Yes!' The word explodes from him like a bullet from a gun. His barrister shoots him a warning look and he takes a breath, looking at the floor, a deep red staining his cheeks. I pray for it to be over, or for the judge to call for a break, but the barrister has more cards to play.

'Yes,' Daniel says again, more calmly. 'She did not show any signs of being out of control. She appeared a bit drunk, but she consented fully to everything we did. She ... enjoyed it,' he adds stiffly.

'Can you account for the fact that when police searched your room, a broken bottle with your fingerprints and DNA on it – the bottle that has been proven to be the one that cut Miss Barton's thighs – and a T-shirt of yours, stained with her blood, were found buried at the bottom of your wardrobe?'

'No, I can't.' His voice is so low I can hardly hear it.

'You can't.' The barrister shuffles some papers around on the table in front of him. 'You have told us,' he goes on, his tone indicating that whatever it was, it was a pack of lies, 'that you had never had any kind of sexual contact with Miss Barton before that night.'

'That's right,' Daniel says, looking up and straight at the barrister in his ridiculous wig. I have a momentary urge to stand up and scream at the ridiculous pantomime unfolding before me. Why do we have these rituals, these protocols that must not be deviated from, these absurd costumes? Is it to intimidate the rest of us, those of us not privy to this world of secret handshakes and Latin phrases? To force us into confessing to things we haven't done?

'So how do you explain Miss Barton's assertion that she had been in a controlling and abusive sexual relationship with you for the three months leading up to New Year's Eve 2006?'

The red blotches have faded from his cheeks and his hands clasp the rail in front of him, the skin stretched tightly over his knuckles.

'I can't explain it,' he says grimly. 'She's lying. I can only assume that she has some sort of ... problems ... That she wants the attention.'

'You have no idea why Miss Barton swears that you and she had been involved in an abusive relationship for three months? That this was not the first time you had raped her? But merely the first time you had done more than rape her? That this time the fact that you had pushed her, and cut her with broken glass, leaving injuries that other people could see if she chose to show them, had given her the courage to speak out about what you were doing to her?'

Daniel doesn't reply; he simply stares at the barrister, his face closed and unreadable. I don't believe in God, but I find myself praying to him nonetheless. Not for the jury to find Daniel not guilty, although I do want that (somewhere deep inside, in my womb, perhaps, where I grew him, I want that regardless of whether he is guilty or not); but what I find myself praying is this: *Please God, let him not have done it.* Which, with a thundering jolt to my heart, forces me to face the unpalatable truth: I am not sure that he didn't.

Olivia

September 2017

Why did Ellen have to dig it all up? It's been hard enough having Daniel back in our lives, after I spent so long shoring up my heart against him. I don't, I won't, believe that he had anything to do with Sasha going missing, despite what I know. Despite what I did. But then I would have sworn he wasn't a rapist until a judge and jury forced me to believe it.

It was a hideous shock, opening the door a few weeks back to find him standing there. I don't expect a ring at the door on a Friday night anyway, certainly not these days. There was a time when friends would pop in at any and all times, saying they were going to stay for one drink, but finding themselves still there hours later, eating a meal I'd thrown together in my famous way, gathering round the piano, singing, talking, laughing. It's been a long time since that happened, though. Over ten years. Perhaps it would have faded anyway; our friends are all ageing, and everybody texts all the time now. Nobody ever calls or wants to meet up.

Daniel's face was a heartbreaking mixture of hope and fear. We stood there for a few seconds, neither of us speaking. I suppose he was waiting to see if I would send him away or invite him in. I simply didn't know what the correct response was; what *my* response was. It was as though someone had paralysed my brain, or put it into a deep freeze, whence it couldn't separate right from wrong, love from hate.

He was the first to break the silence. 'Mum?' he said hesitantly, as if perhaps I hadn't recognised him.

'Yes,' I said, although I wasn't sure what question I was answering.

'Could I ... come in?'

A sort of automatic response kicked in and I stepped back to let him pass. The door closed behind him with a soft thud. Still I stood there, not knowing how I felt.

'Is it OK if we go into the kitchen?' He spoke as if to a stranger, someone who had never been to the house before. My mind filled with images of him clattering into the hall, kicking off his shoes, flinging his coat on to a peg, bursting into the kitchen, helping himself from the fridge. I had to clamp down, lock those memories away. If I started thinking like that I'd be lost. I walked silently into the kitchen and he followed. I stood with my back to the Aga and he faced me, half-leaning against the dresser. Behind him I could see the marks that refused to disappear, where I had ripped off the sellotape that had stuck the family photos to the edge of the shelves. I hadn't been able to bear removing only the ones that had him in them, so I took them all down and stuffed them in an envelope, hid it away in the loft.

'What are you doing here?' I found my voice, although it didn't sound like mine. It was hard, spiky.

'Dad told me about . . . being unwell.'

'He's dying, Daniel. No need to be so delicate. And since when did Dad tell you anything?'

'I didn't know he hadn't told you. We've been in email contact for a while now. Sorry you're finding out like this.'

'Where are you staying?' Despite myself, concern crept in. He heard it; I could see it in the downward tilt of his shoulders.

'With a friend,' he said. 'Don't worry, Mum.'

'Don't worry?' My façade dropped and ten years of pain soared through my body. 'You turn up after all this time and you're telling me not to worry? My worrying days are over, Daniel. I am beyond worry. In fact, I'm beyond everything. I don't feel anything any more. That's what you did to me. That's what you have made me.'

His face twisted, and I thought he was going to cry, but then he shifted his weight off the dresser and moved towards the door.

'I shouldn't have come, I'm sorry.'

I followed him back into the hall, not saying anything in case I opened my mouth and begged him to stay.

'Bye, Mum,' he said quietly, and then he was gone. I wanted to sink to the floor and sob like a child, but I am a sixty-year-old woman, so I went back to the kitchen and poured myself a glass of wine and sat, shaking, at the table to drink it.

I am back there now, drinking again. I must be careful; we can't have two alcoholics in the house. My eyes keep being drawn back to the bare spots on the dresser where the sellotape was, where the evidence of our happy family life used to be. I've been resisting the urge, but the wine has loosened my self-control, and Tony is out at the pub, won't be back for hours. He said he was meeting a friend and I colluded in the lie, knowing that he'll be sitting alone at the bar, engaging anyone who is foolish enough to linger too long next to him in his self-centred conversation.

I have to get the wooden step from the kitchen to reach up and unhook the loft hatch, and even then it's a struggle. It's years since I've been up here. I pull the ladder down, unleashing an avalanche of dust that sticks in my throat and makes my eyes gritty. At the top of the ladder I fumble for the light switch, unable to remember exactly where it is. I snap it on and the loft is bathed in yellow light. There are piles of boxes, and everywhere remnants of a life I cannot bear to think of. A mini shopping trolley lurks in one corner, two moth-eaten bears sitting at drunken angles in the seat at the front; next to it is a wooden rocking horse given to me by my mother when Daniel was little. It had belonged to me as a child, a fact that fascinated him, his toddler brain entranced by the idea of me as a small girl, my hair in pigtails. Once, we spent an entire afternoon going through the albums of family photos that my mother had painstakingly stuck in, photos that went back years, featuring forbidding-looking Victorian ladies in black, high-necked dresses and hats, all annotated in my mother's spidery hand: *Great Aunt Mary, 1906. The baby must be Uncle Cecil.*

The photos from the dresser must be near the top somewhere, from the last time I was up here. There's a brown envelope on top of one of the boxes that's marginally less dusty than anything else. I pick it up and open out an ancient folding wooden chair, sitting down and sliding my thumb under the flap of the envelope. It gives way easily and I reach in and pull out a stack of photos that make my heart flip, even though I knew what to expect. Daniel beams at me from the top of the pile, sitting on a rock at Cheddar Gorge, squinting into the sun, his skin tanned, wearing his favourite *Toy Story* T-shirt. I swallow, dust on my tongue, unsure whether to go on, unable to resist. The next one is Daniel and Nicky, older this time, leaning against the car, the Citroën we had when we first moved here. Their dark hair is blowing in the wind and Daniel is laughing at something outrageous Nicky has said. God, I loved this photo, back when I was a normal woman with two sons who loved each other, a great career, a happy husband, friends; a life. Before Sasha. There's a bitter taste in my mouth that has nothing to do with the dust, and I shove the photos back into the envelope and drop it on the floor.

There's so much crap up here. I don't even know what

some of it is. I have a sudden urge to sort through it, to declutter. Maybe it will be liberating, cleansing – paring our possessions down to the things we truly need. There's no time like the present. Better to make a start, do something positive, than to go back downstairs, finish the bottle and sink into the inevitable self-flagellating hole.

I pick a corner at random, kneeling down, heedless of the thick, sticky grime under my shins. The first box I open is Daniel's old school books. Once I've established that, what I should do is put them firmly into the 'chuck' pile. No one is ever going to look at them. Nobody cares. This thought, though, gives me such a pang that I begin leafing through them. He spent time and care on this work. As I read, I am taken back to the days before New Year's Eve 2006, when one of my greatest concerns was to what standard he had done his homework, or whether he would pass his exams. These books are mostly maths, and as such largely incomprehensible to me. There's a music book too, though, with a composition that I find myself singing, my voice cracking with dust, and pity, and love. When I've worked my way through, I put the box in a pile in the middle that I have allocated for the 'undecideds'.

I must throw some things away. Knees creaking and complaining, I crawl over to the furthest corner. There's a black bin bag here, the corner of a hardback book poking out through a hole. I rip it further and see it's one of a pile of Tintin books. I put the bin bag in the charity pile and move on to the boxes behind it. The first one houses a collection of seemingly random items, none of which ring a bell: a deflated football; two mugs; a satchel, its faux leather peeling off; an untouched notebook. I don't even know who these belonged to. I put the box into the throw pile and move on to the next, which appears to be filled with ancient football magazines. I flick through quickly, assuming it will be simply more of the same. I'm about to put the whole box in the chuck pile when I catch a glimpse of something unexpected, near the bottom of the pile. Something pale pink and shiny. Satiny. I lift the magazines out and place them on the dusty floor beside me. I stare in confusion at the inside of the box. I am looking at a scrap of rose silk, with little lace flower buds sewn into it. I am looking at a pair of knickers.

Ellen

September 2017

He steps towards me, reaching out, and I flinch.

'No, sorry ... it's just, you might want to mop that up before it goes everywhere.' He gestures at the lake of milk.

Something in the movement takes me right back to that courtroom: the smell of furniture polish, the smooth grain of the wood under my fingers as I stood in the witness box. I shudder. He walks past me and pulls several sheets of kitchen paper from the roll on the side and starts soaking up the milk. I take a step back, watching in stunned silence. When the paper is sodden he gets more, and grabs the cloth from the sink to finish the job. I am rooted to the spot, suspended in this completely bizarre scene that, from the outside, looks like domestic harmony, and from the inside feels like a horror film.

'That's better,' he says, rinsing his hands in the sink and drying them on a threadbare tea towel. 'Now, we need to talk. Shall we go through and sit down?'

I follow him out into the hall, taking a snatched look at my bag, which contains my phone, and into the lounge, where we sit opposite each other.

'I'm sorry to barge in like this, Ellen,' he says, leaning forward, elbows on his knees. I shrink back further into the sofa. 'I didn't think you'd see me otherwise.'

Too right I wouldn't. I still haven't spoken, and I'm not sure if I can. The moisture has drained from my mouth, and it's all I can do to keep breathing in and out.

'So the police have been sniffing around. I gather that's thanks to you.'

'I'm sorry,' I whisper. 'Sasha ...'

'I know, Sasha's gone missing. But Ellen, I don't know anything about that. You've got the wrong man.'

'How did you get in?'

'I let myself in while you were out. You don't spend five years in prison without learning a thing or two. You wouldn't have let me in if I rang the buzzer.'

'What ... what do you want?' I manage, my tongue sticking to the roof of my mouth.

'Ha! There's a question, Ellen. What do I want? What I want is to go back eleven years and choose differently, choose better. I can't do that, though, can I? So what do I want now?' he goes on. 'I want the same as you. I want to know where Sasha is. I want the police to stop wasting their time hassling me when they should be trying to find her. You've dragged me into this. I was living a quiet life before you told the police about me. Building bridges with Mum and Dad. Trying to get a bit of life back. But not any more.'

'The only reason I told the police about you was because Karina had seen you in London. So had my mum.'

'Is it? The only reason?' He narrows his eyes, appraising me. I look down. 'Or did you think of me straight away when Sasha disappeared? Did you think of Daniel the rapist?'

I shake my head, not trusting myself to speak.

'You're barking up the wrong tree, darling.' His voice is different, rougher around the edges. No longer the posh boy who went to the Royal College of Music. Has that been gradually worn away by whatever he's experienced over the past ten years, or was it deliberate, an attempt to fit in with his fellow prisoners? 'Was it not enough for you to ruin my life the first time around? Are you intent on doing it again?'

'I didn't do anything. I told the truth.' I need to hold on to this.

'And what about Karina? And Sasha? Were they telling the truth too?'

'Yes.' They were. I'm sure they were.

'And you think you know everything that was going on back then, do you?'

'Maybe not everything.' I think of Karina in the pub with Sasha two weeks ago, deep in conversation; Karina sitting on her bed earlier, hinting that not everything was as it seemed; telling me I didn't know Sasha as well as I thought I did.

'No, not everything, Ellen. For example, I'm assuming

you don't know that Sasha and I were in a relationship in 2006.'

'What?' All the breath leaves my body. I feel like a
fish that's been pulled from the water to flounder on the
deck. 'No. You're lying.' But my voice is weak and I'm
not even convincing myself. I remember the way I caught
them looking at each other, way back at that first party
when Daniel was playing the piano; how he stormed past
me out of her room on New Year's Eve 2006; her face
when I walked in.

'Thought you knew everything about her, didn't you?'
He sits back, self-satisfied. Why does everyone take such
pleasure in pointing out how little I know Sasha? 'We
fell in love eleven years ago, when we lived in the corner
house. Nobody knew, it wasn't only you,' he adds, as if
this will somehow make it better.

My mind spins, trying to grasp what he is saying,
trying to slot the pieces into this new pattern. Trying
to come to terms with the fact that, yet again, Sasha has
lied to me. This is the worst yet. I am Rip Van Winkle,
waking up after twenty years to find everything changed.

'But ... Karina ... What ... ?'

'I didn't rape Karina. Everything I said in court was
true.' He leans forward again, his eyes boring into mine.
'Sasha and I ... things didn't end well between us.
We had a sort of ... fight that night, New Year's Eve.
Something happened that meant it was over for good. I
was so low, so pissed off with her and with everything,
and drunk. Karina was there, and she wanted me, and I

314

didn't try too hard to fight her off. She consented, though. I wasn't drunk enough not to be able to tell. And neither was she.'

'But the cuts on her legs, the blood ... '

'I don't know what happened to her or how those cuts got there, but they weren't there when she left my room. All that stuff about me having a relationship with Karina for three months, none of it was true.'

I try to ignore the small voice in my head that says he is telling the truth. These are the same lies he told in court. I heard him with Karina in his room. I need to focus on how to get him out of here. I try to remember the things I've read about these kinds of situations. Keep them talking – I'm sure that's the advice.

'But Sasha ... she saw you and Karina together, that day before Christmas.'

'She was lying.' His face hardens. 'Like I said, something had gone wrong between us. She was angry with me. And to be fair to her, I think she believed Karina then. She thought she was doing the right thing.'

'Believed her then? What about now?'

'I don't know, Ellen. Where is she? Maybe she knows Karina lied.' Daniel stands up and wanders over to the window, staring out of it, then turns to face me. 'Like you lied. Like she did.'

'I didn't lie.' The fear I felt when he first appeared had abated, but it roars back now, making my skin tingle all over.

'That day you came round to the house on your own,

you said you heard me and Karina having sex in my room. That never happened.'

I don't speak, I'm too frightened, but I remember a banging noise, grunting. Karina saying, *You're hurting me.*

'If you really heard someone with Karina,' he goes on, 'it was somebody else. It wasn't me.'

'They were in your room,' I whisper. 'It was you. It had to have been you.' If it wasn't, then what the hell have I done?

'It wasn't me, Ellen.' He comes and sits down next to me on the sofa this time. 'I need you to believe me.' He takes my hand but I let it lie there, limp and unresponsive. His is clammy. 'If you don't believe me, you'll never find Sasha, because you've got everybody looking in the wrong direction.'

'But . . . if Karina wasn't with you in your room that day, who was she with?'

'I don't know.' He sounds uncertain, and for the first time I can see the boy he was ten years ago, still there under the hard shell of the man he has had to become.

'That's why the police should be talking to Karina, not to me.'

'But if you're right and she lied in court, she's not going to tell the police now, is she?'

'No, probably not. She might talk to you, though. Even if you can't persuade her to go to the police, she might tell you something that could help find Sasha. If there's even a chance of that, Ellen, you have to try.' Something in the way he speaks tells me that, unbelievably, he still

316

feels something for Sasha. Something that has lasted through years of incarceration, through what is, if he is right, a shockingly unforgivable betrayal. I can't waste emotional energy on that now, though. There's something I need to know.

'What were you looking for, last Wednesday night?'

'What do you mean?'

'When you broke in, in the night. What were you looking for?'

'I've never been here before, I swear.' He looks me full in the face. 'What happened?'

'Somebody was in the flat, in the middle of the night. I heard them. They were going through Sasha's things.' The terror I felt that night still lingers, like the smell of onion on my fingers after cooking.

'It wasn't me, Ellen,' he says simply, and like everything else he's said today, it has the disturbing ring of truth. 'Look, I have to go now, but take my number – call me if you find anything out, anything at all.'

I tap his number into my phone numbly, unsure how he expects me to find anything out. When he's gone, my brain skips round and round in circles, trying to get to grips with what Daniel has told me, getting nowhere. Daniel and Sasha were in love. I think of the spin the bottle night when Daniel pressed a chaste kiss on Sasha's lips as we all watched. I run all the conversations I have ever had with Sasha through my mind, reconfiguring them in the light of this new information. I remember every look she and Daniel shared, every time I found them laughing together, and I begin to wonder how I could have been so stupid.

I have been smothered in her lies, like someone buried in the snow for whom death comes not quickly and painfully, but so gradually and peacefully they don't even know they are dying at all.

Olivia

September 2017

I place the knickers carefully on the floor, not knowing
what to make of them, fearful of giving it too much
thought. Underneath, there are a couple more books:
scrapbooks, by the looks of them. Something inside
urges me to throw them away without looking at them,
pretend I never found them, but I can't. The strands of
the past are unravelling, as I always knew they would,
and I am powerless to stop them.

I pick the first one up and open it. I'm confronted by
a page of photos of Sasha, simple family snaps that ring
a faint bell in my memory. Perhaps Daniel put these
together, before our ... discussion on the morning of
New Year's Eve 2006. They could be innocent, these
photos, as far as their relationship could be described
in that way.

I turn the page and my stomach contracts, bile rising in
my throat. I clap a hand to my mouth to prevent myself
from crying out. These photos are different. They have

been taken apparently without Sasha's knowledge, while she was sleeping. Some are close up on her face, revealing every pore, every blemish, every fine hair. In others, the worst ones, the duvet has been pulled back and the photos are of her naked body, her face out of shot. There are close-ups of her breasts, her private parts. Did Daniel take them covertly, or did Sasha know he had these pictures? I knew they had fallen for each other, but naïvely I didn't think things had gone this far. I thought I had put a stop to it.

I put the book on the floor, as if I could catch something nasty from it, unable to banish the image from my mind, the day I first walked in on them.

July 2006. One of those hot, airless days when you can't believe you'll ever be cool again. I'd been rehearsing all morning in a stifling room with no air conditioning. We'd thrown the windows open but it was so still and hot that it made no difference. Every time I mopped my face with a handkerchief, sweat formed again immediately, beading on my upper lip, my forehead, even in my hair. I drank glass after glass of lukewarm water; the pipes must have been near the surface because however long you ran the tap, it never got truly cold. We were all cranky and argumentative, so as things otherwise were going well with the show, and it wasn't going out until September, the director let us go at lunchtime. She advised us to lie in a darkened room and gird our loins for the following day, which was predicted to be even hotter.

I floated along the road, light-hearted at the prospect

of an unexpectedly free afternoon, a very slight breeze making me feel instantly cooler. As I got closer to the house, I saw that Sasha's window was open. Faint strains of music floated out into the shimmering heat, and below, a buzz of conversation and laughter. One of the boys was in there with her. My heart lifted even further; I carried the worry of Sasha around with me in a different way then, and the sound of her being happy, particularly within the family, allowed that worry to recede a little. That was probably the last time I was able to think of her with any equanimity, to associate any positive emotion with her.

I let myself in and put the kettle on, then went upstairs to see if they wanted a cup of tea. I knocked on the door, but didn't wait to be asked in. I just pushed it open. I froze. They were both lying on the bed. Daniel was on his back with Sasha sitting astride him. They were fully clothed, and he was holding her wrists as if they'd been play-wrestling. They were both facing me, their expressions a perfect synchronicity of horror. We all stayed in our positions, like some frightful tableau, for a few seconds. Then Sasha jumped off the bed as if she'd had an electric shock, straightening her clothes, and Daniel sat up and smoothed his hair down. I stood there, mouth opening and closing, a pantomime of someone in shock. It was their faces that gave it away. Otherwise it could have been innocent – they weren't naked, after all, weren't even kissing. But I could tell exactly what was going on, and they knew it. When I'd recovered myself enough to speak, I told them to follow me down to the kitchen when they were *ready*, the word dripping with disgust.

I didn't think it could get worse than that. I knew Sasha's history, what she'd been through with her mum. She'd turned out perhaps better than could have been expected, but she was still trouble: mercurial, temperamental. No good for a boy like him. He was such a talented pianist; he had a chance to make it. Not like Tony, the second bassoon, or even me. He had something really special. Getting involved with Sasha at this point would have been a terrible mistake. She was so demanding, so needy, underneath her cool exterior. I saw how she played those girls off against each other, drawing them into her orbit and pushing them away when they got closer than she wanted. That was the last thing Daniel needed. And anyway, Sasha was living under our roof, and she was only seventeen. I wanted them to be close, but like brother and sister, not like this. I had always striven to be the cool parent, the one who was a friend, not a dictator. But that day, I had to be firm. I had to tell them they couldn't have a relationship, not while they were living under my roof. Neither of them said much, sitting at the table, not looking at each other, faces burning.

The next day she was gone. I was insane with worry until she called the following day to say she was in France. I relaxed for the next few weeks. Daniel didn't say much, staying out most of the time. I let him get on

322

with it. He was nineteen, after all, not a baby. When Sasha got back from France in September, I watched them like a hawk, but they seemed to be staying away from each other, so I thought that was that.

Until New Year's Eve. I went to the supermarket to get the things we needed for the party that evening, but halfway there I realised I'd forgotten my purse. The house was quiet when I let myself back in. Daniel had said he was going out, and I assumed Sasha was in her room. But there was something about the quality of the silence in the house that didn't seem right: loaded, potent. I tiptoed up the stairs, holding my breath. As I crept along the landing, I thought I heard a muffled thud and a giggle from Sasha's room. I knew what I was going to find before I flung open the door, yet still I did it, and there they were under the covers: flushed, full of desire, her hair falling over him like a shining curtain.

This time, they were defiant. They were both adults now, they said as we gathered around the kitchen table once more. They weren't doing anything wrong. I listened with mounting horror as they told me they were in love, about their plans for Daniel to 'put the Royal College of Music thing on hold' so he could follow Sasha to Manchester the following autumn. This couldn't happen. Daniel was so talented, he had a real chance at a career, but if he threw it all in for a ridiculous infatuation, he'd never be able to get it back. It would be too late. I had to think quickly. If I'd had more time, I might have come up with something less devastating, but as it was,

I seized on the idea that came to me as if it were divine inspiration. I'll never forget the looks on their faces, the way the colour drained from them. As soon as I'd said it, I half-regretted it, and later, of course, I would have cut my own arm off to take it back, but it was too late. It was done. It is done, and I do a reasonable job most of the time of keeping it at arm's length. But up here, among the relics of the past, it's not so easy to stop the memories from crowding in. I never told Tony about Daniel and Sasha, thinking it a burden best borne alone.

There's one more scrapbook in the box. I lift it out gingerly. It feels slimmer, less bulky than the first one, and I am relieved to see when I flick through the pages that at least there are no photos in it, only writing. I read a sentence at random: *She's taunting me, the way she flaunts her body. She pretends it's not for me, but she knows I am watching her.* Oh God. I turn the page. *He's been inside her, I can tell. Why does he get everything I want? When will it be my turn?*

I think of Ellen, pleading with me to tell her anything that might help her to find Sasha. Should I show her these? Do they actually change anything, these teenage yearnings of Daniel's from so long ago? No. Best to put them back in their boxes. Pretend I never found them. I go to put the book back in the box but something is pulling at me, something that isn't right. I open the scrapbook again, the one with the writing in it, and look at it while trying not to read the words, unable to bear it. I skim read back and forth over the pages, and then I stop, the blood freezing in my veins. I am a mother: I know my children's handwriting. This is not Daniel's writing. This book belongs to Nicholas.

In a daze, I reach for my phone in my pocket and fire out a quick text. As I press send, I hear someone coming up the ladder behind me. I turn and see a head sticking up through the loft hatch.

'Hello, Mum,' he says.

Ellen

September 2017

Karina won't answer. I keep ringing and ringing, trying to wear her down, but it goes to voicemail every time. It's not even personalised, just a mechanical voice telling me to leave a message. She doesn't want to talk to me, and I wonder if it's for fear of what she might say, the secrets that might spew out of her like a dam bursting.

It's after 10 p.m. on a Friday, which seems a crazy time to go out, but I need answers and I can't wait a minute longer for them. I make the journey once more round the South Circular. I keep the doors locked and daren't open the windows. Someone tried to get into Rachel's car once when she was stopped at the traffic lights. She saw what he was doing and managed to lock the doors milliseconds before his hand reached the handle of the passenger door. Sometimes I worry about what would happen if I had an accident: would they be able to get me out with the doors locked? It always comes back to how I feel, though, and with the doors unlocked or the windows open, I don't feel safe.

I step out into the cool air, pulling my skirt away where it has stuck to the damp skin on the back of my legs. Karina's house looks back at me blankly in the darkness, daring me to ask the questions I am afraid to hear the answers to.

I ring the bell and wait. There are no footsteps, no shape looming through the frosted glass panels on the door. A dog barks inside the neighbour's house, a fierce yapping that would drive me mad if I had to listen to it all day. I know she's in; she just doesn't want to answer the door. I try the bell again, but still nothing, so I lean down and pull open the flap on the letterbox.

'Karina! It's Ellen!'

The dog next door goes crazy at this, jumping up against its own front door, its claws scraping the paint-work, but there's still no movement in Karina's house.

'I know you're in there,' I call through the bristles in the letterbox. 'I just want to talk to you.'

The door flies open and I nearly fall through it.

'Oh, for God's sake, come in then,' Karina hisses, pulling me in and slamming the door shut behind me. In the gloom of the poorly lit hallway I can see that she's still wearing her party clothes. 'Quick, come through to the back. Maybe he didn't see you.' She grabs my arm and leads me past the door to the front room, half-empty glasses from the party still sitting forlornly on the coffee table, through to the kitchen at the back of the house. All

327

the lights are off apart from the light in the oven hood, which casts a dim glow.

'Who? Daniel?'

She sits down at the small formica table in the corner and, without speaking, gestures for me to do the same.

'You think Daniel's watching the house?'

She shrugs in the silence.

'Where's your mum?'

'She's asleep. Why have you come back? What do you want, Ellen?'

'I want you to tell me the truth,' I say simply.

She flakes a small piece of dried food off the table with her thumbnail. 'I already have.'

'I don't think so. Please, Karina. Help me find Sasha.'

'You'll never find her. I doubt she wants to be found.'

'What? What do you mean?' I am getting closer to the truth now; it's a shadow over me, cold but intangible.

'Nothing.' The shutters clang down again. 'You wouldn't understand.'

'I think I might, a bit,' I say cautiously.

She looks at me blankly.

'I've seen Daniel,' I go on.

'What? Where?' She pales further, throwing the red patches of skin around her eyes into stark relief.

'He was in my flat when I got back from your party earlier.'

'What did he want?' Her hands are clenched and shaking in front of her on the table.

'I know it's hard for you, Karina, to have all this raked up again, and I'm sorry to be the one to do it.'

'What did he say to you?'

'He said ... that you weren't telling the truth ... at the trial.' I hate having to use these words, words that cast doubt on her experience. If Daniel is lying, I am siding with a world that thinks it's a woman's own fault if she gets raped, a world that doesn't believe a woman even when she has the scars to prove she has been hurt. A world that prefers to place the burden of proving rape on the victim rather than that of proving otherwise on the supposed perpetrator.

She remains silent.

'Karina, I'm not going to judge you.' Even as I say this, I don't know how true it is. We all make judgements, all the time. We judge the girl who was silly enough to walk home alone in a short skirt; we judge the girl who got drunk and into bed with someone she didn't know and then changed her mind; we judge the girl who kissed a famous footballer twice her age and complained when he stuck his hand in her knickers. We do all this as if the men in question had no choice in the matter, no control over their own actions, no responsibility.

'You will,' she says, looking down at the table. 'You won't be able to help it.'

'What about Olivia and Tony? Tony's dying, Karina. Are you going to let him go to his grave without telling him the truth?' She looks up. I sense a chink in her armour and press my advantage. 'Let's go there now, to the corner house. Tell us all what you know. You should have seen them, Karina. They're broken.'

'What I've got to say won't help them.' She's shutting down again.

'It'll be the truth, though, won't it? That's got to be better, in the long run. Please, Karina.'

'I can't.' She speaks so quietly I can barely hear her.

'I'll ring Daniel then, shall I? Get him round here, see what you've got to say to him?' I hate myself for attacking her like this, but I don't know how else to break through.

'No!' She pushes her chair back, the legs scraping on the floor.

'Then let's go and see Olivia and Tony. I know it's late, but I don't think they'll mind.' I never knew them to go to bed before midnight back in the old days.

'All right,' she says, and behind the reluctance, there's a note of something else, something I can't identify. Is it possible that she still feels the pull of the Monktons, even now?

'Come on,' I say, standing up. 'We can go in my car.'

In the hall, Karina pulls on a wool coat, gone bobbly with age, and zips up a pair of ancient boots with scuffed toes. We don't speak in the car. She sits huddled with her coat pulled tight around her, like a security blanket. We park a few doors down, and she looks at her old house opposite, her expression unreadable. In the orange glow of the streetlamps we make our way up the path. The front door is ajar, but I ring the bell anyway. Nobody comes.

'Shall we ...?' I say, gesturing to the open door.

I push the door further open and peer into the gloom of the hallway. There's a faint sound of voices in the kitchen, but the door is shut so I can't make out the words, or who is in there.

'Hello?' I call.

'Let's go,' says Karina impulsively. 'This doesn't feel right.'

'Look, Karina,' I say impatiently, 'if you're scared of Daniel, of what he might do to you, I don't think you need to be. He doesn't want to hurt you. He just wants you to tell the truth.'

She grabs my arm, her face glowing white in the half-light.

'It's not Daniel I'm scared of,' she says.

'Well, you've got nothing to fear from Olivia and Tony,' I say impatiently. 'Come on.' I pull her in by the arm, down the hall to the kitchen.

We hear a man's voice saying, 'Please, Mum. You have to understand,' and Karina tries to pull her arm from my grasp, but I won't let go, throwing the kitchen door open.

First I see Olivia, seated at the head of the table, her hair loose and tangled, staring at us in horror. She looks up to her right, so I follow her gaze and there is Nicholas, haggard and wild-eyed.

'Don't come in!' Olivia half-rises from the table, but Nicholas pushes her roughly back down into the chair.

I look from Olivia to him and back again in confusion.

'*Go*,' she says urgently.

I take an uncertain step back, but Nicholas grabs wildly for something from a wooden block on the side, and then there's a knife in his hand and he's holding it to Olivia's throat. She gives a small, strangled cry.

'No. Don't go,' Nicholas says to me and Karina, sweat glistening on his forehead. 'Stay exactly where you are.'

Karina

December 2006

I wasn't going to go to the party. I knew I shouldn't, knew it was stupid. If only I hadn't, how different things might have been. At 7.30 p.m. I was still lying on my bed in jeans and a T-shirt, but suddenly something propelled me from the bed, as if I'd been given an electric shock. Defiance pulsed through me. Why should Nicholas stop me from going to a party I'd been looking forward to for weeks? I wriggled into the sparkly dress I'd bought specially, holding it away from the raw spot on my back, the one I'd been trying not to think about.

I rummaged in the back of my wardrobe for the bottle of vodka I'd been keeping there and took a few swigs while I applied my make-up. By the time I left the house, I'd drunk half of it. It made it easier to ring the bell, and when I saw some girls from school in the piano room, I joined them. By the time I saw Nicholas, when I came out of Sasha's room to get another drink, I'd almost convinced myself it was going to be all right. He chatted to me normally as we walked down the landing away from Sasha's room, while we were in earshot. But as soon as we were on the stairs, he gripped my arm, his fingers like iron.

'Don't think I've forgotten, Karina,' he whispered. 'Don't think you've got away with it.' He released my arm and slipped his hand around my waist. 'About *here*, isn't it?' he said, pushing hard against the exact spot where he had pressed the glowing tip of his cigarette just a few days before. I gasped in pain. 'Yes, that's the sort of noise I want to hear you making,' he said into my ear as we reached the bottom of the stairs. He removed his arm and moved away from me into the piano room.

I was filled with a certainty that I'd made a huge mistake coming here. I needed to go home. There was a tiny, silly, scared part of me that wanted to tell Mum all about it, and I half thought I might if I left now. But I'd done that once before when it was Dad who was hurting me, coming into my room at night, slipping his hands under the covers, telling me it was our little secret, and she hadn't believed me then. She'd told me not to be so silly, and when I told the teachers, she made me take it back, say I was making it up for attention. Why would she believe me now?

I rummaged through the pegs, trying to find my coat. Every time I thought I'd got it, it turned out to be someone else's black jacket, and I gave a little sob of frustration.

'Hey, what's the matter?'

Daniel put a tentative hand on my back. I flinched and he snatched it back. 'Sorry.'

'It's OK.' I sniffed. 'I just wanted to get some air. I'm looking for my jacket but I can't find it.' I dissolved into stupid, unwanted tears.

'Don't cry, Karina, come on. Right, stay here, don't move.' He returned a moment later with a wodge of toilet roll.

I blew my nose. 'Why are you being so nice to me?'

'I'm just a nice guy, I guess.' He smiled. 'Plus ... I'm not feeling so great myself tonight. I need something to distract me.'

I didn't tell him what was really wrong, of course. I just said I'd had a bit too much to drink. We stood there by the coats and talked and talked. He got me some water, and after a while, he took my hand and started to stroke it. It felt so nice I started to cry again, so he got me some more toilet roll, and then he put his hand gently on my hair and told me everything was OK. I drank some more wine then, and so did he, and I wondered why I'd never seen how lovely he was before. I don't know if Nicholas saw us talking – I didn't see him go past, although he was there in the back of my mind, the fear of what he would do to me hovering like a black angel of death waiting to strike. Then Daniel leaned forward. I could have stopped him, I should have stopped him, but the wine was making my head swim in a delicious, hazy sort of way, and there was a stinging on my back where the fabric of my dress kept catching on the sore spot, and I thought:

fuck it. Fuck Nicholas. I closed my eyes and I kissed Daniel and it was amazing, and after a while I let him lead me upstairs, because it was better if nobody saw us.

Somebody did see us, though. I slipped across to the bathroom after we'd finished, and as I made my way dreamily along the landing to meet Daniel downstairs, as we'd agreed, Nicholas's door flew open and he dragged me inside. Before I even had time to register what was happening, he had pushed me back on to the bed, all the breath knocked out of me.

'Slut,' he hissed, looming over me. 'I saw you going upstairs with him. My fucking, sainted brother. The musical prodigy. The golden child. First Sasha, and now you. Why does everybody choose him?' I stifled a sob.

'It's too late for tears, Karina,' he said.

'I don't want to do this any more,' I whispered.

'It's not up to you,' he said, lying down on top of me, squashing me so I struggled to breathe. There was a slick of sweat across his face, his breath hot and sickly-sweet in mine. 'What was he like, my brother? What did he do to you? Did he make you scream like I do?'

I stared at the damp spot in the corner of the ceiling, but he grabbed me by the chin and kissed me violently, his tongue large and clumsy, a slug inside my mouth. I couldn't believe I had ever thought I wanted this. I closed my eyes, waiting for whatever was to come next, but then the pressure on my mouth decreased, and he drew back, looking at me thoughtfully. He rolled off me and lay on his back on the bed. I lay motionless, silent.

'Did he use a condom?' he asked.

'No.' Nicholas had insisted I went on the pill when things started between us.

'Is he drinking beer? Are there bottles in his room?'

'Yes.' The room where he had touched me so gently I could hardly feel it.

Nicholas was silent again. 'Is he still in there?'

'No. He said he'd see me downstairs.' He's probably down there now, waiting for me.

'I've noticed recently,' he said, 'that you don't feel the same as you used to. I think you're tired of me, Karina. I think you're scared of me.'

'No,' I whispered.

'Don't lie to me. You are.'

I kept quiet, not knowing what the right answer was.

'There is a way, though. If you do something for me, Karina, I'll leave you alone for ever. I'll delete all the video footage. I'll never ... bother you again.'

I kept my eyes on the damp spot, but my heart was beating faster. I'd do anything, anything at all. I vowed to myself that whatever it was, however hard it was, whatever the consequences, I would do it.

A couple of minutes later, I slipped into Daniel's room and grabbed one of the bottles from the bedside table, averting my eyes from the bed. I took his towel where it was hanging on the back of the door and picked a T-shirt from the wardrobe at random. Back in Nicholas's room, he folded the towel carefully in half and laid it on the bed. I pulled my tights down to my knees, and lay on it, thighs apart. There was a crash and the jagged bottom half of a broken beer bottle glinted in the light. I felt Nicholas's hand on my leg, and then a slicing, shooting pain that made me gasp, and blood running down my thigh. I bit my lip in an effort not to cry out as he sliced into my other thigh and held the T-shirt between my legs for a moment, soaking up the worst of the blood. He gestured to me to pull my tights back up, wrapped the broken bottle in the T-shirt and the whole lot in the towel, then handed it to me. Numbly, I stumbled back into Daniel's room and hid the bundle at the back of the wardrobe.

I vaguely registered Ellen's worried glance as I passed her. I opened the back door and the cold crashed over me like a wave, like relief. My tights were soaked with blood as I sank down, freezing rain dripping on me from the leaves of the mulberry tree, the ground like iron beneath me.

I remember the mascara streaks on Ellen's face as she crouched down and put her arms around me, rocking me as if I was a child. I remember the kindly woman officer, the scratchy blanket she put around me, the swabs. Every time I thought about telling the truth, I reached around and pressed a finger to the raw spot on my back. The funny thing was, the longer it went on, the easier it got, and the harder it would have been to turn back anyway.

By the time I was in court, it hardly felt like I was lying at all.

Ellen

September 2017

A strange sense of something like calm, although it's probably closer to paralysis, has fallen over me. I flick a quick look at Karina beside me in the doorway, and although she's frightened, I don't see any surprise there, and in that moment I understand that she knew it was going to be Nicholas. She never thought Daniel was watching the house. It's not Daniel she is scared of. My brain struggles to catch up, reaching for strands that disappear as soon as I grasp them.

'Sit down,' Nicholas says, somehow short of breath, although he's barely moved from the spot since we got here.

We both hesitate. Should we try and run? What about Olivia?

'Sit down!' he says, more of a sob than a command, but the knife inches even closer to Olivia's exposed throat and she gives an involuntary whimper.

We step forward simultaneously and take our seats on

the near side of the table, next to each other. I'd like to take Karina's hand, to gain some kind of cold comfort, but I'm afraid of drawing attention to myself. Perhaps if I sit still enough, am quiet enough, I will disappear.

Nicholas looks from one to the other of us, the knife still hovering dangerously close to Olivia's neck. Her eyes are bloodshot and she looks grey and tired, her breathing laboured.

'What are you doing here? You're not supposed to be here,' he says, and there's fear in his voice as if events are spiralling out of his control.

I am silent, transfixed by the shining blade, desperate to give the right answer but with no idea of what that might be. It's Karina that speaks.

'We're here to tell the truth,' she says, very low. 'I owe Olivia and Tony that.'

'Well, for a start, *Tony's* not here,' says Nicholas. 'He's in the pub, as usual. Found some private members' club where they let him drink till the early hours, hasn't he, Mum? Where they don't care if it's killing him.'

'Don't speak about him like that.' It's the first time Olivia has spoken. 'After what you've done, how *dare* you?'

'What about her?' Nicholas ignores Olivia and points the knife in my direction. 'What's she doing here? Poking her nose in again.'

'Ellen doesn't know anything.' Karina speaks quickly. I can tell she's trying to sound calm, reassuring, but she doesn't have enough breath and her words end in a gasp.

She swallows, hard. 'I haven't told her. I said I wouldn't tell, and I meant it. Let her go. This has got nothing to do with her.'

'She's been asking questions, though.' Nicholas sounds panicked. 'Why did she have to go rummaging around? Why couldn't she stay out of it?'

'I just want to find Sasha,' I say. 'That's all. I don't care about ... anything else.' I don't know what it is that he doesn't want me to know. 'I'm not interested in the past.'

'Ha! Not interested in it! You're fucking obsessed by it! Still living with Sasha, or living off her, I should say. Still hanging off her every word.'

I daren't speak, terrified of what he might do if I say the wrong thing, whatever that is. I have no idea what he wants, how to play this. Does Karina? I risk a glance at her, but she is looking at Nicholas, her eyes dark bruises in her white face.

'And you,' he says to Karina despairingly. 'Going around, mouthing off about it. With Sasha gone and Daniel hanging around the place, stirring things up, it's too dangerous.'

'It's over, Nicholas,' says Karina. 'I've had enough of lying. But let Ellen go, please.'

'Karina's right,' Olivia croaks. 'Ellen came to see me, asking about Sasha. That's what she's interested in: finding Sasha. She doesn't care about you.'

'I can't. It's too late.' But the hand holding the knife drops to his side and he looks uncertain.

'You can,' urges Karina. 'Just let her go.'

341

'No. She'll go to Daniel, she'll tell him everything.'

'She doesn't know. I swear,' says Karina, leaning forward in her chair.

'Daniel doesn't deserve the truth,' he says, half to himself. 'He's been gone all this time, off doing God knows what. I'm the one who's been here. I've been the real son.'

Olivia goes to speak, but Karina shoots her a warning look and breaks in.

'That's right,' she says. 'You've been a good son. Hasn't he?' She looks hard at Olivia.

'Yes,' she agrees weakly, closing her eyes.

Nicholas sits down opposite us at the table, knife in hand, the patriarch about to carve the Sunday roast.

'It was all Sasha's fault,' he says. 'You two know, don't you?' he says to me and Karina. 'You were in love with her too, in your own way. Who wouldn't be? But she chose Daniel. Of course. Like everyone always chooses him. I saw them together, before anybody knew there was even anything to see. Mum tried to stop them once. Sasha ran off to France, didn't she?' He turns back to Olivia. 'I bet you thought that was it. But they were soon back at it. So you tried again, that New Year's Eve, didn't you, Mum?' Olivia is staring at him, horror-struck. Karina tenses beside me, as if her whole body is clenching in protest, but she says nothing.

'I couldn't hear exactly what you said to Daniel, Mum, but whatever it was, he was in the perfect mood for some meaningless sex with anyone desperate enough to shag him.' He waves the knife in Karina's direction. I flinch, but Karina is made of stone. 'It seemed like too good an opportunity to pass up. Keep Daniel away from Sasha – and get him out of the picture once and for all.'

My mind scrabbles around, trying to pick up the broken pieces of what I thought I knew. Olivia had known that Daniel and Sasha were in love. Daniel didn't rape Karina. Nicholas was . . . I don't know, I don't know.

'It was easy, in the end, just like you,' he says to Karina. 'So easy for you to lie, to let Daniel go to prison. Don't tell me it was just to get me off your back,' he says disgustedly. 'You wanted to punish Sasha, didn't you? That's why you slept with Daniel in the first place. You knew she was in love with him. You were always jealous. And when I gave you the chance to make things even worse for her, you couldn't resist.'

'No,' she says, the word bursting from her. 'I did it because I was frightened of you, not to hurt Sasha. It was the only way I could get you to leave me alone, and you know it. That's how bad it was, that's how frightened of him I was.' I realise she is talking to me and Olivia now, not to Nicholas but about him. 'At first, I was flattered. I thought I was in love with him. But then he started to do things to me, things I didn't like. He hurt me. I tried to stop it but he just hurt me more. He wouldn't stop. I was so frightened of him. And he'd taken videos, said he'd show everyone. I was trapped. You have to understand.'

Olivia looks at her, greyer than ever. 'So you were lying?' she whispers. 'Daniel didn't rape you?'

343

Karina shakes her head, tears in her eyes. 'I'm sorry,' she whispers. 'My dad, and then Nicholas ...'

'Your father?' says Olivia, horrified. 'Not ... what they said at the trial?'

'Enough!' Nicholas bangs the handle of the knife on the table. 'Don't start spinning a sob story, Karina. You're as much to blame as I am.'

'I know,' she says, stronger now. 'And I'll never forgive myself. Never.'

'Mum, I'm sorry you had to find that ... stuff in the loft, but I didn't have anywhere else to store it. I wish I hadn't had to involve you, but you should be thanking me, really.' His lack of self-awareness is chilling. 'I was the only one who could put a stop to Daniel and Sasha, and that was what you wanted, wasn't it?' He looks proudly at Olivia, as if seeking approval.

'Not like this,' she says.

I will her to play along, to keep him happy, and then maybe he will let us go, but I sense a gathering storm.

'I never wanted this. How could you let me believe those terrible things about Daniel? It destroyed me.'

'What, your perfect son?' says Nicholas, his grip tightening on the knife handle. My heart sinks. 'Your golden boy? The concert pianist, the Royal College of Music star, the boy destined for a glittering musical career? That last bit didn't quite go to plan, did it? Oops.' He gives a weird half-smile. 'Even now, he's worming his way back in, isn't he? I can't believe you've seen him, let him come here.'

'I'm glad I did,' says Olivia defiantly. 'I was right, wasn't I? Look what you've done.'

'But you let him in before you found my stuff in the loft,' says Nicholas. 'You were letting him back in anyway, Mum. Why would you do that?'

'Because I love him. He's my son.'

'Your favourite,' Nicholas says dully. 'Always your favourite.'

'Yes,' says Olivia, and I can tell she has gone beyond caring what happens to us, into a place where she can only tell the truth. 'Yes, he was my favourite. He was so much easier to love than you. He had so much going for him. I had to accept the court's judgement, but I knew in my heart that he could never have done what they said he had. I wish to God I had listened to my instincts.'

'No!' Nicholas pushes back his chair and it clatters to the floor. 'Don't say that! I've been here for you, I've visited, and helped you out, and looked after Dad. What has he done?'

'He's been in prison!' shouts Olivia, getting to her feet too. 'And it was your fault! He should never have been there; it should have been you. I wish it had been you.'

For a terrible second, I think he is going to raise the knife and slash her, but instead he rushes from the room, slamming the kitchen door behind him. The three of us look at each other in panicked incomprehension, and then there is an almighty crash. We are suspended, motionless, for a second, and then Karina runs to the door and pushes against it. It opens a crack and then stops.

'He's pushed the bookcase over,' she says. 'Help me!'

Olivia and I join her and the three of us push together, but it's no good. We can't shift the bookcase, which, as well as being full of books, is six-foot high and solid oak. There's no sound from outside the door.

'He's not there,' says Karina. 'What's he doing?'

We stand behind the door, looking at each other helplessly. And then we hear it: liquid being sloshed around, the rasp of a match and the hiss as it flares into life.

'The garage,' says Olivia in horror. 'There's petrol in there.'

There's a bang as Nicholas closes the front door behind him. A crackle as the flames find something wooden and flammable. Karina puts a trembling hand to the door and then draws it back in terror, staring at the palm of her hand, transfixed. Smoke begins to seep under the door. It seems we are all going to stand here in a trance, and calmly let him burn us to death, when something jolts in me.

'The window!' I say, hurrying over to it.

'It's painted shut,' says Olivia. 'We've been meaning to do something about it, but . . . '

'It's been like that for years!' I explode into anger. 'For God's sake, Olivia. Are there any tools in here?'

She looks around vaguely and shakes her head. I run to the dresser and pull open the drawers, flinging the doors open, looking for something, anything. There are some rusty metal skewers and I grab one in hopeless desperation, running to the window and trying to prise

346

it into the painted cracks between the window and the casing. It's utterly futile, but I can't stand here and wait to burn to death. Olivia sinks down at the table and starts to cough from the smoke.

'Put this round your mouth and nose.' Karina springs into life, shoving a tea towel into Olivia's shaking hands. Olivia looks down at it as if she has no idea what it is. 'To protect you from the smoke,' Karina says more softly. 'Here. Let me do it.' She ties it as best she can over the bottom half of Olivia's face.

'It's all my fault,' Olivia says, her voice muffled, as I grab kitchen implements at random and try to force the window open.

'No, Olivia, it's not,' says Karina distractedly. 'It's mine. Break the window. Shout,' she says to me.

I grab the heaviest pot I can see from inside the dresser and heave it up to shoulder level. The window has small panes of glass, each about six inches square. I slam the side of the casserole dish into one of them but it doesn't break. The smoke is getting thicker and the heat is rising. Sweat drenches me and every muscle is clenched.

'Again,' gasps Karina.

'I lied to them. I told them Sasha was Tony's daughter.' Olivia speaks again from beneath her mask. 'I told them they were half-brother and sister.' Her eyes are streaming and she stares dully at the tabletop.

Karina and I gape at her for a second, then Karina remembers herself. 'Again!' she shouts at me.

I heave the pot up and smash it against the glass. This

time a crack appears. I lift it again. The muscles in my arms are in screaming agony but I gather every bit of strength I have and launch it once more at the window-pane. This time there is a cracking and splintering, and a jagged hole appears in the pane. I grab a stone pestle from beside me, one of the previous implements I had tried, and smash out all the glass. I start shouting for help and Karina runs over to join me, our screams shrill and terrified. The kitchen is at the back of the house, so it's unlikely we will be heard from the street, even if some-one is passing by.

'Shhh.' Karina puts a hand on my arm. 'What was that?'

We are silent, but all I can hear, apart from the crackle of the flames on the other side of the door, is the faint sound of traffic from the main road. We start to shout again, but the smoke is getting thicker, making our eyes smart and our voices hoarse, and it's becoming even harder to make ourselves heard.

Out of nowhere, a face looms up at the window. For a second I think it's Nicholas and I jump back, a scream shredding my throat, but it's Daniel, staring horrified through the broken pane at Karina and me, wild-eyed and dishevelled, and Olivia, catatonic and masked at the table.

'Oh my God, Daniel,' I pant. 'You have to get us out of here. Nicholas has pushed the bookcase in front of the door and set the house on fire. We're trapped.'

'Fuck.' He's standing there, staring at us. We have all

played a part in the car crash that has been his life up to this point, and I know he's thinking he could walk away. I may not have lied, like Sasha and Karina, like Olivia, but the defence barrister was right. I couldn't hear who was in Daniel's room with Karina that day, and it's perfectly clear now that it was Nicholas. Did it give him a thrill, taking her into his despised brother's room?

'Please,' I say, holding his gaze. 'Please, Daniel. We're going to die in here. We'll do whatever you want. Please help us.'

He doesn't speak, just turns his back and walks away. I sink to the floor and let my head fall to my knees. It's over. Karina is crying uncontrollably and coughing beside me. I close my eyes against the sting of the smoke. My chest is burning and I try to take shallow breaths because it hurts less. My head is spinning now and everything is blurry.

There's a *thwack*, then the sound of breaking glass and splintering wood. Tiny shards of glass rain down on my head. I put my hand to my hair and brush some of them off. They stick in my fingers, beads of blood blooming from them.

'Get out of the way,' shouts Daniel from outside.

I crawl across the floor, just in time for another assault against the window. More glass flies into the room and I can see that he has an axe. I remember it. Tony used to buy logs from a local supplier and chop them himself for the wood burner. Daniel hacks and hacks, and finally the window splits from the frame and swings inwards, years and layers of paint sprinkling in fragments across the floor.

'Olivia,' I say. She is slumped down on the table, her head at an awkward angle, arms hanging by her side. 'Shit. Karina, help me.'

Karina coughs and crawls towards us. She tries to haul herself up using the table, but collapses to the floor, barely able to breathe. I look towards the window and Daniel's already on his way in. He grabs Olivia under the arms and starts pulling her across the room. I take her feet and help as much as I can. When he reaches the window, he props her up and climbs out, gesturing to me to lift her up to him. Somehow, between us, we manage to haul her out. Daniel drags her away from the house and lays her on the grass. Karina is crawling towards the window now. She's nearly here and Daniel is on his way back.

'Get out, Ellen,' he shouts. 'I'll help Karina.'

I hover in an agony of indecision. Of course he rescued Olivia: she's his mother. But Karina? The girl who has lied and lied again, ruining any chance of a normal life for him?

'Get out,' he shouts again. 'Fuck's sake, I'm not going to let her die.'

He helps me out of the window and springs easily in for Karina. I stand outside the window, waiting, and help him to get her over the sill and on to the grass. We pull her down the garden to where Olivia lies slumped under the mulberry tree.

A moment later, there's a crash from the kitchen and a tongue of fire leaps from the window we have just escaped from, licking the wall outside. As Daniel calls the fire brigade, the three of us stare in dazed horror as the corner house is engulfed in flames.

Ellen

September 2017

Leo wanted to come to the flat, but something in me
didn't want to be alone with him in a confined space.
We've arranged to meet at a coffee shop near my parents'
house. Near the Monktons'. I haven't seen the corner
house since we were driven away in an ambulance a
week ago, smoke in our lungs, exhausted, numb. He is
there before me, sitting at a corner table, a barely touched
coffee in front of him. He jumps up when I come in and
goes to hug me. I stand unresponsive in his arms and he
steps back.

'I heard what happened,' he says. 'Are you OK?'

I sit down, and he retakes his seat opposite me.

'I'm not sure,' I say. 'I've been through this massive,
traumatic thing, which should have been the end, but
I'm no closer to knowing what's happened to Sasha.
Nicholas swears he doesn't know where she is, hasn't
seen her for years, and I think he might be telling the
truth. It's Daniel he's obsessed with really, more than

Sasha. Thank God Olivia texted Daniel when she found Nicholas's stuff in the loft, otherwise we never would have made it out alive. Nicholas was just sitting there, you know. In his flat. He'd gone back there after starting the fire and waited for the police. Didn't even put up a struggle.'

'I can't believe it, Ellen. Nicholas and I were friends. We were pretty close back then. How could I not have seen what was going on?'

'Nobody did. Even Daniel had no idea. Nicholas was always competitive with him, used to make snide comments about his musical talent, but as far as Daniel was concerned, it was normal sibling rivalry stuff. He didn't have a clue what was really going on in Nicholas's head. He was horrified when Olivia told him the whole story.'

'I knew they had a bit of a difficult relationship, but I had no idea Nicholas was so jealous of Daniel, so angry. As for Karina, what she did ... ' He shakes his head in disgust.

'You don't know ... ' There's so much I want to say, but it's not my story to tell. It's an age-old story, one of a little girl whose father did things no father should do; a little girl who sometimes, secretly, wished her father would die, and then one day he did and she thought it was her fault. A girl who was so ripe for exploitation, for ill-treatment, that Nicholas didn't even have to try that hard.

'And Sasha, she must have lied at the trial. She can't have seen them together that day, can she? If it was Nicholas that Karina was seeing, not Daniel?'

'I don't know. I suppose she did. She was . . .' I hesitate. This is not my story to tell either, but now I realise how little I know Sasha, it hardly seems to matter. Daniel matters, but I don't think he'll mind what I say as long as it's the truth. 'Daniel and Sasha were in love. They'd split up the day of the New Year's Eve party. Olivia didn't want them to be together, so she lied to them. She told them Sasha was Tony's daughter, that they were half-brother and sister.'

'Jesus! That's so messed up. Do you think Sasha believed that Daniel raped Karina, and was lying to support her?'

'I honestly don't know.' God, I wish I did. If she genuinely believed Daniel had raped Karina, maybe her lie was understandable, if not forgivable. Although if she believed that, then did she also believe that Daniel had been cheating on her with Karina for three months? In which case, was this her twisted way of taking revenge? Or if she didn't believe that Daniel raped Karina, was her lie to punish him for sleeping with Karina the day she split up with him? Either way, she's a monster.'

'What about you, Ellen? You lied too, didn't you?'

'No!' An elderly woman at the next table looks round in alarm. 'No,' I say again in a low voice. 'I heard them. I heard Karina. They were in Daniel's room.'

'But it wasn't Daniel.'

'No, but I swear to God I thought it was. If I'd had any doubt, if I'd thought for a second it could have been Nicholas, I would never have testified.'

'So what exactly did Karina tell Sasha when they met in the bar that day?'

'Karina saw Daniel in the street and panicked. She was terrified that he was back to take his revenge on her for lying. She knew Sasha had lied at the trial too, so she was the only person Karina felt she could talk to about it. She looked Sasha up online, found out where she worked and waited for her outside. Karina told her Daniel was back, and she also confessed that she had lied at the trial. She didn't tell her about Nicholas, though. She was still too frightened of what he might do.'

'I just can't reconcile the Nicholas I knew with what he's done,' says Leo.

I shudder. 'I can. You should have seen him. And the stuff Olivia found in the attic ... He'd taken naked photos of Sasha when she was asleep, he'd taken her knickers from her room. It must have been him that moved stuff around in her room as well. I guess he took the money from Olivia's bag, hoping Daniel would get the blame, or Sasha, maybe.'

'It's so twisted,' Leo says. 'You must have been terrified.'

'Mmm.' I can't talk about the fire, not yet. 'He broke in to my flat, too, last week. The police said he admitted it. He must have taken the key when he was there the first time, and come back in the night looking for some clue as to where Sasha had gone. He thought Karina had told her the whole truth. He thought she knew what he'd done; he was desperate to find her.' There must have been a part of him, too, that wanted to frighten me, to stop me dragging the past into the light. I'm silent, my mind a jumble of past and present. 'I've got to go, Leo. I'm meeting Daniel at the corner house. He's staying there to look after the place for a while, until it's properly secured and the renovation work has started. Olivia and Tony are staying with friends. I can't blame them.'

'Before you go, Ellen ... ' He stops, smoothing one finger up and down the handle of his cup. I wait.

'I'm sorry, about sleeping with Sasha.'

Oh, that. 'It hardly matters now. I'm honestly not bothered. You were right, I had no business having a go at you about it.'

'I know, but still ... She probably knew it would upset you. I think ... that's partly why she did it, in her own twisted way.'

'What do you mean?' I'm genuinely curious, no longer burning with indignation every time somebody says something bad about her.

'She's jealous of you. Always has been.'

'Why on earth would she be jealous of me?' She was the one with all the admirers, all the hangers-on. The life and soul of the party.

'You had the real relationships, Ellen. She might have had the glamour, the surface popularity, but you had proper, strong bonds – with Karina, with me, with your own family. Even Olivia was closer to you than she was to Sasha. She needed you more than you realise.'

I think of the way she played Karina and me off against

each other, and more recently, Rachel and me, each taking it in turns to be her confidante, her special one.

'Maybe,' I say. But if that's true, then where is she now?

We leave the café together and I watch him walk off in the other direction. He's just gone round the corner out of sight, when something strikes me, and I get a wave of goosebumps down my neck. How does Leo know that Karina and Sasha met in the bar? I didn't tell him. Has he seen Sasha more than he let on? In which case, why is he lying to me?

I stare after him with a growing sense of unease. I still don't have the answers I want. I'm still facing the prospect of returning to an empty flat after I've got this meeting with Daniel out of the way. I take a deep breath. I have to deal with Daniel first. We didn't really speak after the fire – it was a blur of fire engines and police cars and hospitals – but I can't avoid him any longer. I need to apologise, even if it doesn't – can't – make any difference.

The front door is ajar, as it was a week ago. I stand outside once again, suddenly apprehensive. Nicholas is in police custody; he can't hurt me. And yet I linger on the threshold, unable to go into the house that was once the epicentre of my hopes and dreams. The front left-hand side of the house, with the piano room, is largely, miraculously undamaged, but on the right it is ruined – blackened and ghostly.

Footsteps crunch on glass inside, the door is pulled open, and there is Daniel. It's odd to see him and not feel afraid. He's been a sort of bogeyman in my head for all these years, and it's hard to rid myself of that mindset.

'Come in,' he says. 'Careful of the glass. I'm leaving the front door ajar to try and get rid of the smell. Is that OK?'

I nod.

'We'll go in here.' He indicates the piano room on my left. 'There's no damage.'

I go ahead of him. The piano is still there, the sofas are the same old blue velvet, there are books everywhere. It's like stepping back in time, if it wasn't for the acrid stench of smoke. He sits on the armchair and I take my place opposite him on the sofa.

'I'm sorry,' I say, before he has a chance to say anything. 'I know it doesn't change anything, maybe it doesn't even mean anything, but it's true. If I had thought for a second that Karina was lying, I would never ... I could have sworn it was you in your bedroom with her that day before Christmas. I was so sure.'

'I know,' he says. 'I believe you were telling the truth as you thought it was. I believe you thought you were doing the right thing. I don't know why Nicholas took her into my room that day. I guess it was part of his weird ... I don't know.' He looks down. 'I still can't believe what he did to me. I can't believe I couldn't see it, how jealous he was of me. He must have hated me so much, to do that to me. What did I do to him?'

'Nothing!' I say. 'You can't blame yourself, Daniel.'

Still looking down, he says in a rush, 'Ellen, do you know where she is?'

'No! I want to know as much as you do. I just met Leo, actually.'

'Leo Smith?' He looks up.

'Yeah. He met up with Sasha recently. They ... well, they slept together.'

'Jesus Christ.'

'I know. I got the feeling today that ... maybe he knows something, but I'm not sure any more. I don't trust my feelings. I don't trust anyone.'

'Join the club,' he says grimly.

We hear the click of the gate outside. 'Oh, that'll be Karina,' I say. 'I hope you don't mind. She wanted to see you too, to apologise, and to thank you for what you did, in the fire.'

He stands up and strides towards the door, and I'm scared I've made a huge mistake. I didn't lie and he knows that, but Karina did. I take a step after him and go to take another, but I don't take it, because she's there in the room, smiling at me. My knees buckle. I reach out to grab onto something but there's nothing there, and I am falling, the world going black around me like instant night, and the last thing I see is the face that looms over me, golden strands of hair hanging down around it.

Sasha's face.

Ellen

September 2017

When I come round, I am lying on the sofa. Something spiky pokes through the soft material into the back of my legs, and the smell of smoke is more overpowering than ever. I sit up abruptly, the room spinning around me.

'Hey, take it easy,' says Sasha. 'Are you OK?'

Am I OK? The hideous inappropriateness of the question stuns me as much as the fact of her, sitting next to me as if nothing has happened. Daniel comes in.

'Are you OK?' he says in an unconscious echo.

'No.' It's all I can manage as I stare at her in horror.

'I got you some water.' Daniel proffers a water glass, cloudy with smudged fingerprints. I shake my head and he sits down awkwardly, placing the glass on the floor beside him.

'Look, I realise this is a shock,' Sasha says, putting a tentative hand on my arm. I shake it off.

'A shock? That's what you think this is? A shock? A shock is ... I don't know, when your cat brings in a half-dead bird first thing in the morning; a *shock* is putting your hand under what you think is a cold tap and finding it's scalding hot. This is not a shock. This is . . . ' I have absolutely no idea what this is.

'I'm so sorry, Ellen. This was the one part about all of it that I hated: lying to you. I know it's going to be hard for you to believe me, but I swear it's true.'

She is close enough to touch. She even smells the same, a mix of coconut shampoo and cigarettes and something else indefinably Sasha. Tears well in my eyes and I feel myself weaken. I thought I'd never see her again, but she is here, right here with me. Do I want to waste that by being angry with her? There were so many times when she was missing that I thought I'd do anything to have her back safe. Is this the price I am going to pay? Am I going to forgive her for whatever it is she's done?

'God, you really are unbelievable.' Daniel's voice is harsh.

It's like being awoken from a dream, and something snaps inside me. I stand up, move away from her, out of her orbit, towards the door.

'I thought you were dead. I thought I was never going to see you again. Have you got any idea what that's been like?'

'I know, I know.' There are tears in her eyes, but I won't let myself soften towards her. 'Will you let me explain?'

I should walk out. There is nothing she can say that will make any of this OK. But I don't. I stay, and I let her tell me, because there is a stupid, pathetic part of me that wants to hear something that will make this better.

'Oh, please do,' says Daniel, voice dripping with sarcasm.

'I know it was stupid, but when Karina turned up outside work and told me she'd seen Daniel, I panicked. And when she said she'd lied at the trial, that Daniel hadn't raped her, I felt sick. It was as if I'd lost my mind. All I could think was that I had to get away. All those years I thought I had done the right thing.' Daniel makes a noise, an involuntary grunt, and she looks at him pleadingly, as if her eyes can melt him. 'I did. I know I lied, but I thought Karina was telling the truth. I thought I was helping her. Ellen said she heard you with Karina. I believed that was true. That's why I've kept Ellen so close all these years: I thought she was telling the truth, and that made my lie OK. I didn't know she was lying too.' She puts her hand on my arm again, and again I shake her off, appalled at how easily she can shrug me off in trying to appease Daniel.

'I wasn't lying,' I say. 'It was Nicholas I heard with Karina in Daniel's bedroom, but I believed it was Daniel. I made a mistake. It was you and Karina that lied, not me.'

'Well, I didn't know that. I thought if you'd heard that, then Karina must be telling the truth. And if she was, Daniel deserved to be punished.'

'For what? Cheating on you?'

'No! For what he did to Karina.' She has lied to me so much that I have no idea what the truth is. I probably never will.

362

'So you lied in court?' says Daniel. 'You allowed me to be sent to prison?' I can hear behind his words what he has suffered, things I can't even begin to imagine. She looks at her hands, which are clasped together in her lap.

'Where have you even been?' I ask. 'I've been looking for you ... I went to your mum's flat.'

'You've been to see Alice?' There is ice and fire in her voice, but I don't care any more if it's a taboo subject. She can't dictate to me what I can and can't say, not after what she has done.

'Yes. I was desperate. You don't seem to have any idea what you've put me through. I was right to go, anyway. You'd obviously been there, although she wouldn't tell me anything.'

She smiles slightly at this, and Daniel gives a disbelieving laugh.

'I'm glad you're finding something to smile about. Fucking hell, Sasha.'

'Why did you go to her?' I persist. I will not allow her to deny me the answers I've been seeking.

'She owed me,' she says simply. 'After what she did to me, what she put me through. I needed somewhere to go, and I knew she'd know somewhere. She'd always found a way to let me know where she was living.' I think of Olivia's address book. Alice kept her updated too. Maybe she cares more than she lets on. 'It cost me, of course.' Sasha goes on. 'She needed to get away from her boyfriend; things had been ... difficult.' I think of the suitcase in Alice's flat, and the devastation I saw when I went back there. 'So I gave her some money to go back to Hebden Bridge – she's got friends there still,' she goes on. 'She called a friend of hers who has a flat in Worthing that she doesn't use very much. It was available, and she said I could stay there for a bit. I couldn't risk telling anyone where I was. I needed to get my head down. I wasn't thinking straight.'

'It didn't occur to you that the police would get involved?' enquires Daniel coldly. 'That they might question me, having been told I was back in London? And that this would be the very last thing I needed, after everything you'd already done to me?'

'You have to forgive me,' she says. 'Both of you,' she adds, looking at me beseechingly.

'Why did you come here first?' I say slowly.

'What do you mean?' Her composure falters, as if it's a question she wasn't expecting.

'If you're so anxious for me to forgive you, if lying to me was the worst bit, why didn't you call me to tell me you were coming back?'

'I didn't think I could explain properly over the phone. I needed to see you.'

'Why are you here, then? Why aren't you at our flat?'

'I thought . . . ' She trails off.

'You've seen on the news that Nicholas has been arrested, realised what his role was in the whole thing, and thought it lets you off the hook. But it's Daniel you've come for, isn't it? Oh, I'm sure you would have made your way round to me eventually, but I could wait. Good old

Ellen, dependable old Ellen, she'll be all right. What is it – are you frightened of Daniel, still thinking he's going to make you pay for what you did, like in his letter? Or is it something else? Are you still in love with him?'

She flinches.

'Oh no,' I say with brutal satisfaction. 'He's your half-brother, isn't he?' She flushes. I sneak a glance at Daniel. He's like stone. 'Well, you know what?' I feel like Nicholas with his knife, swiping and slashing. 'Daniel already knows this, so I'm sure he won't mind me telling you. You and Karina weren't the only liars back then. Olivia lied too.'

'What do you mean? Lied about what?' she whispers.

'Tony's not your father. She made it up because she didn't want you fooling around with her precious son, messing up his music career.'

'What?' Her knuckles clasp the sofa's edge, bleached white with the pressure.

'Yep, the whole thing was a lie. If you'd bothered to challenge her on it, you could have found out. You and Daniel could have stayed together, and he would never have slept with Karina.'

'Fucking Olivia.' The venom makes me draw back.

'Don't you dare.' At last, Daniel is roused into speech. 'Don't you dare blame Mum. Yes, she told a stupid, unforgivable lie, but you know what? She was right about you. You are a poisonous, selfish bitch.' I catch a glimpse of the man who spent five years in prison. 'You say you were scared of what I might do to you – but what about

Karina? What about Ellen? You didn't give a shit about them. You just went running off, leaving them to face whatever was coming.'

She looks at him and her mask drops for a second, and I see what's left of her love for him, and fear, and hatred too. She knows he is completely lost to her, that there's no way back for her with him. She turns to me, and it's so calculated I almost can't believe it, but I have to because she takes my hand and squeezes it, imploring me with her beautiful eyes.

'Ellen, you have to forgive me. You have to understand. You remember how scared we were when we got those letters.' Daniel has the grace to look ashamed. 'When Karina told me she'd seen Daniel, I destroyed them in a panic. I didn't know what he was going to do. He was angriest with me; I knew he was. Because we'd been . . . together, you know? I knew he wouldn't be so angry with you.'

'What about Karina?' I say coldly, withdrawing my hand. 'Surely he'd be angriest of all with her? She was the one who started it all. Or did you not care about her?' She had never cared about Karina; I can see that now. Karina was too sarcastic, too spiky. Not enough of an acolyte. Not like me.'

'Of course I cared about her,' Sasha says. 'But not as much as I care about you. We've got something special, haven't we? Please don't throw it away, Ellen.'

'How many times did you sleep with Leo?' I ask conversationally.

If she's taken aback by the sudden change of pace, she hides it well. 'Only two or three times. You don't mind, do you? It was nothing serious.'

'I couldn't give a shit if you were swinging from the chandeliers with him on a daily basis.' This is a lie, of course, but I won't give her the satisfaction of knowing it hurt me. 'What bothers me is that you had me thinking he might have hurt you, killed you, even. Did you tell him at the time that you'd seen Karina in Café Crème?'

'I might have mentioned it, yeah. I think I saw him the next day. I didn't tell him what she'd said, though.'

'Even today I was questioning how he knew you'd seen her; I was looking at him with suspicion. That's what you've done: you've made me into this anxious, fearful person who can't trust anyone. God, I even suspected Matthew from work of doing something to you, just because he was at the studio having a meeting. You want me to forgive you but it's too late, Sasha. It's you who's thrown our friendship away, not me.'

Her face drops and I feel a throb of triumph at having the upper hand. For a second I consider letting her back in, just to experience what it would be like to have something over her for ever. It's only fleeting, though. The prize wouldn't be worth the pain, the loss of self-worth.

'I think you'd better leave now,' Daniel says to her. 'I don't ever want to see you again.'

At the door, she halts. 'You'll change your minds,' she says, but with an unfamiliar uncertainty. 'You'll be back.'

We hear her footsteps on the broken glass and then

the smack of the door as she slams it behind her. Daniel and I look at each other in the space she leaves behind.

'Karina'll be here soon,' I say. 'Don't be too hard on her, will you?'

'I've been so angry with her for so long,' he says. 'Sometimes, in prison, it felt like my anger was the only thing keeping me going. But now I know what Nicholas did to her, well … she's been through enough. I won't make it any worse for her. What she really needs is a friend.'

'So do I.' I've been dependent on Sasha for so long. I have felt cut adrift without a rudder this past week, and that hasn't gone away, but now I also feel strangely weightless, with a sense of limitless possibilities opening up ahead of me. The thing I feared most when she disappeared was that she was gone, that I'd never see her again. I know now, in this moment, that I was right. I will never see her again.

I am free.

Ellen

January 2018

The flat is tiny, the kitchen and living area all in one, and it takes me about half an hour longer to get to work, but it's light and airy – and it's ours. I can just about cover the rent and bills on my own. I'm happy for Karina to contribute as and when she can.

There's a chance she'll be facing another trial, but if she does, at least this time she will be telling the truth, and there is a freedom in that. Her fate is in the hands of the Crown Prosecution Service, who are currently deciding whether she should face prosecution on charges of perjury and perverting the course of justice. We've been unofficially told that there's a good chance they'll decide not to prosecute, given the abuse she was suffering from Nicholas at the time of the trial, and her resultant mental state, but it's by no means set in stone.

I keep remembering all the ways in which we were friends, before the arrival of Sasha and the Monktons; how we would laugh until our stomachs hurt. Sometimes

I can make her laugh now, and although she'll never be the same, she already looks younger than she did the day she opened the door to me a few months ago, a cornered animal. She says she's prepared, as much as she can be, for the possibility of a prison sentence. If the worst does happen, I'll be here when she comes out, in our little flat. Our home.

Sasha is living alone now, and I wonder how she finds it, with no one to make her look good, no one to bolster her opinion of herself, no one to play games with. I hope she's struggling. What Karina did was terrible; I can't deny that. But at least there were mitigating circumstances – she was being abused, after all, just not by Daniel. Sasha, though – what's her excuse? Was she punishing Daniel for sleeping with Karina? I guess I'll never know.

As for Daniel, he'll never get those lost years back, but I hope he can find some peace, rebuild his life, mend the relationships that were shattered all those years ago. At least Tony knew the truth before he died.

We've been warned that Daniel has the option to sue Karina, but he says he has no interest in punishing her. What matters to him is that his conviction has been quashed. That he is innocent.

I can hear Karina now through the paper-thin walls, clattering up the stairs and bursting through the door.

'Mum's agreed to pay for it!' she says, practically dancing with delight.

'Your training?' Karina wants to train as a counsellor for

370

people who have suffered abuse, but has been struggling to find the money for the course.

'Yes. She hasn't said so, but I think it's her way of acknowledging what he did . . . my dad, I mean.'

I know Karina was hoping for more from Dilys, for her to admit she had done her daughter a terrible wrong in not believing her, but maybe fully admitting the truth would just be too hard for Dilys to live with.

'That's fantastic. I'm so happy for you.'

'Thanks. I know it'll be years before I'm able to practise, if I ever can at all, but at least I'm working towards something, something that could make a difference. All these years I've been treading water, stuck. I thought that was it for me; that was how I'd always be. At least now there's a chance of something better.'

Telling the truth has set Karina free and I need to learn from that. I may not have lied at Daniel's trial, but I've been lying to myself for years about my relationship with Sasha. Pretending the way we were with each other was normal, that it was OK to be so over-involved in each other's lives. Pretending she cared about me as much as I did about her. Well, I can't pretend any more. The only reason she kept me around was because it validated her lie. As long as I had heard Karina and Daniel together, what she did was all right, but the moment she knew the truth, she was gone. All she thought about was saving her own skin. She never cared about me, and telling myself she did was the biggest lie of all.

It's so easy to lie to yourself, because you're never going

to get called out on it. No one's ever going to say: hang on, that's not right. There might be a small voice in the corner of your mind that speaks in the dark of the night, when all the other noise has died down, but it's easy to ignore, especially when the sun comes up and the world starts again. You fill your days with work, family, friends, hobbies, socialising, and soon you can't hear the voice at all. I can blame Sasha as much as I like, but I also have to acknowledge the part I played in our dysfunctional relationship.

I turn my attention back to Karina, who is still babbling excitedly about the course. I want to freeze this moment for her, because it feels like the first time in forever she's been happy, looking forward to the future, and I fear what's to come for her if the CPS does choose to prosecute. I take my lead from her, though, smiling and chatting as though my life depends on it, and perhaps it does.

Maybe that's all we have to do, all we can do: face the truth of our lives with equanimity and grace. Karina, Olivia, Sasha – they're all living with the consequences of their lies. Now I have to find a way to live with the truth.

Acknowledgements

It takes so much more than just a writer to make a book. Immense thanks are due to the following people:

To my super-agent Felicity Blunt, for her unfailing support and dedication. Felicity, I can't believe how lucky I am to have you in my corner. Also thanks to the brilliant Melissa Pimentel and the foreign rights team at Curtis Brown.

To my amazing publishing team at Sphere, especially my editors Lucy Dauman and Lucy Malagoni, as well as Cath Burke, Kirsteen Astor, Emma Williams, Thalia Proctor, Sara Talbot, Rachael Hum and the whole team who have worked so hard and been so supportive.

To Ognjen Miletic for his patience in the face of my dim questions about all things legal, and going above and beyond with his incredibly helpful suggestions as to how to tell the story I wanted to tell without making any glaring errors. If I have made any such errors, they are mine and mine alone!

To Robin Nickless, for his invaluable advice on police matters. Again, any inconsistencies are entirely down to me.

One of the most surprising and wonderful things about my midlife career change has been the unexpected new friends I have made. It turns out crime writers are the nicest people. To my squad, aka the Ladykillers – Steph Broadribb, Fiona Cummins, Emily Elgar, Caz Frear, Karen Hamilton, Jo Jakeman, Jenny Quintana, Amanda Reynolds, Laura Shepherd-Robinson, Laura Smy and Caz Tudor – for the support, the wine, the lunches and so much more. It means so much to have you as fellow travellers on this crazy journey.

To my CBC classmates, for their continued friendship and cheerleading.

To all the reviewers and bloggers who work so tirelessly for no reward other than to spread the word about books they have loved.

To Claire Marshall and Natasha Smith, my first readers, and first port of call in a crisis.

To Susie Osborne, Amanda MacNaughton and Debbie Nash, who have been there to help me out time and again. And of course to Frankie Osborne (without whom none of this would have been possible!).

To Hattie, Jane, Naomi and Rachel. Love you, girls.

To my family – my parents, Murray and Cecilia and my sister, Alice, and to Lisa and Andrew, and Mark and Elle, for all their support.

To Michael, Charlie and Arthur, who mean everything to me. I love you.

And finally, thank YOU. When I wrote the acknowledgements for my debut novel, I didn't thank my readers because I didn't have any then, and it seemed presumptuous to assume I ever would. I am now lucky enough to know the extraordinary joy of readers getting in touch to tell me they have enjoyed my work. Thank you from the bottom of my heart for buying this book, or borrowing it from a library or a friend. I hope you like it.

The addictive *Sunday Times* bestselling debut from Laura Marshall

'Engaging characters, good plot – intriguing from first page to last!'

'Addictive, thought-provoking and truly hits home'

'Kept me on the edge all the way through'

'Hooked me in from the start'

'Absolutely brilliant, I could not put it down'

'Wow. What a story. Couldn't put it down'

'If you like a story that makes you think and keeps you guessing this is the book for you'

'One of the best books I have read in a long time'

'Brilliant book and with an unexpected twist at the end'